THE FIRST IMMORTAL

Angel Blood

Stone Palatin

First Edition
November, 2016

ISBN 978-1-943492-21-3 (hard back)
ISBN 978-1-943492-18-3 (soft cover)

The First Immortal: Angel Blood is a work of fiction and fantasy based largely on characters described in The Old Testament. All events depicted, as well as names, places, events and incidents are either the product of the author's imagination or are used fictitiously. Any resemblance to actual persons, living or dead, events or locales is entirely coincidental.

It was written for a twenty-first century audience and the author has taken some license in his descriptions, including measurements of time, distance etc. in order to convey the essence of the story to the reader.

Cover art by Elena Kalashnik

ELM GROVE PUBLISHING
San Antonio, Texas , USA
WWW.ELMGROVEPUBLISHING.COM

Here's what Amazon readers said about
The First Immortal: Dark Angel
(4.9 out of 5 stars in 25+ reviews!)

"...a gripping adventure in a Biblical setting replete with monsters and magic."

"Mr. Palatin entertains and enlightens with his vivid (take) on the Genesis plot."

"The multiple storylines are jam packed with love and betrayal, hate and wars, prehistoric beasts and giants... Star Wars type weapons and genetic technology interwoven between myth and the Bible."

*"An area of Biblical history that has always been of great interest...
Lovers of fantasy will most definitely be satisfied !"*

"5.0 out of 5 stars from the first page to the last page, I was completely hooked. Great read!!"

"The author paints vivid landscapes and epic action scenes in an uncharted world that has been long ignored... Some of the most imaginative moments have simply been lifted from scripture and depicted literally..."

"Well written, fast paced and full of action... a great read for anyone who grew up with comic book heroes and graduated to action adventure and more sophisticated fantasy stories."

"This book is AWESOME!! I got kind of upset at the end, because the second book isn't coming out until later this year! I totally would have set this one down and picked up the next one and started right in!"

"Not many books about the first humans on earth even if it is fictional. You can almost imagine, reading this book, how the beginning might have been."

"This book explodes in creative thinking..."

"I can't wait until it is made into a movie."

Again, for my loving wife, Angela.

Introduction

While these tales are intended as entertainment and fantasy, they strive to stay true to the Biblical narrative, even to the point of sometimes leading the reader to a more difficult understanding.

The names of the characters are often the original Hebrew names, and while somewhat Americanized, they do not roll easily off the tongue. The reader may also find some names confusing, for example Enoch, the seventh generation from Adam and the main character in our story, shares the same name with Cain's first son, Enoch, for whom Cain built the first city recorded in the Bible. Just note that the City of Enoch, Cain's capital, is named after Cain's son Enoch – *not* the same Enoch as Adam's seventh generation descendant.

The author has taken the position, in this tale, that all life began some 6,000 years ago, so dinosaurs, prehistoric beasts and humankind all live together when the incursion of the watchers or fallen angels occurs and leads to the creation of giants, twisted beasts and Nephilim.

The power of sound is alluded to in the Bible when it is related that the earth was created when God spoke. The Bible also speaks of nefarious ones who have mastered "dark sayings" – another allusion to the power of the spoken word and sound.

The "super human" qualities of size and life span are a logical extrapolation of God starting out with perfection, as the original creation occurred without sin. The bodies of Adam and Eve, as well as all the animals and vegetation, had not yet tasted the degrading qualities of sin. It would take some time for the ravages of disobedience to manifest themselves in earth's biosphere.

Map of Lands

Atlantis
LANDS OF NEPHILIM
WILDERNESS
THE GREAT GORGE
Carmel
LANDS OF ADAM
Abelton
LANDS OF ABADON
Euphrates River
Lucifer's Pass
Caves of Halief
City of Light
LANDS OF CAIN
City of Enoch
Tigris River
Garden of Eden

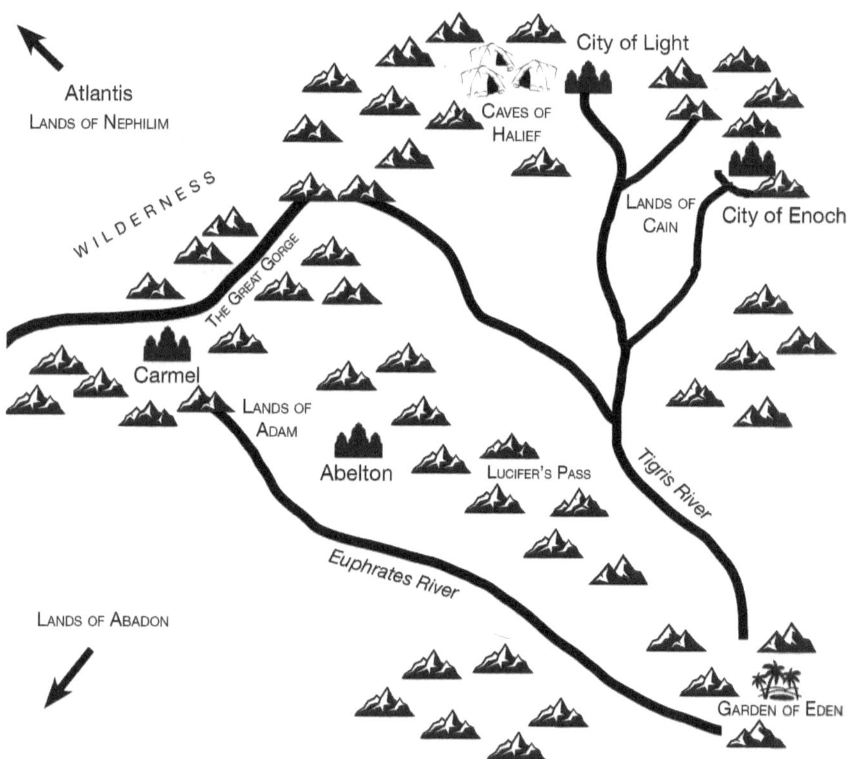

Family Tree

Adam
Cain
Abel
Seth
Other sons
and daughters
Enoch
Enos
Irad
Cainan
Mehujael
Mahalaleel
Methusael
Jared
Lamech
Enoch
Jubal
Jabal
Naamah
Tubal-Cain
Methuselah
Lamech
Noah
Ham
Shem
Japheth
THE FLOOD

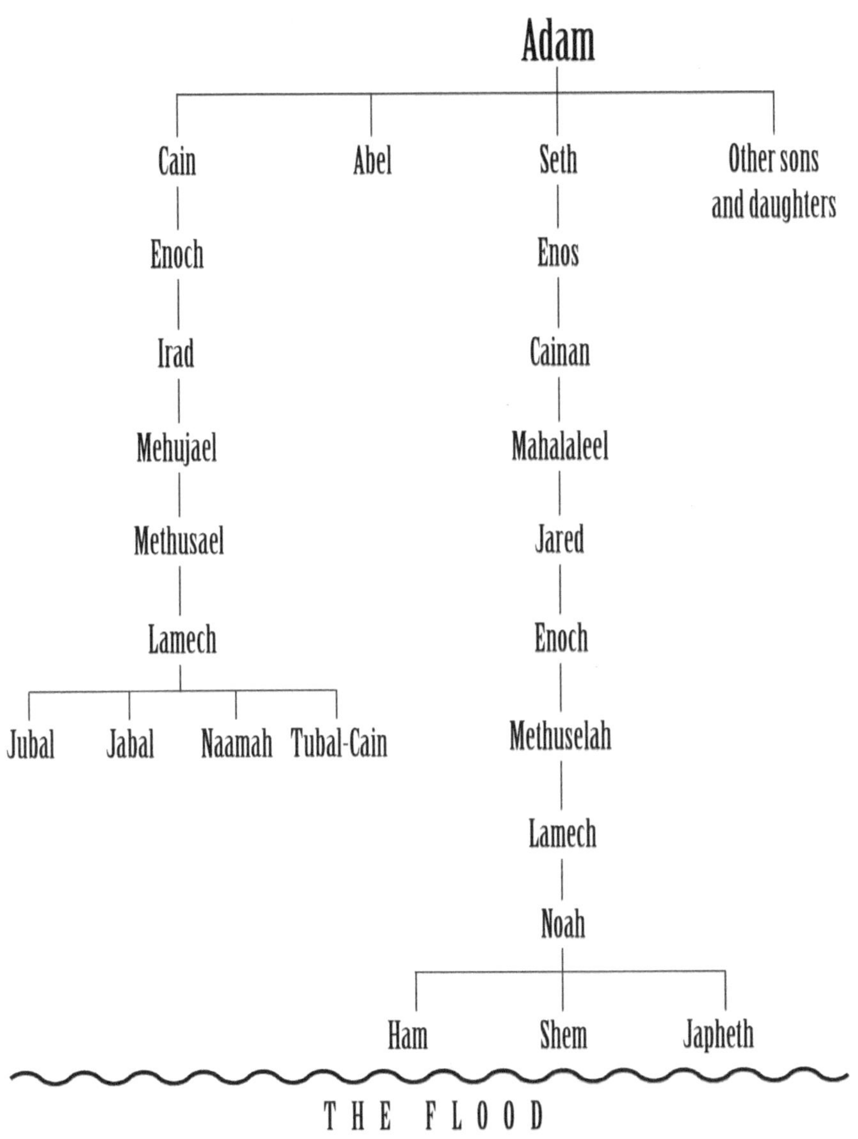

Prologue

Angela tossed and turned in the still night, a million thoughts running unchecked through her mind. She tried to put some order to them in an attempt to regain control. She had come so far since those innocent days in the village of her youth, enjoying her special bond with all the woodland animals – a bond that would later change the course of history.

Ruefully she recalled winning the contest to find the most beautiful, most comely young woman in her land to provide to the Dark Lords – a race of fallen angels that lusted continually for human female flesh. While most winners coveted such a position, Angela found nothing desirable at all in the honor.

To her horror, her attempts to ignore the Dark Lords' advances had only attracted the attention of Lucifer himself, who desired her for his bride.

Then came the miraculous rescue by Enoch's band of raiders from her caravan of doom towards the City of Light, the abode of the Dark Lords. The strong attraction she and Enoch had felt was unusual – the Adamic tribes usually shunned the children of Cain, but love had found a way to blossom.

Meanwhile Cain's obsession with securing eternal life led him to an unholy alliance with the Dark Prince Lucifer. Kidnapping his own mother, Eve, did not yield the location of the Tree of Life, as she was stolen from him before he could rip the secret from her. While Eve lay captive in the City of Light, something dreadful happened – death by disease was introduced to the City of Abelton.

The alliance of Cain and Lucifer put Eve in this terrible predicament, as they led their armies to secure the entrance to the Garden of Eden and plunder the fruit of the Tree of Life for Cain and his select followers, in order to gain immortality like the Dark Lords.

Adam and Enoch, along with all the Adamic warriors, raced

across the lands to try to cut Cain's force off from this prize, and Angela had no idea of their success or failure.

And even though she had rallied the remaining women and children to stand up to the assault of Cain's son Lamech, driving them from the gates of Abelton, Angela couldn't help feeling helpless and alone,

Enoch, where are you?

Angel Blood

Even Immortals bleed. In this second installment of The First Immortal trilogy, the action packed tale of Enoch resumes with The Dark Lord attempting to uncover – and counterfeit – the secret of his fantastic powers.

The Nephilim – Hades, Poseidon and Zeus – master many of the dark arts of old to create new and resourceful ways to dominate the Dark Lords – as well as mankind – in their attempt to become The First Immortals.

What will be the fate of one woman who gives in to the debauchery of the Dark Lords and betrays her own human race?

Belhah is about to find out!

Chapter 1

Eve's frail and lifeless form was adorned regally with exquisite white linens, jewels and precious metals. Her honey blonde hair, now noticeably grayed, was perfectly combed, her body perfumed and spiced, her ashen and sunken skin oiled to make her as presentable as humanly possible.

Angela, the new daughter-in-law of Eve by virtue of marriage to Enoch – Eve's grandson seven generations from Adam – along with Luna, Angel, the sisters of Enoch and the high governess all stood behind Eve. A rich bed of purple, gold and white that displayed the former Queen and the First Mother of all who were living to her loyal descendants. Not one of the women showed the age that had mysteriously crept upon Eve, wasting away her life energy. They stood ramrod straight, imposing and with grim purpose. Incense burned all around the periphery of the massive courtyard of meeting in front of the royal spire, infusing the air with the rich scents of frankincense and myrrh. Horns and stringed instruments played in the background as a celestial-like choir of Adamic women and children sang a solemn and mournful anthem. The song wound its way to its conclusion and the entire court-yard, packed beyond capacity, turned their attention as one in silence to Angela, now the great deliverer.

Angela strode forward to the speaking platform of the majestic gathering place, which was now overwrought with grief. Adam had de-signed this platform to project and amplify the speaker's voice so that it filled the entire courtyard, yet the people of Abelton stayed deathly qui-et anyway – so hushed that the smallest sound or shuffle could be heard.

Angela was clothed in the regal robes of white silk, encrusted with a rainbow of precious gems and crystals set in silver and gold, given to her by Eve. Underneath the softly billowing folds, she wore the polished amber armor and breastplate Enoch had taught her how to use and acti-vate with the spoken word of faith. As she reached the platform she lifted off her amber and silver helmet and shook out her long flowing locks of golden blonde hair, her bright, brown eyes sparkling with authority.

She surveyed the huge gathering before her. The warriors of the last remaining cities of Adam – Abelton and Carmel – were still absent, occupied in chasing and trying to stop the armies of Cain. All the women and children of both great cities had joined to engage in a surprising defense against the combined siege of Lamech, the son of Cain, and Apolodon – the high Dark Lord who had allied with him. Their forces had been shattered and scattered by Angela's ingenious defense and they were now in full flight back to their homelands far to the east.

For a moment Angela's eyes fixated upon Trulock and his band of rogue giants, each thirty feet in height, now battered and bloodied by the recent engagement, but standing proud to have helped in the defense of the city. She gave a slight nod of appreciation, which Trulock returned. He had come to respect this woman warrior who was the spitting image of the deceased Queen, only with bright yellow blonde hair and of course full of life and strength.

Angela cleared her throat and began. "Descendants of the First Mother, I salute you!" She raised her fist in the air and tens of thousands silently joined her as they raised theirs as well.

"Eve would not want anything to diminish your great victory in the defense of the city she gave her life for. The last word she uttered before her fragile body gave up its last breath was this – "

She looked around and paused, "She said to me, 'Fight!' And fight we did!" Angela again raised her fist in the air and fired amber energy blasts in rapid succession, causing the smell of electricity to singe the air.

A spontaneous roar of victory erupted from the somber crowd and as Angela reveled in the din, she was amazed at the release of pent up emotions that were freed by their response. Eve had been their First Mother, the only queen they had ever known for five hundred years. She was formed directly by the hand of God, perfect in beauty and grace.

The withered corpse beside Angela now shared none of Eve's elegance and poise. It was a poor shadow despite their best efforts to prepare her.

Angel Blood

As tall as Eve was she was still a full foot shorter than Adam as she and all of their offspring benefited from their rich gene pool and the fantastic environment this freshly created Earth gave them. Adult males were well over ten feet tall and many females grew past nine feet themselves. Death from old age and disease were unknown to these robust progeny of Adam and Eve as their regenerative cellular structure could carry them to nearly a thousand years before it broke down, permitting their demise.

That is why Eve's death was so startling, so unsettling. Not only was it the first of its kind, but it had also taken their most precious, most beloved, most beautiful member. Each individual in the somber crowd had to wonder if death could claim them in the same way.

Something had taken hold of Eve when she was held hostage in the City of Light, that pale glowing abode of the Fallen Ones – the legions of Lucifer. Lucifer's twisted magi and wizards were experimenting with combining angel blood with flesh and producing horrible monstrosities.

The Fallen Ones lusted constantly for human women. Those who could manifest themselves in the physical form were all male and few had taken the path of pleasing each other.

The cities of Cain, Eve's first son, had bargained with the Dark Lords, offering their women in exchange for an alliance and dark secrets, in order to gain an advantage over the lands of Adam. This unholy collaboration had led to the current dilemma as all the men of Abelton and Carmel, the two remaining kingdoms of Adam, had rushed to intercept Cain to prevent him from taking hostage the highest treasure of the Garden of Eden, the Tree of Life.

No news had returned about the success or failure of that mission, but their absence had given Lamech, fifth generation of Cain, an apparent opening to waltz in unopposed and seize both kingdoms, enslaving all the remaining women and children.

Never before had women raised a hand in war. They had submitted helplessly to the victors, subject to whatever the conqueror's desires were for them, be it murder, rape, enslavement or mating. Angela had raised the fighting spirit of the abandoned women and led them to battle for their futures. The surprising resistance had flummoxed Lamech, catching him completely by surprise. The engagement resulted in the routing of the unsuspecting troops of Cain's heir.

The tumultuous roar quieted and Angela threw back her head, shook her hair and continued, "Never forget what you have accomplished this day."

She reached out to a small child of less than 10 summers and beckoned him to the stage. He crawled up with her and she proudly raised his hand. The lad had ridden a giant cave bear and participated in the massive charge of wild beasts that attacked the rear of Lamech's forces and began the rout, decimating the men crewing the massive siege engines and catapults with all of their ammunition stocks. The shock of that attack spread through the rest of Lamech's forces, and they trampled over each other to flee from the tidal wave of fur, teeth, claws and talons.

"We have found that with God's help and the word of faith, we will never be helpless again!" shouted Angela.

Again their voices cheered and the young boy smiled as he looked up at Angela, then over the crowd. Angela shaped the cascades of sound and channeled their roars to activate the golden energy shields that protected the walls of their city. The amber covered walls literally pulsed with power.

Angela continued, "Yes, Eve would have been proud of you. Surprised by your ferocity, perhaps a tad unladylike – " a knowing laugh flowed through the crowd. Eve was always the lady, elegant and proper – but proud nevertheless. "We gather here this morning to lay our Great Mother to rest. She was the giver of life to all of us present and she never stopped giving of herself. This great city bears the stamp of her design and imagination. You and your children and your children's children were taught in her schools. We owe her our deepest thanks and appreciation."

A murmur of acknowledgment rippled through the throng as each thought of what Eve had meant to them. It was immeasurable.

Angela paused and let the little rider return to his mother below, nodding to him in thanks.

"We know not the fate of our sons, husbands and fathers, but we pray for their successful and safe return. They were vastly outnumbered and faced a formidable foe. We cannot assume anything. Cain's armies could appear to our south, or Lamech could reorganize his troops and return before our men can. We must be prepared."

She took a deep breath and continued, "My scouts tell me we have at least a few days of respite with Lamech in full retreat and no sight of anything from the south. So let us mourn this day the passing of our queen. Tonight we shall light her funeral pyre to consume this lifeless flesh to prevent her body from becoming a possession of the lesser demonic lords. Tomorrow we prepare our city to stand, to stand strong until our men return!"

Once more, a tumultuous roar of champions erupted from the multitude and Angela encouraged their outpouring of defiance, pain and grief. After they quieted Angela waved her arm towards Eve. "Come and pay her your respects, then after the sun sets, we will send her back to God."

Chapter 2

Adam woke with a start and wiped the perspiration from his brow. He had removed his amber armor to sleep and wore the simple white linen tunic designed with Eve's rainbow of gems and his royal golden robe wrapped around him. He desperately clutched its folds until he located a small lump tucked away in its midst, the heart-shaped golden fruit of the Tree of Life.

Adam breathed a silent sigh of relief as his hand clutched around the last remaining fruit that promised eternal life to whoever consumed it.

The Creator had forbidden humankind from ever eating of this Tree of Life and had protected it from man by placing two Cherubim and a living, flaming sword at the gates of the Garden of Eden. However, the combined sortie of Lucifer and Cain had succeeded in getting one piece of the fruit out before the gates were forever shut to man and the Garden of Eden drawn up into the heavenlies.

Adam had tried to stop them, but reached the portal too late to prevent Cain's forces from pouring in. All he could manage was to follow Cain in and confront him. Adam had been successful in stopping Cain from eating the fruit, but in the ensuing struggle the huge sword of fire had destroyed Cain while the lone fruit had fallen into Adam's possession.

He hid it from everyone, desperate to get it back home to Eve, his lovely wife who was suffering horribly from some evil she had contracted while held hostage by the Fallen Ones. If he could get her to partake she would be cured and perhaps this act of sacrifice would finally restore the lost sense of closeness and intimacy that lingered over he and Eve ever since Cain had murdered Adam's favorite son, Abel.

"Trouble sleeping?" asked Enoch softly, startling Adam in the pitch black of a starless night. Enoch was seven generations descended from Adam. At ten feet tall he was dressed in his hunter-scout furs over amber armor. He carried a black obsidian blade that he strove tirelessly to polish and clean.

Adam cleared his throat and muttered, "I had a troubling dream." He was suddenly uncomfortable around Enoch and worried if Enoch could see into his thoughts. Enoch was always so close to God, it unnerved him at times.

"Perhaps if you share your dream with me, I could interpret it for you?" offered Enoch. He was eager to get at the root at what had been bothering Adam ever since they had won the battle at the Garden of Eden, preventing Cain from capturing the fruit of the Tree of Life.

"Thank you my son, I'm sure it was nothing," Adam deflected his offer, not wishing to add any more connection to his already painful thoughts.

Enoch nodded silently ,but after a few moments he spoke again, "Are you worried about Eve?" He mentally slapped himself; of course Adam was worried about Eve. She had been deathly ill when they had left to intercept Cain. What a stupid question. He quickly added, "I'm sure the healers have found something to help her."

Adam fingered the smooth rounds of the fruit in his robe. "I'm sure God will reward their efforts," he said, unconvinced.

Enoch continued, "I didn't see Lamech or Apolodon at the Garden, did you?"

Adam responded, glad to be on another subject, "You know we were all pretty busy. I could easily have missed a lot of people."

"I suppose," hesitated Enoch. "I just pray for the women's safety as they were left unguarded. You don't think – ?"

"No! Cain's total focus was to take the Garden captive and pass out as many eternal life passes to his supporters as possible. He would have wanted that first before he tackled our cities," stated Adam. It had been a risk to leave the cities unguarded, but he had to meet Cain's army with every man he could muster to have a prayer of stopping him.

Enoch nodded in hesitant agreement. "Even so I can't wait to get back to Angela and share the great victory God has given us," he said, attempting to raise their spirits in celebration. Adam just quietly nodded and turned away.

Enoch wondered to himself, "After so great a victory, why does it still feel like we lost?" He also turned away and began to seek God for his answer.

Chapter 3

Belial had landed his winged mount next to Lucifer who was plodding ahead of Cain's shattered army on one of the few remaining fire breathing dragons that survived after Cain's failed attempt to secure eternal life.

This Dragon was a deep, rich, red hue, trimmed with black at the edges of its rock-hard scales, claws and wings. They trudged on in silence for a long while, hooded figures shrouded in the mist of defeat.

"They were strong," whispered Lucifer, in a low melodious voice. Every word he spoke had a songlike quality to it; the musical instruments woven into his body gave background and depth to his voice, giving it a hypnotic quality.

Belial started, drawn out of his own silent scheming. "My Lord?" he asked, returning to the present.

"The Angels – they were stronger than I remember," Lucifer almost sounded a note of respect that unnerved Belial; he had not seen Lucifer this melancholy before.

"They got lucky, that is all. Did you see how hastily they retreated? They moved the entire garden into the heavenlies to escape us!" said Belial proudly, trying to put his best spin on the situation. Belial looked into Lucifer's eyes, trying to see that old spark of defiance so prevalent in his master in the past. Lucifer's handsome face drew up in a scowl.

"I have allowed myself to grow complacent and lazy, meddling with these creatures of flesh," he muttered. His music grew louder and angry in its chords.

Belial licked his lips as if tasting a delicious morsel. "The women are quite beautiful and pleasurable," he said as he reviewed his collection of bed partners in his mind.

"They are but a distraction," spat Lucifer. "They made me weak with their demands, playing on my lust and desire."

Belial stayed silent, he did not like the direction in which the conversation was going.

"Women have only caused me grief and trouble for a moment's pleasure," complained Lucifer. "And all these half breed children are a constant headache. They don't obey me and everyone wants his own way; they are insufferable," he continued.

"What are you saying my Lord?" Belial hesitated.

"We must refocus ourselves, at least until we conquer these pesky Adamites," Lucifer proclaimed. He was still smarting from Adam's unsettling intervention that had ruined his plans for an eternal ally in Cain.

"How so?" Belial murmured, struggling to keep up with Lucifer's twisted thoughts.

"I will not risk myself personally again until I am sure I can defeat them. I will work on subjugating the human race until they're all worshipping me. I will be an angel of light to those who receive me, a roaring lion to those who oppose me. They must all eventually serve me so that we can overthrow the Creator as one, united force. To win He must admit His failure and destroy us all, and in so doing, He undoes Himself!" Lucifer exclaimed in powerful exultation at his new plan.

Belial nodded in agreement, glad to be off the subject of giving up his harem. He eagerly proposed, "I will organize our ranks to accomplish this. I will assign a spirit to every human to guide him into submission. I will choose higher spirits to each position of power, to control and guide their governments to follow your will. I will assign even higher spirits to rural towns, cities and nations. They will all influence the leaders to accomplish your will. I will offer unbridled lust, riches and power to those who serve you, and you alone." Belial schemed as he planned his strategy, leaving ample room for his own advancement in power.

"We must be strong to accomplish this," agreed Lucifer as he turned his hypnotic gaze upon Belial, shaking him from his plans. "Do you love me?" he demanded of Belial.

"My Lord, I serve you. Of course I respect you and follow you," he said nervously.

"But do you love me?" demanded Lucifer again.

"I suppose I do, my Lord," stuttered Belial.

"Then let us swear off these fleshly women and their traps and desires. Let us seek pleasure only from each other, then show our strength by taking only the strongest males and humbling them before us. Swear to me Belial, be my consort and first in my kingdom!"

Belial winced before the piercing, hypnotic stare of Lucifer's bright flashing red eyes. The thought of giving up the luscious women he had collected these hundreds of years, balancing against being offered the highest position of power in the land. "What choice do I have?" he thought as he returned Lucifer's penetrating glare.

Belial lowered his head and responded, "I submit myself to you and we will rule this world together." But in the back of his mind he thought, "He can't watch me all the time, I will find a way to enjoy all my pleasures."

Chapter 4

"Lord Lamech," said Belial, bowing, while Lucifer acknowledged with a nod.

Lamech stood in quiet shock, next to his Dark Lord General, Apolodon.

"So you are sure Cain's been killed?" Lamech demanded, unsettled by this sudden reversal of fortunes that appeared to be going in his favor. "What about Cain's curse, his mark, did it not protect him?"

Lucifer spoke, "The creature that struck the deathblow was not of this earth, but of the heavenlies and thus immune to the curse of Cain."

Lamech looked out of his traveling royal coach, high upon a gigantic behemoth, a creature that resembled a walking mountain with a tail and neck as tall as the cedars of the forests, and surveyed the remnants of the two retreating armies. His force had somewhat regained their formation and order. But all their siege engines and machines of war had been lost in the surprise retreat forced on them before the walls of Abelton. On the other hand, Cain's heavy weaponry was still intact, but their numbers were decimated. Almost all of the fast striking palace guard with their T.rex-like mounts had been lost. However, between them they comprised a most formidable force, easily five times what the Adamites could muster.

"If we can trap them in the open field, before they get back to their strongholds, we can crush the Adamites once and for all," said Lucifer, banging his fist down on Lamech's map table for emphasis.

Lamech turned to Irad, Cain's second in command, and asked, "How is the morale of your troops? I do not want another forced retreat in such a brief period of time. Our armies might lose all faith in us."

"They are itching for a good fight, a chance to redeem themselves from this past battle," said Irad supportively. He had never yearned for the top spot of command, and was grateful to see anyone else making decisions.

Lamech pursed his lips. He had not gone into any detail on his own hasty withdrawal from the battle for Abelton. A quick victory would do much to erase the embarrassment of being routed by women and children and cement his role as Cain's successor.

He could trust Apolodon's complicity of silence, as he would be just as hesitant to go into much depth with any of his peers, also fearing humiliation.

"Show me their location," ordered Lamech as they gathered around his map table.

Lucifer was wearing bright golden armor encrusted with a rainbow of precious gems and crystals; his head was adorned with a golden helmet shaped like a pit viper with ruby red eyes. His face was pale as fine porcelain, but gave off an unearthly glow and his long flowing hair was ghostly white.

Belial and Apolodon shared the same glowing skin tone and white hair, as did all the Dark Lords in their incorporated, fleshly state.

Belial had the black hooded cape of a Dark Rider, while Apolodon had on his full ruby red suit of armor, covered by a midnight black robe.

Lucifer pointed to the map below them and informed, "My scouts show me they are here, still several days' journey from Abelton," displaying a long valley, shielded from them by the mountains. "If we send our fastest cavalry around the mountains from the south to the north, we can drive them to here."

Lamech rolled his eyes and blew air from his mouth, "This is blocked from us by mountains. Our main force could never cross the mountains and could never catch them in time by going around."

Lucifer shot a narrow beam, like a black laser, that burned across the mountains shown on the map, causing the obsidian clad Lamech to start backwards for an instant in surprise. "What if I created a pass right here? We could intercept them before they reach the security of their amber walls."

"How could that be?" questioned a dumbfounded Irad. Lamech was glad Irad voiced the question, as he was thinking it but didn't want to look foolish in front of the Dark Lords.

"My powers have grown since the Garden of Eden has been removed from this earth. You leave the new pass to me, just be ready to march your main force through," promised the archfiend of Hell.

Lamech pondered his options and surveyed the Dark Lords huddled around the table. Something was different with Lucifer and Belial. Lucifer seemed stronger, more powerful but Belial just seemed... strange. His gaze made Lamech feel uncomfortable, "I will follow this plan on one condition," stated Lamech.

"Of course Lord Lamech, name your condition," bowed Lucifer in a slightly condescending way.

"Keep your friend here from staring at my ass," demanded Lamech, pointing an accusing finger at Belial.

Chapter 5

Zeus gently raised himself from the embrace of the two almond eyed beauties. One of them was softly snoring, her naked breasts rising and falling in slumber. He chuckled as he remembered how he exhausted them and their screams of passion that waned to soft moans, then to sleep. He carefully covered them up so as to not tempt his brothers if they happened by.

Zeus walked quietly back to his traveling desk and turned on the glowing crystal lantern. He reviewed the plans he had drafted for the city of Atlantis. He had solved the issues of fresh, clean water in abundance, year-round production of fruits and vegetables, sewer elimination, heating and cooling.

He needed to consult with Poseidon to work out the port facilities. Poseidon was designing huge vessels that would traverse the seas and carry massive amounts of cargo across the waters. Zeus had to get accurate dimensions on these behemoths for his docking facilities.

One of the girls moaned softly in her sleep and rolled over in his bed. Zeus noted how these further reaching tribes had begun to pass on similar traits to their offspring as the gene pool began to isolate itself due to the limited choice of mating partners. This last little town that had been assimilated on their march to the sea had primarily yellow coloring, dark hair and those lovely almond shaped eyes. There were exceptions of course, but Zeus was fascinated by the possibilities of creating entire nations of singularly identifiable peoples.

They would be easier to control as each nation would feel isolated and afraid of the different looking neighbors. Keeping your subjects divided and at odds with each other meant coming to a dictator for assistance and deliverance. Zeus had already created a class of bureaucrats that lorded their position over the populace and would tread on their own kind for a little more power or recognition from him or his brothers. They did most of the governing work of for him, keeping him free to cultivate his designs and pursue new women.

Hades had petitioned him for a second entirely underground city, full of experimental facilities, prisons, torture chambers and grand halls for education and courts. Hades gained pleasure from causing fear and pain, so much so that Zeus had to bridle his lust for butchery to protect the morale of his own followers. He had bargained with Hades, with help from their teacher and mentor Belshazzar, to feed Hades a steady stream of convicted criminals, making examples of anyone who showed too much independence or leadership potential. The justice system was a sham to enforce the god's will and give the illusion of fairness and righteousness, but Hades had to be fed. So Zeus's bureaucrats were constantly scrambling to find some new enemy or threat to their power who could be put away in chains.

"Zeus!" exclaimed Belshazzar in greeting as he walked into the canvas walled chamber of Zeus's royal tent. Zeus held his finger to his mouth hushing Belshazzar as he walked him further from the bedchambers.

"The sun has been up for some time now," Belshazzar frowned. "You need to get these lazy girls up and out of here!"

Zeus laughed, "They worked hard all night my teacher, give them another few hours to recover."

Belshazzar shook his head, clearly disapproving of Zeus's behavior. "We have much work to do, my son. You should not allow these foolish girls to occupy so much of your time," he fussed.

"What good is a kingdom without subjects?" said Zeus, spreading his arms wide. "I must keep my subjects satisfied."

Belshazzar gave a quick wave of his hand in frustration, tired of arguing with Zeus about this. He moved on to the point of his visit. "Have you given any thought to your defense systems?"

"Defense against…?" Zeus raised an eyebrow.

"You can't expect Lucifer to ignore us for long. If he succeeds in overcoming the Adamites and enslaving the descendants of Cain, he will eventually attempt to crush any challenges to his rule. If, on the other hand, any of the sons of man overcome the Dark Lords, they would also eventually see you as an obstacle to eliminate," explained Belshazzar, frustration rising in his voice.

Zeus motioned to Belshazzar to follow him outside and walked him over towards a steep cliff of solid stone. He began, "All three of these armies depend too much on flesh and blood, tooth and claw. I have discovered a better warrior."

He raised his hands and called forth to the giant face of the cliff. A thunderous rending and crushing sound sprang from the wall of rock, creating an avalanche of sound. A towering form wrenched itself out of the confines of the stone and strode forward to Zeus, a good forty feet tall with hardened muscles in its arms, chest and legs.

"I call it a golem," said Zeus gleefully. "I can animate stone, iron, crystal, bronze, water, you name it. Each golem has its strengths and weaknesses, but an army of these should be a match for whatever any- one throws our way." Zeus waved his hand and the massive creature crumbled back into a pile of boulders.

The two sleeping girls had been violently awakened by the din and stood wide-eyed in amazement at Zeus's display. The shock of the collapse of stones broke their stunned silence and they ran, screaming, back to their own tents.

"Looks like I have you to myself, finally," muttered Belshazzar, eager to see them go.

Zeus shook his head, "These mortals are so easily frightened."

Belshazzar challenged him, "You are dealing with their lesser kind out here on the outskirts of humanity. Don't make the mistake of thinking that the Adamites would be so simple minded."

Zeus pouted a little. It was hard for Belshazzar to remember Zeus was still very young, as quickly as he had grown and matured. "But this is good progress," he added, wanting to encourage the child-god to continue on this path.

Zeus's pout dissolved. "Hades and I have been working on weap- ons for the spirit realm as well," he bragged. "One never knows when one might entertain angels unaware."

Belshazzar touched Zeus on his broad shoulder. "You call my kind mortal, and well you should as we are but dust and the Creator tells us to dust we shall return. But remember, you too are half mortal and you cannot be sure that you too will come to an end."

"That's why the spiritual weapons are so important," explained Zeus, already light years ahead of a surprised teacher. "We will need to assault the heavenly realm and lay claim to the Garden of God that has been removed from this earth. In that garden is the Tree of Eternal Life. Once we eat of that fruit, our mortal bodies will be completely transformed to immortal, and no one will be able to stand against us!"

Belshazzar stood open mouthed, observing the young half-breed of angel blood in human flesh. At this young age he was already over thirteen feet tall, muscularly well developed and certainly sexually active and mature. Zeus wore a loose-fitting linen tunic that displayed his powerful form. Even more impressive was the way Zeus assimilated knowledge and created and shaped it in new and formidable ways. And now it seemed his ambitions were kicking into high gear.

"Well, good," stammered Belshazzar, trying somewhat unsuccessfully to keep his surprise in tow. "Keep up your studies and quit wasting so much time with that," he said, pointing below Zeus's waist.

Chapter 6

Belhah admired herself in the full-length mirrors of Lamech's royal coach. She was far more beautiful than either of Lamech's two wives, with her caramel colored skin, light amber eyes, long, straight jet-black hair and perfect athletic curves. Her beautiful skin was marred only by the fresh scar across the breast from the knife of Adah, forcing her to accept this life of consort to the royal family and betray the city of Abelton that had taken her in. Belhah had come from the villages of Cain and never really quite fit into the righteous lifestyle of the clans of Adam.

Angel Blood

She rubbed the healing salves from a blend of medicinal plants into the scar seeing it lessen the lesion every day. Soon her skin would be flawless again, but she could not see how she would be anything more than a third wheel, one of many sex toys for Lamech and his two lustful wives.

She cursed her rotten luck. Was she always to be second best? She was second to Angela in beauty when they were selected as brides to the Dark Lords, as Lucifer had chosen Angela over her. Then when Enoch's band freed them from the Fallen Ones, much to her regret, that conniving bimbo had sunk her claws into Enoch, the leader and future heir to the throne of King Adam, while she had to settle with Mahalial, a nice enough guy but a simple warrior with no ambitions to power.

Now she had landed in the house of Lamech, certainly an ambitious man and heir to the throne of Cain, but she was nothing more than a sex slave. A puppet of Adah and Zillah, at best third in Lamech's affections and after her newness wore off, maybe less than that. She craved power, a castle, a kingdom of her own, servants, riches.

"Good morning my pet," purred Adah, coming up next to her and stroking her bare skin. "What thoughts are running through that pretty little head of yours?"

Belhah faked a smile and lied, "I'm just wondering how long it will take for the scar to fade away." Well, maybe half the truth.

Adah laughed a throaty laugh and said, "Believe me honey, with that body no one is looking at your scar. But keep treating it twice a day and it will fade away in a couple of weeks."

She spanked Belhah's naked backside and commanded, "Now go draw my bath and be ready to attend me, oh, and draw one for Zillah as well. We must be fresh for Lord Lamech. After we finish, clean yourself as well, you never know if Lord Lamech will call for you." She grinned as if Belhah should be grateful for that privilege.

Belhah feigned another smile and headed off to her task.
"Oh, this is not going to do," she muttered. "This will not do at all!"

Chapter 7

Adam sat astride of his snowy white war unicorn, a massive beast with a long flowing mane and hair on its legs from the knee down. He was adorned in his white robes with Eve's royal design of multicolored gems and jewels emblazoned upon it as well as in the trappings of his mount. His amber armor and weapons were packed and he rode with just his belt of black obsidian sonic blades, each one razor-sharp. He looked with dissatisfaction at the speed of progress his weary army was making. He had to get back to Eve as quickly as possible.

He again fingered the fruit in the pouch of his robe, trusting his secret was still secure. If he could get this prize into Eve's system, she would be healed from the deadly illness and no one would know of his disobedience to God in obtaining it. He would rededicate himself to be the loving husband to her and make up for the lost years.

"Lord Adam," announced Enos, "scouts are approaching."

Adam shook himself from his thoughts and readied himself. "Send them to me," he motioned.

Seth approached on his towering giraffe-like mount, all legs and neck.

"Lord Adam," greeted Seth.

"What news?" asked Adam.

"A large force of light cavalry, followed by heavier cavalry is tracking us from the south," Seth announced.

"Will they catch us before we make Abelton?" Adam questioned, courting despair. He did not think his force was ready for another en-gagement so soon and he craved the protection of his amber energy walls around the fortress of Abelton.

"If we double our pace the rest of the way, we should make the city ahead of them, but it will be close in getting the entire army safely behind the walls," worried Seth.

"The way is clear ahead?" Adam asked Enos. Adam's subordinates could sense his desire to avoid a fight, most unlike Adam, but they excused him knowing how concerned he was for Eve. They too wanted to reunite him with their queen and prayed somehow she could be healed.

Enos declared, "Our scouts see no force between us and the city."

Enoch spurred Maverick, his massive, muscular saber-toothed tiger mount, forward into the circle of command. He still wore his amber armor, covered by the tan skins of a scout and hunter, prepared for a fight at a moment's notice.

"Lord Adam," he interjected. "Let me take my men to a position between the pursuing force and our main army. We will fight to cause a delay and give you the extra time you need to safely enter the city walls. Just be ready to receive us in haste when we break from the battle and follow you in."

Adam considered his options: Turn his exhausted troops to face these new opponents or use their last bit of energy to gain the safety of their walls and be reunited with their families. It really wasn't much of a choice, he reasoned.

"Take your men and slow them down," agreed Adam. "Give us as much time as you can, but then break off and reform closer to the city. Do this as often as they will fall for it and we will make all haste for the city. When you hear the horns of Abelton, you will know we are in and ready to receive you. At the blast of the horns, break away for the gates and we will be ready to cover your retreat," said Adam, clasping his hand on Enoch's shoulder. "May God's blessings be upon us!"

Enoch replied, "Godspeed to you!"

He patted Adam on his back, causing Adam's robe to jostle and Adam felt the weight of the fruit of the Tree of Life nestling against his body.

Suddenly God's blessing seemed distant to him.

Chapter 8

The pathway was a good one hundred yards wide. Lucifer could have made it broader but there were limits to his powers and he sacrificed breadth for speed. The pass was already ten miles cut through solid rock and he would have to gamble that enough of Lamech's army could burst through the opening, appearing to the forces below to have materialized out of a solid mountain peak, to secure the pass exit and establish a stronghold. Then the rest of the forces could come through.

Lucifer and his Dark Lords worked furiously, cutting huge blocks of stone with their black energy blasts while the human magi and half-ling mages levitated the blocks out of the pathway.

Lamech's combined armies of giant sauropod beasts, giants, trolls, ogres, twisted creatures from the Dark Lords' genetic experiments and the Cainite troops all inched their way in a mass behind the excavation crews. The dark army filled the ten-mile long freshly cut pathway and was still funneling in from the other end.

Lamech, fully decked out in shiny black obsidian armor and scarlet regal robes, rode high above the anxious forces on his lumbering behemoth. He cut a striking figure before his troops, his long black hair flowing in the mountain breeze. Atop his kingly coach set upon the huge back of his gargantuan steed, he turned to the royal aid who accompanied him. "Give me the new dragon helmet," he commanded. "I'll try it out today," he stated as he took the newly crafted golden helmet. Fashioned after the head of a dragon, its open toothed mouth encircled his face.

The narrow confines of the path and his desire to see what was happening placed him closer to the front of the formation than he was used to, but there was no way around it.

He turned to his three sons, Jabal, Jubal and Tubalcain, each similarly clad in reflective black crystal armor and scarlet robes. "I have designed each of you a unique helmet as well," he declared as he passed out similar open-mouth dragon helmets of golden metal, each one with a different pose. His sons donned the helmets, completing the foursome.

"With Cain gone, our family shall rule undisputed. I have longed for this moment for decades and now it has fallen in my lap. I will not lose it, ever. You will be heirs to my kingdom and together we will crush all who oppose us. We shall be known as the Clan of the Dragon and we shall be indestructible!" boasted Lamech, his chest swelling with pride and utmost confidence. His eyes flashed with the same fire that enabled Cain to humble his foes and force this world to submit to his will, with just the power of his gaze. No champion had been able to resist Cain save Adam. Lamech had inherited the same fear-invoking glare that turned his opponents' knees to jelly. In fact Lamech boasted his power was seventy times as strong as Cain's.

"Jubal, take your position with the scouts and sound your trumpets when the way is cleared for our charge. Tubalcain, when you hear the trumpet sound, lead your troops quickly into the breach and secure the opening for me to pass with our main column. Jabal, press the rear of our forces to follow quickly into the pathway and onto the field of battle, we can have no stragglers or confusion. We need every soldier and creature through this pass, engaged with the enemy. Is that clear?" Lamech ordered with great intensity.

The sons nodded in understanding and turned to mount their flying leather-winged pterodactyl-like steeds. Each flew off to his assigned task.

Lamech felt the earth tremble beneath his mount and smelled the raw static energy manifested in front of him as great blocks from the mountain, carved on either side. Rock dust wafted in the air and his army crept forward, ready to charge.

This would be the defining moment of his new kingship. Everything must be perfect.

Chapter 9

Enoch's first delay tactic worked to perfection. He and a score of his sabertooth riders had allowed themselves to be discovered and baited the lead element of light cavalry into chasing them after a mock stand to engage.

Enoch's feigned retreat led through the middle of heavy woods on both sides and when the last Cainite scouts entered the path between the woods, the hidden Adamites on either side fired their razor-sharp black crystal blades and flung their piercing spears, throwing the pursuers into disarray.

Enoch promptly reversed his retreat and signaled a charge, combining with the forces on both sides of the woods to smash into the disorganized column which had suddenly gone from predator to prey.

Giant claws from the tawny battle cats swiped men left and right from their raptor-like mounts. Built for speed, their slender bodies were no match for the powerful felines and the lizards' bodies were pierced by the sabertooths' massive incisors and powerful jaws.

Many of Enoch's band were blade throwers as well and black obsidian blades buried themselves into the flesh of the shrieking Cainite riders. Enoch blasted away with his amber sonic energy bolts, knocking down both riders and mounts as his men made short work of the stunned enemy.

Within moments the survivors sounded the retreat and bolted back to their lines, a shattered remnant of the force they were before.

Enoch's troops quickly reformed and lined up across the breach of the woods, many melting back out of sight. Enoch fought back a choking fear when he saw the masses the retreating scouts fled to. They were like locusts, covering the plains. Enoch saw scouts furiously waving their arms and pointing their direction. A collection of giants and three horned armored beasts complete with mounted archers and spearman took the front lines.

He heard the sounds of drums setting a pace for their methodical advance.

"Well," Enoch said to Mahalial at his side. "At least they've slowed down some."

Mahalial grinned and readied his own saber-toothed mount, patting its massive furred neck.

Enoch motioned his men to listen to his commands over the drums of the enemy and their earthshaking advance. "Everyone stay absolutely motionless for a few moments!"

Enoch shouted a command of illusion and vibrated an image of each warrior, filling the space around them. "Now back away slowly and leave your image behind," he instructed, and soon a likeness was all that was left blocking the path as Enoch's force melted away.

"We will let their heavy units chase these images and when they pass we will hit their unprotected flanks from behind them," instructed Enoch as they took up their positions of ambush.

Enoch kept retreating the image of his troops backwards through the woods and the armored archers, giants and spearman shot their arrows, threw their spears and stones in an attempt to strike down these ethereal foes, as they were seemingly unaffected by the Cainite missiles.

Behind the massive armored front came the lighter, swifter animals, raptors, four-legged quick-moving lizards and some of the faster T.rex-like mounts of the palace guard.

The Cainites squinted cautiously into the darkness of the forest as they slowly advanced behind their protecting armor. Something was not right. The ground was littered with arrows and spears but no bodies of their enemies were to be found. The quiet was also unsettling, surely their armored wall should have engaged the Adamites before them but there was no sound of battle, only a stillness that built their fear, despite their superior numbers.

Suddenly, on either side of their advancing column ram horns blared out their deep signal to attack. Human shouts and the roars of prehistoric cats plunged from the silence and Enoch's band tore into the lightly armored troops, causing devastation and panic on both flanks.

The Cainite trumpets sounded, desperately calling the armor wall backwards, in an attempt to shore up their inability to push back the bigger, stronger onslaught of fur and fangs. Confused but obedient, the armored units turned back to join the threatened light cavalry and reunited only to see Enoch's forces once again vanish into the surrounding terrain. Enoch looked behind as Maverick picked his way up the wooded hill. The Cainites were definitely shaken and completely stopped, for now.

Chapter 10

Angela shivered with an unnatural chill as she remembered her own death. When she had been brought back by the Angels she saw with spirit eyes how the lesser Fallen Ones had fought over her lifeless body, striving to inhabit it. She remembered the Caves of Halief and the ghastly creatures that dwelled in the underground and she knew she had to destroy Eve's body.

Nothing would be so demoralizing to the Adamites as to see this wasted wreck of their former queen, eaten away from within, stumbling around with the perverted mind of a demon.

"Build it high and build it strong, worthy of the High Queen of this earth," she had told Trulock, the leader of the band of renegade giants who had joined them to repulse the attack on Abelton.

Trulock's giants had done an admirable job, cleverly stacking and cutting the funeral pyre to make it stand over thirty feet tall, with a soft bed of tinder at the top.

Angela stood with the high governess, Angel and Luna, granddaughters of Eve, all dressed in their royal finest, brilliant white linens and Eve's design of multi-colored gems and crystals.

Angel Blood

The entire population of Abelton and Carmel seemed to have turned out for Eve's funeral procession– from the royal courtyard where her body had been displayed, to the towering funeral pyre on a tall hill outside the city.

Death did not come often to Abelton and certainly not by disease or old age. The inhabitants of this new earth lived lives of nearly one thousand years. Adam and Eve were now well over five centuries old and until Eve's demise, many considered her the most beautiful woman on earth, without a hint of age or decay marring her perfect features.

The oxygen-rich atmosphere of the pre-flood earth where over eighty percent of the planet's surface was covered in lush vegetation with no icecaps, was combined with a massive body of water vapor suspended in the atmosphere, blocking the deadly ultraviolet rays of the sun. This, combined with incredible cellular regeneration capabilities with the human body so close to God's original design, made aging and dying from natural causes most alien to the Adamites. Adam and Eve's DNA held all the richness and diversity of the human race, able to produce all sizes, shapes, shades and colors of humans, much like the original ancestor of the canine species lent itself to a large number of vastly different progeny, yet all still dogs.

"Sound the horns," commanded Angela, wife of Enoch and defender of Abelton, arrayed in her regal splendor. After several long mournful blasts, Angela and the three other leaders walked four abreast at the head of the procession. Trulock gathered Eve and her funeral bed and walked behind them, followed by all the citizens in the courtyard, out of the amber city.

Angela's mind raced with many thoughts as they slowly marched out of the city walls. Where were the men? Had any survived? What had killed Eve? Would it happen to more of them? Would Lamech's armies come back? What would life without Enoch be like and how long could they hold out in this world without their men? Why had God let this happen?

The future was too much for her to bear and she felt the weight of responsibility and the unknown crashing down on her. She began sobbing with grief and loneliness, abandoned by her husband and her best friend Eve, who had treated her like a daughter when she had been a newcomer and alien in her husband's native land.

Angela touched her belly feeling the little life that had started within her. Enoch must return, a child needs a father.

Luna saw Angela's body shaking and put her arms around the great high warrior of the city, letting her drown her sobs against her chest.

"All we can do is live each moment to the best that we can and trust God with the outcome," she whispered to Angela as they marched towards the funeral pyre.

Angela nodded between sobs and responded, "Well, He better fix things because there's an awful lot wrong right now."

Chapter 11

Adam felt an unexplained tremor in the ground beneath them. As he jerked his head around, trying to locate its source, he heard the blast of trumpets coming from the mountaintops to his right. He looked at Enos and Seth in befuddlement and they return his puzzled gaze. The column had made good time and it seemed they would have no trouble reaching the security of Abelton ahead of the chasing army. Enoch must have succeeded with his delaying tactics.

Suddenly Adam smelled the sulfuric scent that betrayed the use of demonically inspired black energy. "The Dark Lords!" he yelled, panicking and searching the skies – perhaps an aerial attack? Usually he was attuned to the danger of the spirit world and alerted to attack by a sort of God-given sixth sense, but this had caught him totally by surprise.

The tremor grew to a crescendo of sound and vibration and the mountaintop to their right exploded with a shattering spray of rocks and dust, vaporizing itself. Adam's column stopped suddenly, stunned and motionless at this awesome display of power.

Through the haze and smoke of what used to be a craggy mountain peak, something was moving. Adam squinted through the fog, trying to discern what was happening.

Then, completely and impossibly, forms began boiling forth from the flattened mountaintop, driving forward with great speed towards the unprotected flank of Adam's column. With no time to ready themselves Adam's army was about to be cut in half and his limbered machines of war and their crews would be destroyed. Adam cursed the coming destruction and flung an accusation towards the heavens. "God, why have you forsaken us? You allow evil to triumph?" He spurred his mount towards the tidal wave of enemy flesh and shouted, "On me, on me! We must try to turn the attack!" As Adam rode into battle on his snorting war unicorn, its snow-white main billowing in the wind, he directed his fellow riders, hopelessly trying to right their formation to meet the onslaught. At the same time he was dimly aware of the small weight in his pocket, thumping against his side.

Tubalcain excitedly led his troops towards the heart of the Adamite column. He saw them vainly attempt to turn to meet his force, but the heavy wedge-busting mammoths were too far to the front and would never make it in time.

His accompanying Dark Lords had shielded his charge with black energy and the few amber blasts that were flung at them dissipated into nothingness.

The Adamites seemed stunned and disjointed and he reveled in the expectation of a slaughter. Like a red-hot flow of blazing magma his massive dinosaur riders crashed into the vulnerable formation, crushing and stampeding through them to the missile launchers and catapults. The crews were caught still struggling to unlimber the weapons from traveling mode and somehow get them into the battle.

They had no chance. Stunned and surprised by the unexpected attack they were overwhelmed by the dark forces.

Now even more troops clattered through the new mountain pass.

In horror, the realization came to Adam that this was not just a delaying ambush. The entire Cainite Army might lie above them, waiting to spill out and swallow them whole.

Somehow, someway, he had to fight his way to that pass and stop the hordes pouring through.

Chapter 12

Truloch gently laid Eve's skeletal corpse on the soft bed of kindling atop the gigantic funeral pyre, then gingerly stepped down and stood back.

Angela had calmed herself but her face still showed stains of tears. She strode to the base of the pyre and took a flaming torch into her now steady hands, then turned to the masses that thronged below her. The women and children of Abelton and Carmel, many dressed in their amber armor of war in honor of their recent victory, were closest to the foot of the tall hillside.

Further from its base and closer to the surrounding forest she saw the vast animal army that had helped them rout the armies of Apolodon and Lamech, slowly creeping from the woods. Giant cave bears, grounds sloths over twenty feet high, great apes, rhinos, sabertooths, great black-maned lions and great horned animals, revealed themselves in honor of Eve's passing.

As she scanned the massive crowd below her she realized they must go on, they were the world's hope and they needed comfort and encouragement just like she did.

"Descendants of Eve!" she started, waving her arm across the people of the two cities. "And my furry friends who so ably helped us defend our city!" The great apes and the Alphas of the animals' kinds nodded to her.

"We stand today at a great crossroads, the passing of a generation," she paused to let the enormity of this thought sink in. "Although we pray for the safe return of our men, we can only know for sure that God is our help, our ever present source, our protector and our provider."

She swallowed and choked back her tears. "There is a life beyond this world, I have seen it. And though the pain of death is awful and real while on this earth – and we will miss and be missed by our loved ones – the hopes of being reunited someday are real and worth all the pain, suffering and challenges of living an honorable life that pleases our Creator."

She thrust the torch into the midst of the pyre. "Love God, love each other. We will miss you Eve."

Chapter 13

Adam watched helplessly as thousands of his men were slaughtered. He saw the end of his descendants at hand and the rise of the line of Cain and their unholy progeny of angel flesh and demonic seed now free to populate the earth unhindered, giving rise to all manner of wickedness and violence.

What had a life of struggling to honor God accomplished?

He dodged a clumsy blow from a half-breed giant and spurred his powerful unicorn forward, driving its deadly spike into the chest of his opponent while slicing open its neck with his black crystal blade. He pulled free of the collapsing bulk and charged forward. God expected too much from him, He just didn't understand how difficult it was to blindly trust Him, to obey Him. A lumbering troll swung his spiked club at Adam and he dove from his mount to avoid a crushing blow, rolled to his knees and fired three black ice daggers pulled from his belt, all striking the creature in it's unprotected neck. The troll clutched at the spurting wounds, pointlessly trying to staunch the flow of its half-breed blood as it crumbled to the ground.

As Adam stood to remount his one-horned steed, now splattered with gore, a gleam of gold from the ground caught his eye. In a flash he felt for the fruit of the Tree of Life, that heart-shaped golden meat that would heal his Eve from the ravages of disease. It was gone! Once again he scanned the ground, feverishly looking for the origin of that golden light. There, underneath the hand of the fallen troll. He desperately pried up the heavy extremity and there, back within his grasp, lay the golden fruit.

The world slowed down around him and the sounds of battle faded away. For that instant in time, it was just he and the answer to the prayers God had denied him. He stretched forth his hand in seemingly slow motion. His spirit moved within him. How could he expect God's blessing by disobeying Him? Did he think he could hide his actions from God? Was he smarter than God? Did he learn nothing from the Garden?

Adam came to himself and whispered, "Eve, forgive me, I place you in the hands of God. I cannot please God by disobeying Him, even for another chance with you."

With that he fired a powerful blast of amber energy and the last fruit of the Tree of Life, pilfered from the garden of God by Lucifer, then Cain, and then by Adam, disintegrated into vapor and rose into the air.

The mist rose above the battlefield, leaving behind an unsuspecting Adam. Distracted by his thoughts, his helmet was smashed from behind by an opposing foe, knocking him senseless and face down in a field of blood.

The hazy mist wafted to the north, floating high above the struggling armies towards another plume of smoke far in the distance. Then, as if guided by unseen hands, the mist was grabbed by a billowing breeze and rushed to the hilltop where a huge fire was growing.

Chapter 13 ½

Lucifer was exalted in the apparent collapse of Adam's forces. His brilliant plan to crush Adam's exhausted army between the remaining forces of Cain and the combined strength of Lamech and Apolodon's columns was succeeding with total perfection. Adam's defeat would be absolute when he discovered his beloved Eve was gone forever.

"Lord Lucifer," announced his scouting wraiths, "We bring news from Abelton."

"Yes, yes, what is it now?" asked Lucifer, halfheartedly listening but not wanting to take his eyes off the carnage taking place below.

"They burn the body of Eve, we will have nothing to embody for your pleasure."

Lucifer's mind flew back to his assault of Eve in her dreams: that perfect body, her intoxicating smell, the sparkle of her brilliant blue eyes, and his moment of ecstasy spending himself inside of her while she was helpless before him. He sighed, "That will be a shame. She was truly the most beautiful of all women and I will miss her."

He smiled to himself. Another part of God's prophecy was falling short. With Eve gone it limited her seed to only those offspring she had already produced and none of them seemed capable of producing a Messiah, a King among Kings. Of course, there was the youth that had battled Belial. Perhaps he was one to keep an eye on for a while. Maybe he would assign Belial to make sure that one was drawn to their side or destroyed – just to make sure – although he expected none to survive this ambush.

"Strange," mused Lucifer as he watched over the battle raging below. His eye caught a wisp of vapor or smoke of some sort, appearing to move against the wind, towards Abelton. "I guess the winds below blow differently than up here."

He dismissed the oddity and continued to press the advantage his troops had to eliminate the Adamic force below.

Chapter 14

Angela watched the fire lick its way up the oil-soaked logs and tinder of the massive pyre. Her grief was overwhelming and she steeled herself for when the flames would reach the top and begin to consume the wasted body of her friend, her confident, her teacher, her ancestor, Eve.

The crackling heat was intense as the massive pile of fuel fed the flames and Angela had to step back from the stifling blaze.

The smell of smoke lay heavily in the air and Angela shielded her eyes to catch a glimpse of the top of the pyre, now billowing clouds of smoke into the atmosphere. She squinted as a lighter mist descended through the dark rising plumes and settled around the resting body of Eve.

"What in the – !" exclaimed Angela as she waved Trulock over to her. "Lift me up, hold me high!" she commanded urgently. Truloch quickly obeyed and Angela was just able to peer through the billowing smoke and catch a glimpse of Eve's body.

It appeared as if Eve's chest moved and the hovering mist flooded into her nostrils and mouth as she made a gasp for air.

"How can this be?" stuttered Angela, Eve had been breathless for days!

Eve's face began to fill out, her sunken cheeks rising and her sagging clothes begin to expand as Eve's magnificent form returned. Angela gasped as she saw Eve's eyes flutter and then open wide.

"Had the Dark Ones taken her?" she questioned to no one in particular. That would be a fate worse than death!

"Get me closer Trulock!" Angela yelled. She would have to disable the creature long enough for the flames to devour it. She drew her obsidian blade and leapt from Trulock's hand on to the top of the flaming pyre. She would only have moments to cripple Eve's body before the smoke and flames overcame her as well.

She landed next to Eve and raised her blade to take off Eve's head. Eve lifted herself by her elbows, raising her torso halfway off the bed of smoking tinder, exposing her graceful, porcelain neck to Angela's blade. As Angela swung her blade downward she saw a flash of startled recognition in Eve's now restored eyes and realized the beauty of Eve's flesh had been renewed.

"Wait!" she exclaimed to herself. The bodies taken by the fallen ones retain their wounds. Eve had been restored to health. Something else was at work here.

"Angela?" asked a hesitant Eve as Angela's blade stopped at Eve's throat, causing a slight trickle of bright red blood.

"Eve, is that you?" she coughed as the smoke surrounding them got thicker.

"Who else would I be?" coughed Eve as well. "What's happening here?"

Angela sheathed her sword and quickly helped Eve to her feet. "I'll explain in a moment, right now we need to jump!"

Angela and Eve burst through the wall of flames and smoke at the top of the pyre and fortunately Trulock was quick enough to snatch them from the air before they hit the ground.

A gasp of amazement swept through the startled crowd as Trulock gently placed the two regal women on the ground. Eve glowed with health and vigor and now the two were like twins in face and form, with only Eve's honey blonde hair and blue eyes distinguishing her from the dark eyed, bright yellow haired Angela.

"It's a miracle!" exclaimed Angela, looking at an almost a mirror image of herself in the centuries older Eve.

"I work out," quipped Eve. "I've been trying to get you youngsters to join me." She suddenly became serious. "The men need our help!" she exclaimed. "They are under attack to the south of the city. We must hasten. Even now we might be too late!"

Angela stared glassy eyed at Eve, "How do you know this?"

"Trust me, mount up every soul that can fight and we must leave! Now!"

Queen Eve was back and with a vengeance!

Chapter 15

Enos rushed to Adam's side and lifted him halfway off the ground. "Lord Adam!" he urged, shaking him out of his stupor.

"Form around me!" Enos ordered and a troop of mammoth cavalry pressed back the snarling, snapping sauropods and their riders to give Adam a small pocket to recover.

Adam shook his head and muttered, "I've been such a fool! I have put us all at greater risk for my selfish needs."

Enos helped him to his feet, "Lord Adam, we serve you regardless of whatever you think you've done. You are our King, our father, and we will follow you to our doom."

Adam stared glassily at the loyal Enos and for a moment thought he felt what God felt when His children showed their devotion and respect. He shook his head and uttered, "I am not worthy of your devotion," then dropped his eyes.

Enos looked in horror at the devastation occurring around him. Now was not the time for Adam to have an attack of conscience. Enos, in desperation, slapped Adam in the face and shook him. "You must be the King this day that you should have been before! We need your best, now!"

The sounds of battle began to rise in Adam's ears, his awareness returned and he came to himself.

Enos helped him as he struggled to his feet. Adam retrieved his blade and clambered back onto his unicorn, now pawing and snorting in defiance of the foes around him. Adam's mind cleared and he once again assessed their tactical situation.

The dark army was still pouring through the mountain pass like water through a spigot. If they were to stand any chance at all he would have to find a way to shut off that flow before they were totally engulfed. Almost as he thought it Enoch's delaying force appeared, racing along the right side of Adam's shattered flank, immediately seeing the need to staunch the tide of combatants spewing from the mountain.

The powerful saber-toothed tigers quickly sliced through the unprotected left flank of the dark forces pouring down from the mountain. Within moments they had the fighters before them either felled, slowed or backed up, congesting the troops behind and causing a log jam at the mouth of the pass.

"Form on me!" shouted Enoch to his amber energy shield partners. They stretched across the one hundred yard wide opening, activated their sonic shield and a huge amber arc appeared. It started pressing the evil forces of Cain backwards into the pass. Enoch's armor was growing white-hot as he channeled all of their combined energy into the wall, trying to give the forces below a chance to survive. He turned to Mahalial, "Get down there and tell Adam he must defeat that force quickly while I hold these back. Warn him that a huge force is still following him and he must flee to the city as quickly as he can."

Adam saw the outpouring of reinforcements had ceased and the amber shielding was plugging the gap. "Attack!" he shouted to his heavy mammoth led cavalry as he pushed to reach the back half of his column that had been isolated by the ambush. Even with Enoch's help with preventing new troops in, they were still outnumbered and Tubalcain was doing an admirable job of blocking Adam with his massive behemoths, giants and trolls while his more mobile forces kept up their advantage of surprise against Adam's more vulnerable units that crewed the heavy weapons.

Mahalial fought his way to Adam's side and conveyed Enoch's message. "Lord Adam! The force we delayed is not far behind us. If we don't break through to the back of the column soon, they will be caught between both forces and annihilated!"

Now that the pass was blocked, more of Enoch's troops were shearing off and assaulting the bridgehead of forces commanded by Tubalcain, but the progress was too slow and Adam feared half of his force would be lost.

Seth yelled down to Adam from the high vantage point of his giraffe like mount. "I can see the dust kicking up on the horizon. Their southern army will soon be upon us!"

Adam furiously blasted amber sonic energy bolts, trying to punch some sort of hole through to the soon to be trapped men, but the combination of massive armored bodies, black crystal shields, and dark energy absorption shielding were thwarting his best efforts.

Adam knew Enoch could not hold forever and each second he delayed sounding retreat for the front half of his column – while giving the back half hope – risked losing them all if Enoch's shield faltered or the pursuing southern force came within range.

"God," he prayed out loud as he continued blasting and stabbing at the enemy forces. "This is all my fault for disobeying you and stealing from the Tree of Life." He ducked beneath the spiked tail swinging to impale him and blasted its rider from atop the beast, down into the boiling fray. "Take vengeance on me, but let my men live!" He spurred his steed forward and speared the dismounted rider in his chest. Above the shouts and clashes of battle Adam heard the distinctive, deep long blast of ram horns sounding a charge. Adam glanced around in confusion. He had not ordered such a command. Were the Dark Lords trying to confuse his men by imitating their command signals?

Seth pointed to the north and announced in dread, "Another force to the north, just beyond the crest of this rise." He shook his head, "They have us trapped but we should go out fighting!"

Adam squinted through the foggy mist of battle and declared, "Wait! There appears to be an amber hue ahead of this approaching force and they used our signal horns. But who…?"

Four brightly glowing amber figures draped in flowing, white regal robes raced towards them on glistening white unicorns, all emblazoned with the royal colors of Abelton.

Angela, Eve, Luna and Angel led the charge, long flowing hair billowing from golden helmets. The ram horns continued to bellow and behind the glowing riders came a horde of great beasts of prey, cave bears, great apes, lions, and saber-toothed tigers, as well as giant sloths, war unicorns, rhinos, mammoths, stags, moose, bulls and buffaloes, each with a small amber glowing rider protecting it with a sonic shield.

Adam also saw a score of giants in their midst, aiding in the charge.

"They are ours!" shouted Seth, "It is a miracle!" he gushed.

Adam's heart skipped a beat as he recognized Eve out of the four-some. The way she was riding and how she filled out her suit of armor showed she was definitely no longer sick, but totally, completely recovered. His chest filled with pride as they thundered towards them.

"Clear a path!" urged Adam and his men fought furiously to form a point of attack into the Cainite forces, allowing the momentum of their charge to do its force shattering work. The point was cleared and into it pierced the power and might of many tons of fur, flesh, tooth and claw, smashing apart the shocked Cainites that tried to hold the line.

Eve pulled up from the charge and ran to Adam's side, clinging tightly to him as he smothered her face and lips with kisses.

"I'm so sorry!" they gasped simultaneously between frantic kisses. They both laughed and Adam said, "I've been so selfish, I don't want to waste another moment of life at odds with you."

Eve sobbed with relief, "And I should have been a much better wife to you, I love you Adam, I always will."

They enjoyed one more long deep embrace and Adam marveled that she looked more beautiful than he even remembered her, almost like their days in the Garden.

Adam surveyed the field after tearing his eyes away from her and said, "We have much to share but first I must get these men home to Abelton. It is still there, isn't it?"

Eve smiled and said, "Oh yes, and what a story you'll hear."

Chapter 16

"What's the holdup?" shouted Lamech as Jubal swooped out of the sky on his pterodactyl and landed on Lamech's plodding behemoth. Lamech impatiently observed his forces had stalled before they could exit the mountain pass.

"A troop of Adamites on sabertooths surprised us at the mouth of the pass. They sliced through our flank and are now damming up the entrance with a sonic shield," reported Jubal.

"Call for the Dark Lords!" bellowed Lamech, furious with the delay. "We must break through to support Tubalcain and catch the Adamites between our two forces!"

Lamech's signalers blew their brass trumpets in a call for the Dark Lords. Belial and Apolodon soon arrived on winged mounts and Lucifer materialized in front of Lamech's royal coach high above on his lumbering beast.

They all appeared a bit drained and Lamech still did not like how Belial looked at him. "What do you require from us now?" snapped Lucifer, clearly annoyed that he was disturbed.

"The pass is blocked," stated Lamech.

"Impossible!" stated Belial flatly. "I was there when the Lord of Light brought the final rock down," he boasted. Lamech curiously eyed Belial's expression towards Lucifer and pushed those thoughts out of his mind. "It is not blocked by stone, but by an Adamite amber energy shield. I need dark energy to bring it down and I need it now!"

Lucifer sighed, "We just moved ten miles of mountains to allow you to surprise your foes and you couldn't even secure the foothold?"

Lamech's ears turned blood red at this rebuke in front of his son. He touched the hilt of his sword in fury but Apolodon restrained him and shot him a "What the hell are you thinking?" look.

Lamech regained his composure and said slowly, "We do not have the power to break this shielding quickly, if we do not break it down immediately all your work will be in vain." He stood quietly, smoldering, and stared at Lucifer.

There was an unnatural silence in the room, a stark division of power between Lucifer and Belial on one side, and Lamech, Jubal and Apolodon on the other.

Lucifer's fists pulsated with dark power, throbbing in the shadows. Apolodon stepped between the competing parties and attempted to mediate.

"Gentlemen, we have all gone through incredible trials and struggles to get to this point. Nothing has gone as we planned, so we're all upset. Unless we pull together, we shall fail again."

The crackling sound of static electricity and the smell of sulfur began to dissipate and Lucifer exhaled, his pale white flesh glowing with a luminescence that contrasted with his flashing red eyes. The background of musical resonance that accompanied Lucifer constantly lessened in intensity and mellowed out to a more symphonic tone.

"We have expended much energy and are not at full strength. Can you reorganize your troops and give us some physical pressure against the field, catapults, hammers, rams, etc.?" requested Lucifer.

"Make it so!" Lamech ordered Jubal, then to Apolodon, "Bring up the siege engines from the rear lines."

Lucifer nodded in agreement and turned to Belial, "Gather the Dark Lords and all the mages and magi. We shall amass all the force we can muster."

Chapter 17

With the new push of fresh troops, the Adamites were able to punch a hole in the Cainite encircling force around the last half of the bisected column. They created a protected route to withdraw the survivors and fight an orderly retreat towards the city walls.

Adam ordered the fastest troops back to the city to man the defenses, then sent his heaviest troops to give them a head start in the race for safety. The following southern Cainite army had made contact with the remaining initial force that had burst from the mountainside to surprise Adam and they were reforming for another attack.

"Where's Enoch?" Angela cried desperately as she rode by Adam's side, firing blasts of amber energy to slow the advancing hordes.

Adam shouted, "He's holding back the reinforcements on the other side of that pass up there!" pointing to an amber glow on the mountainside.

The press of the southern army had reached beyond the mouth of the pass and Tubalcain was reestablishing control over the passage foothold.

"We must reach him and give him an escape route!" screamed Angela as she desperately tried to organize an assault force to fight its way up the mountain. Suddenly the smell of ozone, sulfur and heated air accompanied a throbbing vibration at the top of the mountain. A huge black cloud engulfed the glowing amber shield and with a crackling burst of black lightning the amber bubble exploded into a shower of rock and dust.

Adam, Eve and Angela looked in horror at the devastation on the mountainside. In a shout of victory the Cainite forces again boiled forth from the smoke and fog of the explosion, adding to the already superior numbers of the dark army below.

Adam steeled himself and commanded the rest of his riders and troops, "Head for the city, run!"

He turned Angela and said, "We can do nothing for them now, don't let his sacrifice be in vain. Come!" He grabbed the reins of her stallion, "We must go!"

Eve also touched her shoulder and urged her, "Remember the life you share, Enoch would want both of you safe now."

Angela watched the mountainside in stunned silence as it now was swarmed with dinosaur riders. She turned her face towards Adam and nodded her quiet agreement. "Sound retreat!" She shouted to her animal commanders and once more the ram horns blew. The other Adamites turned and raced to the protection of their city walls.

All those trained in shielding put up a retreating amber force that hindered the advance of the enemy and created a separation between the two opposing armies. As the retreating armies approached the security of the energy charged walls of Abelton, massive projectiles flew over their heads into the pursuing Cainites, effectively negating any chance they had of catching the retreating tail of Adam's forces.

Adam stayed until the last warrior had crossed through the gate and Angela's animal army had melted back into the vast surrounding forest. He circled his arms around his head, signaling the gatekeepers to close the massive gates as he clattered across the threshold.

Chapter 18

"There it is!" expressed Belshazzar proudly, as they crested the rise and looked down on a majestic valley, rich and green working its way down to a crystal blue sea. Towering cliffs eventually gave way to gentle beaches and several rivers and waterfalls twisted their way to the sea.

Zeus, Poseidon and Hades dismounted and gazed in awe at the beauty of the location.

"Behold Atlantis," smiled Belshazzar as he waved his arms slowly across the valley.

Zeus drew in a breath and exhaled, whistling at a high pitch, "You have chosen well Belshazzar."

Poseidon gazed at the sea and exclaimed, "I never dreamed it could be so beautiful, the drawings don't do it justice."

Hades looked at the solid bedrock and saw endless possibilities for subterranean chambers. "Yes, it is a most desirable site," he said as he looked at the seaside caves. "My work is already started!"

"There are all manner of sea creatures that we know very little about, my children," taught Belshazzar as he picked his way down the rocky hillside. "Let's begin our new adventure!"

The column had grown to about thirty thousand men, women and children complete with animals, wagons and tents. A good start for an empire, Zeus thought, as he patted the backside of a passing young woman. She squealed in delight as Zeus lamented that he would have to share some of the women if he wanted to grow their population.

"Set up camp between the two rivers," ordered Zeus and the columns of worshippers and settlers unwound themselves down the steep hillside. "Tomorrow we start building."

Chapter 19

Enoch awoke in a cold dark cell. The floors pulsated with dark energy and the air stank with sulfur. He wore nothing but a loincloth, stripped of his amber armor. He tried to stand up but his legs could not support him. He tested each leg and collapsed both times. By their irregular feel he surmised they were both broken.

Enoch was amazed that he was even alive. He remembered straining to his limits to hold his amber shield in place to give Adam one last chance to escape to Abelton and the security of its defenses. He had felt an unearthly power building up against him on the other side of his barrier, crushing his attempts to withstand it, then the explosion, rocks piling up on top of him and then blackness. He wondered if he had given Adam enough time. "Lord God," he muttered, "I pray they are safe, that what I did mattered. I ask you to guard them, be their shield, their comfort and strength. I lift up Angela to you. Protect her from the assaults of the Evil One, form a barrier of supernatural thorns around her and let her know I love her," he winced in pain as he adjusted his battered body. "Oh, and if you can, free me from this prison," he sighed, falling into a fitful slumber.

Time passed, he knew not how much, and he awoke again. There was a skin of water and a crust of bread on the floor by the entrance. He was extremely thirsty, but rationed the water, unsure how long he would have to make it last. He crawled to what felt like the lowest corner of the cell and relieved himself. "Lord God, do not forsake me in this hole. Grant my freedom and put me back with my family." He prayed again, seemingly with no response.

Lucifer glanced at Belial, "Your prisoner is awake. Do you feel the disturbance in the heavenlies?"

Belial nodded his head, "He tried it before. I have dispatched spirits to squelch any response. No messengers will get through," he stated confidently.

Lucifer observed his tattered forces, recently split from Lamech's army of flesh and bone, now headed back to the city of Cain while he and his Dark Lords returned to the City of Light.

Their alliance with the Cainites had neither the will nor the strength to marshal a concerted siege upon Abelton, now fully defended by the warriors of Adam. They agreed to leave Adam and his forces holed up in their fortress. The Cainites were exhausted and were missing the comforts of home, so the campaign was ended, a missed opportunity.

"I don't know why you didn't just kill him," mused Lucifer. "I sense you are playing with fire."

Belial sensed melodies of irritation emanating from Lucifer's body – another feeling, perhaps jealousy?

"He is nothing without his armor," he assured. "I will study him and find out what gives him such power."

"Well if you are studying him, how do you know he is nothing without his armor?" ridiculed Lucifer.

Belial waved his hand through the air effeminately. "Don't quarrel with me. Can't you give me a little trust?" Belial complained.

Lucifer rolled his eyes, Belial was acting too much like his dissatisfied wives. Maybe his plan for spiritual rebellion against God's design was not without its flaws.

Chapter 20

Adam and his commanders, as well as Angela and the female leaders, all stood on the lofty vantage point above the huge city gates. They watched as the last of the enemy forces vacated the fields of battle. It seemed they lacked the desire of an all out siege against the now fully defended city.

Likewise, Adam did not intend to pursue them with his exhausted men, so he let them go in peace, weary of violence and bloodshed. There were tears of joy and of sadness as families were reunited or discovered their losses. Adam himself was equally torn, amazed and grateful for Eve's miraculous return to health but saddened by the grief he saw Angela going through for his grandson Enoch.

He was at a loss for words to comfort Angela, so instead he turned to Eve and hugged her. "I guess the healers discovered a cure," he offered as an explanation of her recovery.

Eve stared out at the now empty plains below. "Actually, I died," she stated, then looked up into Adam's disbelieving face.

"You what?" he exclaimed.

"The healers could do nothing. I was lost in the blackness of fog and pain, wasted away to skin and bones. I couldn't move, I couldn't speak. I remember rising above the smothering sea of despair to utter one word to Angela, then I passed out into utter darkness. The next thing I remember was Angela ready to cut off my head as I awoke upon a huge burning funeral pyre," she spoke in a tone of hushed amazement. She saw Adam's concerned look and quickly stated, "She could only assume my corpse was being animated by the unincorporated Fallen Ones who seek a body to inhabit. But when I spoke to her and she realized it was truly me, she rescued me from the fire."

"When did this happen?" asked Adam thoughtfully, and still with some amazement.

"Just today. We raced to battle as I sensed you needed us," Eve said, reaching up and touching Adam's face tenderly. Adam kissed her softly.

"Just at the time I destroyed the last fruit of the Tree of Life," he realized. "I had no idea."

Eve looked up at him, puzzled. Adam held her. "Cain is gone, perished in his quest for eternal life."

Eve gasped with pain then searched his eyes. "Did you?"

"No, he met his end by a weapon of the heavenlies, not by my hand," Adam explained. "He succeeded in securing a bag of fruit from the Tree of Life and as he was struck down, one of the fruits survived and fell, along with me, outside of the portal to the Garden of God. God forgive me, I took it and hid it, thinking I could heal you with it."

She stroked his face, "Adam, I would not want to live forever without you. I would be content to meet my end."

"When I realize I risked everything because of my disobedience, I destroyed the fruit and placed you in God's hands." he whispered, holding her tightly.

"By being willing to lose me, you saved me, my husband," Eve lovingly gazed into his eyes and her heart melted inside with renewed love for her husband. She kissed him long and hard.

Angela watched Adam and Eve acting like two love-struck children and her heart ached for her own man. She felt her abdomen in sorrow. She had never been able to tell him she carried his child. Now this seed was all she had left of him.

"I will tell the child everything about you," she said to the heavenlies. "I will let him know how brave you were and how you sacrificed all so that we could live." She rubbed her stomach and patted it. "You should be very proud."

Adam walked over to her, "I am sorry for your loss, Enoch was always the best of us."

Angela let loose the flood of tears that she had done so well holding back, causing Eve to rush over to console her. Eve looked at Adam and said, "Angela carries Enoch's child."

Adam's face showed both surprise and satisfaction. "We'll make sure the Cainites are gone, then return to recover his body. He deserves our greatest honors."

Angela nodded in agreement, slowing her tears and squaring her shoulders.

Angel and Luna strode forward into the circle and Luna stated, "Angela led us in the defense of the city."

Angel added, "She anticipated an attack and called all the women and children from Carmel to us so we could all support each other."

Luna chimed in, "And when Lamech threatened our city, Angela taught us the words of faith to activate our own amber armor so we could fight back."

Angel interjected again, "And she has a remarkable way with animals; it's as if they can read each others' minds or something."

Adam remembered when he was in the garden and pure of heart, he could speak to the animals as well, but that gift had faded from him since they left the garden.

"Lamech is a terrible man," stated Luna. "He slaughtered an innocent hostage to try to force us to surrender."

"But Angela led us out of the city and we rescued the other hostages, she led the charge of the forest animals and routed Lamech's forces!" beamed Angel. "She is a hero!"

Adam looked with renewed appreciation at Angela. "Indeed she is," he declared. "You've been busy, very busy in my absence," he remarked in wonder.

Angela said humbly, "I didn't know what else to do so I just called on the Lord."

"And he answered," completed Adam, remembering what Enoch had told him as a youth. Then again in grateful acknowledgment he repeated, "And he answered."

Chapter 21

"Enoch, wake up!"

Enoch moaned in his uncomfortable sleep, his legs still aching in pain.

"Enoch, it's me!" A soft voice urged him and gentle hands caressed his chest.

"What? Who are you?" he muttered as he fought his way back to consciousness.

He awoke to the deep brown eyes of Belhah looking intently into his sleepy gaze. She was ravishing, her face and lips exquisitely colored and her eyes and eyelashes large and inviting. She smelled heavily of lilac and cinnamon, and her loose robes were very revealing.

"Enoch, are you okay?" she looked concerned.

"Belhah, they have captured you too? How many others have they imprisoned?" he asked urgently.

"They attacked the city while you were gone, threatening to enslave or destroy all of us," she began, still keeping her hands on his chest and shoulder. She started to sob and put one hand between her breasts, drawing his attention to her plunging neckline.

"It was awful. We tried to fight but they were just too powerful."

Enoch looked back to her face, "What happened?" he asked, not wanting to hear but needing to know.

"Lamech is a horrible man," she cried. "In the end he demanded a willing sacrifice to save the city." Her sobs became more tortured and she moved her robe back so that it slipped off her shoulder and exposed more of her breast. "I – I volunteered to go but you know Angela – she had me restrained and she went out herself." She sniffled and wiped her eyes. "He raped her repeatedly in front of everyone, then pierced her heart with his sword, cutting it out for everyone to see." She broke into tears at this revelation and buried her face in his chest.

Enoch held her in shocked silence.

"She was so brave. I wish I could be like her," she whined.

Enoch took the news stoically, although his heart collapsed inside of him. "And what of the Queen Mother?"

Belhah continued to sob, "Also dead, as are many of Adam's troops. Alas, Mahalial, my husband was also killed at the battle below the mountain pass. You almost saved them all, my lord, if you had just lasted a little bit longer."

"How long have I been here?" asked Enoch, dazed by the news.

"About a week. They are quite afraid of you and I thought they were going to let you starve, till I volunteered to come in and care for you." She patted his legs. "Both of your legs are set and your other injuries are cleaned and healing nicely."

"I'm so sorry for your loss, Belhah. It must've been horrible to face such a trial and lose your love," he comforted her apologetically with a hug.

"I am blessed to be alive," she stated.

They sat in long silence, Belhah content to share the warmth of her body with him. She smiled to herself as she snuggled against him. The first part of the Belhah's plan was going well. She was taking advantage of feigned grief to gain physical closeness. There would be time to grow more intimate in the weeks ahead.

After a while, she whispered softly, "I will take care of you Enoch. We will get through this together."

Chapter 22

Trulock and his giants, along with huge, powerful mammoths, sorted through the rocks and debris at the mouth of the newly cut mountain pass. The expedition had been foraging throughout the area for the better part of the day, and Enoch's body was not to be found.

Trulock scratched his head. "The explosion was pretty severe," he stated, unwilling to consider out loud the possibility that Enoch's body had been completely disintegrated. "Could he have been thrown far away from here?"

Adam pursed his lips and surmised, "We have covered a far greater radius than any blast area suggested by the energy burns on these rocks. And if he were wearing his armor, at least it would have held up against any dark energy blast. I can only assume that they have moved the body."

Mahalial questioned, "Body? How can we even be sure Enoch is dead? If they had his dead body, they would have surely mocked us with it when they chased us into the city," he observed.

Adam slowly agreed with Mahalial's logic. "So the only reason they would move him, and keep it secret from us…"

"…was if he was still alive," finished Trulock.

Adam looked to the east, where the strongholds of his enemies lay and the countless miles of treacherous lands between them. Where would they have taken Enoch if he were still alive? Adam worried. If he ever found Enoch would his depleted army be able to free him? The enormity of such a quest overwhelmed him.

"Not a word of this to anyone until I have some time to figure out what to do, I don't want to get Angela's hopes up," Adam commanded.

Mahalial leapt upon his saber-toothed tiger and trotted off down through the mountain pass, without a word.

"Mahalial," shouted Adam, "where do you think you're going?"

He paused and looked over his shoulder at Adam stating, "The two people I love the most lay in the hands of the enemy. I go to free them and I go alone." With these words, he rode off, despite Adam's protestations.

Chapter 23

Zeus's golems were tireless automatons, excavating, disposing, constructing and finishing the infrastructure of sewers, foundations, roads and buildings of Atlantis. He could create thousands of them at a time. Their only limitation was lack of independent thought. Someone had to be there to direct and command them with the proper vibration authority frequencies.

For general labor and grunt work they worked perfectly, and he used the adoring Cainites for the finer, craftsman duties.

"Zeus!" Poseidon addressed him. "I need channels dug in the bay," he complained. "These rock golems keep getting stuck in the sea floor."

"Well, when is the last time you saw stone float?" mocked Zeus. "You shouldn't be ordering them into the water in the first place."

"Then how am I to get my harbor built?" whined Poseidon.

"You do it in steps," explained Zeus, rather impatiently. "We're finishing the foundry now. We can make large tools of metal utilizing levers, gears, hoisting mechanisms and scaffolding to dredge lanes out." Zeus worked up a sketch displaying a series of machines that could accomplish the task. "Take these plans to the foundry and have them start on these for you."

Belshazzar looked over the busy hive of activity in amazement. How the triplets – Hades, Poseidon and Zeus – had imagined such a city was beyond him. When he had first dared to whisper the idea for a separate kingdom for the child prodigies they had taken the idea far beyond his expectations. They were unique among all the inhabitants of the earth, the children of the fallen Cherub Lucifer, the highest order of angels and the highest of the Cherubs, conceived in the womb of Eve, the finest source of human potential there could ever be.

Early on as their teacher and instructor he had realized their potential was far greater than anything his master Apolodon had ever envisioned. Apolodon simply saw mighty warriors that could tip the balance of power from Lucifer to himself. Belshazzar foresaw so much more and much of it was taking shape right before his eyes.

They were still adolescents, unaware of how best to control their emotions, and certainly inexperienced in the ways of their father, but they were definitely becoming wise men of great renown. Belshazzar had to balance their selfishness, ambition and lust for life with enough logic to control their desires to reach a greater goal – a delicate balancing act indeed.

"You've made great progress, my young pupil," Belshazzar complimented as he stood by Zeus.

Zeus's back stiffened imperceptibly and he turned to Belshazzar. "Perhaps not a student much longer," he shot an icy glare back at Belshazzar. Then he smiled and slapped the startled teacher on the back. "Just messing with you, old man," he laughed and went back to his work.

Belshazzar was momentarily shaken, but then relieved. "Perhaps I should start referring to them more as peers," he mused to himself.

Chapter 24

Angela stuck to the shadows in the sleeping town, slowly and quietly working her way to the city walls. This early in the morning there was little foot traffic on the roads, but what few people were out would be watchmen and guards and she wanted no one alerted to her movement. Her long blonde hair was bound on top of her head and covered by her black, hooded cloak. She wore her battle armor as well, but it was covered by the dark cloak and reflected no light.

She worked her way to the edge of the city wall, where the mountainside met the gigantic amber covered structure. She waited until the watchman turned to cover the other part of his rounds, then dropped a light silken rope, tied off with a releasable knot, down the outer face of the wall.

She quickly slid down the rope and flicked it with a strong wrist action, loosening it from its mooring. It dropped silently beside her. She pressed her back up against the wall, shrouded in the darkest shadows. Angela gathered the rope rapidly into a loop and stuffed it beneath her cloak holding her breath, her heart racing.

She heard footsteps above her walking to the edge of the wall and stopping directly above her. She stayed motionless as she felt suspicious eyes upon her and after what seemed like an eternity, the footsteps resumed, walking the other way.

After the footsteps receded into the distance she quickly picked her way along the base of the mountain, sticking to the cover of shadows and rocks, pausing in silence as the watchman returned to her side of the outer wall.

After a number of pauses and restarts she worked her way to the edge of the dark woods and began to move with greater speed and less caution. When she reached the familiar clearing where she and Angel had mustered the animal army to surprise and route Lamech's attempted siege of Abelton, she paused and whistled a signal.

She waited, breathlessly, trying to remain calm.

Earlier that day in the city council she had lost the argument, to marshal the army and march upon whomever had taken Enoch or his body away.

Adam had said the men were still too tired and needed time to recover from their last campaign. He also pointed out that they knew little if anything for sure and needed to gather more information. Without coming right out and saying it, he hinted that she was being impetuous and hasty in her course of action and needed to learn patience. Probably all good arguments she thought, for everyone else – but not for her. She could not sit and do nothing, so she was going to find out what happened. To hell with patience.

After a few moments the trees rustled, then branches parted and the huge great ape that had joined her army earlier swung into the clearing, soon followed by another, then others, until a good score of the massive animals towered over her.

"Thank you for coming," she addressed the alpha male. "I suppose I should give you a name if we are to become 'brothers' and battle again."

The great ape bowed to her.

"I will call you MaSaad, for you are my fortress of hope," she said.

MaSaad arose and waited to hear her request.

"I need your help in a most dangerous mission," she started. "My mate," she touched her belly, not yet showing any sign of the life within, "and the father of my unborn child, has been stolen from me by horrible men. I must find him and bring him home," she said as she walked up to MaSaad and holding out her hand as an offering to him. "Will you join me?"

MaSaad reached down and offered his hand as well, agreeing to go with her. He turned to his pack of followers and translated the quest to them. They grunted and acknowledged their intentions to join.

"I can't thank you enough and I will never be able to repay you," she stammered.

MaSaad held his finger to his lips and mimicked the hush sign, then lifted her up and nestled her on his hairy back.

"We go to the site of battle, south of Abelton, to the last place we saw him alive."

The pack of great apes rushed from the clearing with a grace and speed that belied their great size and bulk. Angela felt the cool mountain air billowing past her face and thanked God for MaSaad and his followers. At least someone was taking her seriously.

As the sun started peeking over the eastern horizon the apes reached the foot of the freshly cut mountain pass. The morning sunlight crawled over the scene of Enoch's last stand, revealing a fifty yard radius of blackened marks of sheer energy formed in a broad semi-circle beginning at the center of the pass and extending to the very edges.

She dismounted and began to look for some trace, anything that could lead her onward. Suddenly from behind the cover of some rock, she spied movement and ducked to her knees, twirling to face the unannounced threat and activating her amber armor.

The great apes fanned out, snarling and ready to charge, with their fangs bared.

Trulock stepped out from his cover, followed by his score of giants. "You didn't think we would let you go out by yourself, did you?" stated Trulock.

Angela's armor hummed off and she dropped her guard, turning to the apes and making a sign for friend. The apes' postures relaxed and Angela pushed back her hood, releasing her golden locks. "Well, what are we waiting for?" she beamed.

Chapter 25

Enoch couldn't help but notice how exquisite Belhah looked and smelled each time she came in to check on him. Her hair and body smelled of fresh oil and spices. Her breath was sweet and fresh. She always spoke softly, huskily, almost seductively, no longer the angry young girl he had known from the past.

"Lay back and let me unwrap your legs to check their progress," she declared softly but with authority.

He winced a bit as she gently maneuvered the mending limbs and examined his wounds. "The bones are knitting together nicely, but we need to keep them immobile a little while longer, then start you exercising to build up your muscle."

"Do you know why they are keeping me here?" he queried, growing restless and impatient. "What are their plans for me?"

Belhah placed her soft warm hands on Enoch's firm chest and stomach and patted him. "They tell me nothing, other than they want you healed and well." She smiled and looked deeply into his eyes, her face just a little too close as his senses were seductively assaulted by her beauty and scent.

Enoch turned away. The news of Angela and Mahalial's deaths was only weeks previous and he still grieved horribly. But Belhah seemed to have moved on quite nicely. It bothered him.

"So what do you do when you're not caring for me?" he asked, knowing she must have access to privilege as she always appeared with her hair and face perfectly attended to and wore ravishing new outfits each day.

"A man of some wealth has taken a fatherly liking to me," she grinned. "He gives me whatever I want as long as I pose in the nude for his paintings." She struck a seductive pose for him. "He must have some stature in the city for when I heard about you and volunteered to care for you, he was able to pull the right strings."

"So we are in a Cainite city?"

"Yes, it's kind of weird isn't it? Enoch a prisoner in Enoch," she giggled and then quickly added, "except for the being a prisoner part." She busied herself now with sponge bathing him on his newly acquired bed.

Enoch said, "I don't think you have to do that, I can handle this chore myself."

She pouted, "Well okay, but it's not like I haven't seen you before. I bathed you while you were unconscious."

Enoch stopped her resumed scrubbing by gently holding her hands. "Well thank you, but it's different now that I am awake."

She lifted her hands and said, "Okay," and started to gather her things.

Enoch sensed he had offended her. "I'm very grateful for your care and dedication. You have been incredible," he said hurriedly.

"You are not attracted to me, you think me dark and hideous. That's okay, I always felt that way next to Angela," she huffed and got up to leave.

"Quite the contrary," admitted Enoch. "You're a stunning beauty, but, Belhah, Mahalial was my closest friend and he's been dead for only a few weeks. Don't you grieve for him?"

Belhah drew in a large breath, causing her breasts to strain against the top of her low cut gown, then exhaled quickly causing them to suddenly retreat again. "He had been gone for months already in the campaign to intercept Cain at the garden. I have been alone for a long time," she moaned.

Enoch asked a deeper question, "Did you love him?"

Belhah answered quickly, perhaps too much so, "Of course I loved him. What we had was very special and it will always be. But I have had to face the fact that he is gone now and I can wallow in self-pity or I can try to move on." She sat back down at his bedside and put her soft, warm hands gently on his bare chest and shoulder. "Enoch, I have always admired you and if God has seen fit to throw us together like this, well… But I can see I was wrong."

She stood again, "I can see I've offended you, if you desire another nurse I will tell them I have displeased you and have them replace me," she said, turning for the door, holding her breath to see how he would respond to her withdrawal.

She got to the door, opened it and fought the urge to hesitate. She did not want to appear to be giving him a chance to change her mind. He would have to fight to keep her now.

"Belhah, wait," called Enoch from behind her.

"No, I'm sure you will be better served by another. I have presumed upon our friendship and I should go," she said as she kept moving to close the door. "Guard, he is through with me now," she proclaimed, letting her voice crack just a bit.

"Belhah, wait!" called Enoch again from behind her. "You're right, we are two friends captive in a foreign land. We should not abandon each other."

Belhah turned as the guard approached her. "Are you sure?" she demanded.

"Yes," Enoch relented.

"Then I will see you again tomorrow," she said as she briskly left the room, the prison door slamming shut behind her.

Chapter 26

"The trail leads to here, then splits – one side northeast to the City of Light, the other eastwardly to the city of Enoch," stated Trulock. "We need to choose a direction."

Angela stared intently one way and then the other. If Enoch lived, both kingdoms had reason to hold him. But Belial, she knew, desired revenge of a personal nature and Lamech would obtain great leverage in forcing Adam to capitulate territories and wealth.

"We could split up and try to gather information from the local tribes," she pondered.

Suddenly a voice projected from behind them. "As though giants and huge apes would not be conspicuous. No offense intended."

Mahalial nodded in deference from atop his sabertooth as they padded down to Angela's group.

"Mahalial!" shouted Angela.

"May I make a suggestion?" he asked as he came alongside Angela and Trulock, his mount sniffing the giant suspiciously. "Sorry, all the giants he knows are evil."

"It is so good to see you!" gushed Angela, thrilled to have found another ally. "What is your suggestion?"

"Do you have anything of Enoch's?" asked Mahalial.

Angela's face fell. "When I left the city, I had to travel light to climb down the wall," she despaired. "I have nothing."

There was a moment of silence, then Trulock spoke up. "I have his spare suit of armor and his royal robes and tunic," he said reaching into his back pouch and producing a bundle. "I thought he should be dressed for the part when we found him," he explained. "It's not stealing," he defended himself.

Angela gently touched Trulock, "No, that was a marvelous idea, it's not stealing," she agreed.

Mahalial took the bundle and asked, "Did he ever wear these?"

Angela asserted, "Well of course he did, I recognize them well."

"Good. Gather your apes around my sabertooth," he said, and proceeded to give his tiger a nose full of the bundle, then passed it to MaSaad, mimicking with his hands the smelling motion.

MaSaad inhaled deeply then passed it on to his troops. The last one handed it back to Mahalial. "Now fan out, and find me that scent!" he commanded.

After a few tense moments of covering the trampled ground in both directions, his tiger stopped still and gazed directly eastward, one of his front paws lifted, motionless. MaSaad came over quickly and inhaled deeply and pointed down the eastern path too.

"To the land of Cain," Angela concluded.

"We know they will head for the capital city of Enoch to rest their army. I suggest we take a more sheltered route, as this merry band of rescuers," he looked at the giants, the great apes, himself and his tiger, and the fair headed princess wearing a suit of amber armor and riding on the back of a gorilla, "would be rather difficult to explain."

Chapter 27

Apolodon was enraged. Belshazzar and the triplets were gone – vanished; no note, no message, no nothing. He pondered what deception was being foisted upon him. Had Lucifer discouraged his pet project and stolen them from him?

He stalked around in his throne room cast in rubies, onyx and gold, stomping in his ruby red crystal armor, venting his rage.

But if it was Satan, why had he not been accused already? Certainly punishment would have come by now. And Lucifer had been very distracted by this alliance with Cain; did he even have time to notice?

Apolodon sat down in a huff and continued to ponder the situation. He pulled on a signaling rope and a loud, deep gong sounded. From outside his chambers entered a tall slender woman, her shaved head and nude body covered in gold – one of Apolodon's servant maidens. He liked his servants far better than Belial's dark wraiths. Belial had no taste.

"Check with the gatekeeper and see if any columns of a good size left the city in my absence. Oh, and bring me my dinner before you go," he ordered.

Was Belshazzar capable of absconding with the lads? He was close to them. Damnation. He should have executed the swine after the birth like he had planned. But the servant had bought himself some time by offering such a well-planned education for his subjects.

There was a third option, he thought. But it was almost impossible to conceive. Could the boys have figured out their own potential power and convinced or coerced Belshazzar to help them escape the plans he had to use them to overthrow Lucifer?

Though he shared that notion only with Belshazzar and bound him by oath to never speak of it to anyone else, they could have arrived at that conclusion themselves.

His doors opened and two additional golden serving girls helped the first one serve him dinner. He admired their naked curves as they set his table before him. Well, whatever or whoever convinced the satanic offspring to leave, he would have to find them and bring them back.

He would have to eliminate Belshazzar and take a more active role in the upbringing of his pawns. Apolodon took off his snake-like helmet and was preparing to enjoy his meal when one of the servant girls walked a bit too close. He pulled her to him and buried his face in her ample breasts, feeling a familiar stirring in his loins.

"Leave these two with me and go check with the gatekeeper," he ordered his head maiden. Unlike Lamech, he carried no women with him when going to war and his desire was unfulfilled. "Perhaps dinner can wait," he sighed as he hoisted both golden beauties, one over each shoulder and headed to his royal chambers, shedding ruby armor as he went.

Chapter 28

Eve nestled in Adam's arms, enjoying his warmth as the morning sun worked its way into their bedchambers. They had made love through the night with such frequency and passion that she felt like a young newlywed.

She kissed him and watched him slowly come awake, his eyes fluttering and opening up to her deep blue orbs. She smiled and kissed him again.

Adam rejoiced at the renewed interest of his soul mate and he smiled and tasted her sweet lips again. For a moment, all was right with the world.

"My Lord Adam!" sounded a voice from outside their chambers. "I must speak to you."

Adam sighed. He looked down at Eve as she pouted, kissed her and said, "Sorry, I must be a King for a little while." Then to the voice outside he said, "I'll be there in a moment."

A few minutes later Adam strode into his throne room and observed Luna and Angel waiting for him. "We're sorry to interrupt you this early, Lord Adam," apologized Luna.

Adam motioned with his hand for them to continue.

Angel added, "We were concerned about Angela so we both went to sit with her last night. After a while she assured us she was fine and she shooed us away. This morning we went back and we can't find her anywhere!"

Adam asked, "Have you checked with the gatekeepers? Perhaps she is out walking to clear her head, she does love nature you know."

Luna chimed in, "They have not seen her either and…"

"and what?" asked Eve as she had hastily wrapped a robe around her and entered the throne room behind Adam.

Angel added, "And he said the giants' camp outside the city was abandoned as well."

"Foolish girl," swore Adam as his peaceful morning was shattered. "She's disobeyed me and is off hunting for Enoch's body."

Eve came alongside Adam and gently touched his arm with her delicate hand. "Would you not have done the same for me?" she spoke softly.

Adam had to admit, he had done quite a bit more.

Chapter 29

"So he is not yet intimate with you?" Belial demanded impatiently.

Belhah defended herself, "He was truly in love with Angela. He still grieves for her supposed death."

Lamech observed Belhah's beauty and understood little about love, only lust and opportunity. "Maybe more than his legs are broken down there," he offered.

Belial ignored Lamech's comment and continued, "What little we know about his unusual power is that it springs from his amber armor and his purity of heart. We have his armor, but before we can totally quench his spirit we must debase his heart and see if that robs him of his power for good." He walked around Belhah, making his point.

"You claimed you could seduce him and begin leading him into debauchery and licentiousness. Can you still do this?" he asked, looking unconvinced as he waited for an answer.

Belhah cleared her throat. No one had resisted her charms for this long before. She had conquered every man she had ever desired, but Enoch was proving to be difficult.

"He will drop his guard, he's just a man," Belhah declared, mustering as much confidence as she could.

"You have one more week," declared Lamech. "After that we will forgo all this deception and intrigue and just crush his will the old-fashioned way, or he will die in the trying."

Belial licked his lips and smiled at Lamech, "I love it when you get forceful."

Lamech's skin crawled as he looked disgustedly at Belial. "Get about your work, girl. One week!" he barked at Belhah, then turned abruptly and left the room.

Chapter 30

The fire had burned down to a mass of red embers, just large enough for Angela and Mahalial, as the giants and great apes accompanying them had no need of such creature comforts.

Mahalial tossed another log into the pit sending a shower of glowing sparks into the air.

"Do you think that they are both still alive?" he questioned as he settled down into his coat of skins.

"I feel Enoch is, I just know I would sense it if he were truly gone. Belhah is resourceful; she's a survivor and beautiful. I would bet gold that she lives as well," she answered hopefully.

Mahalial picked at something in his teeth. "The women back at Abelton are not kind in the stories they tell about her," he said as his eyes burned into her.

"Many of them are jealous of her beauty," she defended. "I would pay them no mind."

"They say she led a group out to surrender to Lamech – to become willing slaves – and that one of her retinue was slaughtered because of her actions," he recounted.

Angela sighed, "She was doing what she thought best to survive. Who could have believed a girl like me could do anything to save our city?"

"You believed," Mahalial stated.

Angela held her silence for a while.

Mahalial threw another stick into the fire. "Look, I know Belhah is no angel and she has made some horrible choices, but I love her and I know somewhere deep inside her, when all is settled, that she loves me."

Angela wondered at his devotion, positive in her own mind that it was totally undeserved. "Well, that is all anyone can ask for in this world, to love and be loved. She is a very lucky girl," she smiled, trying her best to be as convincing and supportive as possible.

Mahalial grunted and returned to silence.

Angela stood up and stretched, gathering her cloak around her. "I'm off to see how Trulock and the others are doing."

Mahalial absently nodded, lost in his own thoughts.

Angela walked the perimeter of their makeshift camp. She felt so sorry for Mahalial, but hoped against hope that she was wrong and

Mahalial was right. He had such an unwavering belief in Belhah, she prayed he would not be heartbroken if his love was misplaced.

Trulock was sitting on the hillside, staying as concealed as a thirty foot giant could, mapping out their course for the next day's march.

He turned as his sharp ears detected her approach and silently nodded to her. After a few moments of quiet he asked, "Have you a plan to enter the city?"

She shook her head, "I'm reasonably sure Mahalial and I could disguise ourselves enough to get through the gates, but I don't think any kind of ruse would get a score of giants and another score of thirty foot apes past them."

Trulock thought for a while, then he touched Angela's amber gauntlet. "Have you ever used these to cut through metal?" he queried.

"Enoch taught me how to vibrate a line through iron, but brass is harder."

"Iron will do," said Trulock as he bent over and drew his plan in the dirt.

Chapter 31

Atlantis was stunning. Already it had roads, sewers, water and power. Zeus had manufactured a series of crystals, tuned to the vibrations of the sea waves, that illuminated the entire city. He provided mechanisms for all kinds of tasks, all run with sonic energy.

The number of buildings was growing, all-towering crystalline structures with fantastic views of the sea and the valley. Poseidon's harbor was almost complete as great metal behemoths cut and dug out his channels and pounded in the necessary pilings for docks.

Poseidon's first ship was to be launched today and he had designed systems to use the wind and sonic energy to propel it forward onto the seas and beyond.

Hades had used Zeus's golems to cut huge underground tunnels and labyrinths under the city and it was rumored his experiments and torture chambers were running at full steam.

The three brothers continued to amaze the people they had gathered with signs and miracles, exhibiting their power over dark beings in the spirit world. Zeus, in particular, had mastered how to manipulate and animate the elements.

Belshazzar watched with some amusement as Zeus formed two tiny warriors out of iron and set them in a small arena. They both charged each other and began pounding on each other with little iron fists.

"I'm trying to get them to use swords like swords and not clubs. This is proving harder than it looks," Zeus pondered.

"Will they be able to protect the city?" asked Belshazzar.

"Within limits, yes. They are not yet capable of independent thought, thus they have no initiative, so their ability to react to changes on the battlefield is very limited," Zeus frowned. "They will always need commanders, which means we must entrust our defense to men as well," he admitted.

"You seem to have your human subjects well in hand," observed Belshazzar.

"That is also trickier than it looked like at first," complained Zeus. "Sure, I can have any woman I desire, either by force or by promise of gain and yes, the people fear me and obey me when I command them, but is it willingly that they serve me? Do they truly love me?"

Belshazzar snorted, "What's love got to do with anything? As long as they obey and do your will that is enough, eh?"

Belshazzar didn't like this line of thought and reasoning. To be truthful, he didn't understand love himself. He never experienced either giving or receiving it. Oh, he had women before, but they were bought with payments or gifts and he tired quickly of such foolishness and instead dedicated himself to the study of knowledge and the black arts. Pleasure was temporary, power lasted.

Zeus continued, "But love seems to be the cornerstone of trust and loyalty. How can I trust my subjects to be loyal and do my will when I'm not there to pay them or scare them into it?" he debated. "Only the worst of them crave power and control over the rest, so my bureaucrats end up being swine, driven by lust and greed."

"Well, that is the kind of government you want. It is easier to control – you know what motivates them!" Belshazzar declared. "You're doing the correct things to build the kingdom, don't get sidetracked with this love foolishness. It can only lead to pain and disappointment."

Zeus nodded in absent-minded agreement. "I suppose," he said, but he couldn't ignore the void he felt in his heart.

Chapter 32

Lamech twirled his practice sword in formidable arcs above his head, then drove hard with considerable fury against his foe. His barrage of blows was parried, so he changed tactics and dove at the feet of his instructor and thrust upwards into his groin area. The sparring partner anticipated the move and leapt high into the air, striking the thrust aside, barely.

"Excellent, my Lord Lamech," he said, removing his helmet. Judah was the kingdom's best swordsman. He was a master trainer and been hired to work exclusively with Lamech. Lamech had a special visor made for himself that covered his eyes to rob him of his traditional advantage inherited from Cain, his Medusa-like, paralyzing glare. Lamech realized some of his opponents could be unaffected by this power and he wanted to be skilled enough to win in such a fight with weapons only.

Lamech laughed as he removed his helmet. "I almost had you!" he grinned.

"You're progressing nicely, but you have more to learn. You need to develop more agility and balance if you are to compete against the Adamite form of fighting," noted Judah.

Lamech nodded. The Adamites relied on quickness and speed above all else. Their blades were black crystal and would shatter if struck by a Cainite metal blade, but that had not been an advantage in real battle conditions as they had thought it would be. The Adamites simply dodged and weaved until they found an opening and thrust their blade home with deadly force. It simply was not practical to completely encase his troops in armor and still keep them mobile.

"Tomorrow we will begin work with crystal blades and it would behoove you to gain instruction on how to use dark energy effectively in battle also," chided Judah.

"I know, I know," said Lamech impatiently. "You know I do have an army and sorcerers to defend me as well?"

"None of those will be of any use if an assassin comes to call," reminded Judah, "then it is man on man, up close and personal."

Judah sheathed his practice sword, "Tomorrow at sunrise, I will continue your training."

Lamech held up his hand, "I'll be here," he promised while tossing his sword to his servant.

Lamech left the training center and peeled off his sweaty garments, heading to his royal bathing pool.

He was pleased to see both Adah and Zillah frolicking in his bath and stepped into the warm water to join them.

"And what have you two ladies been up to this morning?" laughed Lamech.

"As if you have to ask?" mocked Adah as she looked mischievously at Zillah and licked her lips.

"Sometimes I wonder if you two even need me," Lamech pouted, exaggerating his mock sorrow.

The nude beauties swam over to him and began fondling him. "Have no fear my Lord, you have ways to pleasure us that we do not possess!" His wives rose from the waters and snuggled their naked bodies against his as they kissed his chest, neck and lips.

Lamech smiled at the pleasure - hungry women. "Which one of you wants to go first?"

He laughed as Zillah pushed Adah away and jumped on him, encircling his neck with her arms and his hips with her legs.

"It's good to be the King," he groaned.

Chapter 33

Adam had not lived in the city when Angela rose to her leadership position and defended Abelton against the siege of Lamech and Apolodon. So he had vastly underestimated the love and support she engendered from the women who had been left behind there.

Every officer and warrior who had a wife, sister, mother, daughter or girlfriend was being accosted by his significant other as to why they were not mounting up to pursue Angela and protect her.

Adam's quandary escalated when a troop of women declared they were going with or without his support.

Adam gathered the ruling council and rose to address them. "Gentlemen, I have asked several guests into our council today as they apparently played a major role in the defense of our city," he said as he gestured towards Angel, Luna and the high governess.

"Not apparently… they did," corrected Eve as she walked into the chamber, attired in her splendid royal robes of white, embellished with her design of a rainbow of jewels and gems. Her presence in a room always commanded attention.

"And of course, you know Eve," Adam added.

He began, "I've called this meeting of the council to best organize our response to Angela's apparent disappearance."

Luna interjected, "We all know she's going after Enoch."

Adam tried to object, "Now we don't know that," then he caught Eve's eyes and gave in, "but that is the most likely explanation."

He cleared his throat, "Now I saw the explosion at the top of the mountain and I find it highly unlikely that anything could survive that blast." He started walking and continued, "However, Angela has taken hope that since Enoch's body remains unfound he could still be alive but held captive by some foe."

Angel and Luna chimed in, "She's not the only one who feels this way."

"Well, now we find ourselves with at least two of our number, both Angela and Mahalial, running into harm's way trying to find Enoch or his body. We do know they are alive and at risk, so we should plan a response," said Adam.

Enos declared, "The men of Carmel shall muster at your command." He bowed his head to Adam.

Seth agreed, "As will the men of Abelton."

Adam held up his hand. "If any truly are hostage, a large show of force would only hasten their doom. I propose that I take a small entourage and attempt to reason with Cain's successor Lamech, find out his intentions and his price for returning Enoch's body," Adam stated.

"But what's to stop him from taking you hostage as well?" cried Luna, obviously distraught.

Adam smiled warily, "Lamech will find I am not so easy to capture. If I'm alone and I don't have to worry about what will happen to my men, a weakness of mine will be eliminated."

The room filled with sounds of protest until Adam lifted up his hand to quiet them. "My mind is made up. I will not sacrifice the people of the city with a direct assault on either the City of Light or the fortresses of Cain."

Eve grasped his hand and shoulder and desperately gazed into his determined eyes, "I don't want to lose you after we have finally found our way."

Adam met her gaze and declared, "It is time I started acting as King." He held her hand, "The King must think of his people, not just himself."

After the room cleared Eve cornered Seth and Enos quietly. "Adam is indeed brave, but I will not lose him if I can help it. Let him and his group gain a day's advantage, then we will follow. Send your scouts to monitor his progress," Eve said as Enos nodded and hurried away to his task.

She then turned to Angel and Luna, "Do you think the animals would muster to our cause?"

Angel and Luna grinned in dual accord. "Would they! The animals and their riders have been relentless in demanding new adventures. We go now to prepare them."

Eve turned and smiled as she saw Adam finishing his instructions and walking over to her. "I don't want you to worry. I will be very careful. The odds are whoever has Enoch or his remains just wants a reward. If I cannot negotiate a release we can always try another tack afterwards," Adam smiled his best reassuring smile, trying to comfort her.

"I will do my best not to worry," said Eve sweetly. "Now give me a kiss and get on your way."

Chapter 34

"What are they?" asked Angela as she peered out from behind the protecting bushes.

Mahalial shook his head, "I've never seen such before."

Large stone golems were digging into the side of a mountain, filling carts up with ore that had shiny streaks of metal in it.

"They look like they are made of pure stone!" whispered Angela. "How can they even move?"

Trulock muttered, "There is evil magic at work here, this is not natural."

At forty feet tall, the stone golems towered over the giants and great apes by a good ten feet and would be formidable opponents in a fight just by their sheer size and solid constitution.

Angela and Mahalial had so far successfully led their band deep into Cainite territory, sticking to the woods and shadows and staying unnoticed. This mine was certainly the property of the Cainites and these creatures were pilfering Cainite gold, which made them thieves and enemies of Lamech but not necessarily friends of Angela and Mahalial.

Judging by their single-mindedness and blank expressionless stares, Angela felt they would only serve their master, whoever that could be.

Mahalial must have been paralleling her thoughts, "Whom do you think they serve?" he whispered.

Angela pondered, "If we had the time we could see where they deliver those carts of ore." She quickly discounted the idea, "Another day perhaps."

"Let's give this place a wide berth," muttered Trulock as he motioned to his giants to stay low and retreat deeper into the woods.

Suddenly, a clear blast of silver trumpets shattered the air and Trulock signed for everyone to hit the dirt.

Angela's eyes grew big and she mouthed, "Cainite trumpets!" to Mahalial, who pressed a finger to his lips to shush her.

A band of black armored giants marched upon the working golems, forming a half circle around them, trapping them against the face of the mine. They bore the standard of Lamech, a golden dragon etched on a fluttering black flag.

"Nice artwork," admired Angela. Mahalial hushed her again.

"Who dares to steal from Lord Lamech?" demanded the giant in charge. The giants looked like children compared to the stone golems and clearly felt nervous with this reversal of roles.

The golems kept cutting the vein in the mountain and loading the carts.

"I command you in the name of Lord Lamech to stop and tell me who your master is!" shouted the commander of Lamech's policing force.

Nothing.

The commander turned to his men and motioned them to stop the loading. Four of the giants stepped in front of the carts and drew their huge metal swords and maces, interrupting the path of one of the burdened stone goliaths.

The golem kept moving towards the cart with his load.

The commander ordered, "Smash his leg, that will get his attention!"

Two of the giants lifted their massive hammers like maces and struck the stone behemoth on his foot, smashing several of his toes into dust.

Suddenly, as if some silent signal had gone off, all of the golems changed instantly from working mode to attack mode. With surprising swiftness for their large bulk they caught the startled giants and began pulling them into pieces. The giants were as helpless as rag dolls in the hands of the larger golems and their tortured screams betrayed their utter terror.

Angela shielded her eyes against the slaughter until the last of the bellowing stopped and the giants lay in a bloodied collage of separated body parts. The golems expressed no emotion or elation and just returned to their task. The one with the smashed toes was now walking with a noticeable limp.

The secluded band of Adamites looked at each other in amazement and hushed awe.

"What power!" murmured Mahalial.

They stayed in silence for a while longer, until Trulock whispered Angela, "I think we might be able to use that armor, now that they have no need for it.

Chapter 35

Belhah's visits became longer and longer as she tended to Enoch, dressing his wounds and caring for his health and well-being.

She had starting taking all of her meals with him, laughing and sharing intimate conversations, always letting her hands linger on him, greeting and departing from him with hugs and kisses on his cheeks.

She had him transferred to a larger, better equipped cell and had it fitted with many creature comforts.

Enoch began to welcome her visits and her company, although he marveled at how much pull she had through her new owner. They had just finished taking a few laps around his cell on his newly mended legs.

"You are doing so well!" she said excitedly and put both hands on his face, pulling his startled lips towards hers as she gave him a quick kiss on his mouth, smiling at him. "I'm so proud of your progress," she said as she nestled into his arms and pulled them around her. "I feel so safe with you, so protected," she purred.

Enoch enjoyed her warmth as she burrowed into him.

"You have been so diligent in helping me," he admitted, wrestling with conflicting feelings. He still ached for Angela and wondered why he had been spared here in the enemy's lair, but he appreciated the beautiful Belhah's attention. She was a semblance of home.

He missed her when she was gone from him and looked forward to her smile and affection when she returned. She was worming her way into his heart.

"Enoch?" she asked softly, snuggling closer into him.

"Yes Belhah?" Enoch answered, enjoying her scent and closeness.

"You know that slaves can never marry, the masters do not allow it," she said as she turned and looked into Enoch's eyes. She raised his hand to her lips and softly kissed it. "If someday we moved past our losses of the ones we loved and chose to love each other, we could never be 'officially' married as slaves. Would loving and committing just between us be acceptable to God?" Her eyes were wide and vulnerable, misting with tears.

Enoch brushed the start of a tear from her eye. "If that day comes, I'm sure God would understand."

She smiled and her eyes brightened as she kissed his lips, lingering on their softness as she draped her arms around his neck pressing her firm breasts into his naked chest.

After a few moments she relented and buried her face against his strong muscles. "No rush, no hurry," she murmured breathlessly as she held him tight. "But I want you to know that I am ready to be yours, heart, soul and body if you ever desire to take me."

She got up quickly and smiled her most alluring smile at him, then turned to leave. "Whenever you're ready," she said bouncing out the door as the guards closed the heavy metal opening behind her.

"Just four more days," she counted to herself, "this is going to be close.

Chapter 36

Hera was appalled at her sudden loss of status. As Cain's wife she had enjoyed the best that life could offer. She had the royal palace Cain had built for her, opulent furnishings throughout, servants to wait on her hand and foot, the finest jewelry and gems, regal clothes and robes, and the best wine and food in the land.

At just under nine feet tall she had the slanted, almond shaped eyes and her skin was light brown. Her hair was jet-black and long, oiled with the finest spices, bouncing and shiny when she shook her head or strode from place to place. Her eyes were jade green, and she took great care to keep her figure lean and seductive.

Cain had been a difficult man to keep a harness on, so she had experimented and perfected many pleasures to keep him interested at home. Now he was gone and she was being ignominiously removed from her home and reinstated in a tiny shack on the outskirts of the city.

She shouldn't have burned so many bridges, she thought. Her haughty spirit and cruel demeanor had stripped her of any friends and her family had long since washed their hands of her.

Without Cain she was nothing and it was finally sinking in. Thank the gods that she'd worked diligently at enhancing her physical beauty and appearance. She could still attract a powerful man, but she needed a fresh start, in a place where no one knew her by sight or reputation. That wouldn't be here, in the city now ruled by Lamech.

Hera looked at her small retinue consisting of two giants, two triceratops-like three horned beasts of burden, and her own lizard-like, four-legged mount. The giants were slow witted but loyal, they took her insults without understanding.

"Is everything loaded?" she asked impatiently.

The giants looked at each other and nodded uncertainly.

"Well then, let's leave this place and find our new future," she urged her little band forward, leading them out of the city gates.

As they plodded forward, leaving behind the city of Enoch, the city named for her and Cain's son, she thought hard about the past and the future.

Cain had become obsessed with his quest for the Tree of Life. It was his undoing. But if what he said was true, Hera's five hundred years of life might be leading her to an end, a return to dust and death. If only he had returned with that fruit, she could have enjoyed true immortality, ruling as Queen forever! She shook her head in defeat. "I will find a new man and make him the most powerful ruler on earth. Then I will take my vengeance on these thankless peoples," she vowed.

Chapter 37

The bright light of the sun blinded Enoch as he stumbled, his still healing legs unsteady, as his guards flung him into the sandy floor of the training arena.

"You wonder, perhaps, why you are still alive?" questioned Lamech as he circled Enoch, his voice dripping with disrespect.

"Well I can tell you I'm not sold on the idea, but stripped of your amber armor you seem to be just a man, like the rest of us," Lamech continued as he tossed a training sword of wood down at Enoch's feet. "Others in my kingdom seem to think you might have some value so for now you live," he concluded as he chose a training sword himself out of the racks and hefted it in his hand, cutting the air with swift arcs.

"My trainer, Judah, tells me I must improve in the style of your people to become a better swordsman."

He sprang into a defensive position. "So today, you will be my sparring partner," he grinned like a cat cornering a mouse.

"Are you ready?"

Enoch remained silent and left his sword on the ground.

Lamech circled warily and warned, "I would not stay unguarded." When Enoch still did not respond Lamech swept his sword across the backs of Enoch's legs, knocking him heavily on the ground.

"Now get up and train with me," he commanded.

Enoch slowly got to his feet, but did not pick up the sword. Lamech struck him on the shoulder, then spun to his backside and struck a sharp blow on the back of Enoch's head, again knocking him to the ground.

"Tsk, tsk, tsk," Lamech strutted around the fallen Enoch. "As I anticipated, you are not being cooperative." Then to his guards he called out, "Bring out his nurse."

Enoch turned his head and saw Belhah being dragged into the training arena. Lamech walked over to her as she struggled, ripping off her linen tunic.

"Wait!" cried Enoch as he struggled to his feet.

Lamech grinned at Enoch then struck Belhah on her shoulder and spun, striking her again on the back of her head, sending her falling, face down into the sand of the arena. "Stand her up!" he ordered.

Then he snarled at Enoch, "Every blow I land on you, I shall land on her, so quit playing the fool and let's start training!" he laughed, twirling his sword in his hand.

Enoch snatched his sword and hefted it in his hand. It was a cumbersome blade, with none of the weight and balance of his own crystal foil and his legs were weak from inactivity. He had only been walking on his own without help for a few days.

"You may stop beating helpless little girls," said Enoch as he watched Belhah's frightened gaze, clutching her torn tunic to her naked breasts, her hair disheveled and face smothered in sand.

"I thought you'd see it my way," chuckled Lamech and he began his assault anew. Now that he had Enoch engaged, he was far more difficult to strike. Even hobbled as he was, Enoch dodged, weaved and ducked under the best-aimed blows, often jabbing his own blunt point into Lamech, knocking him off balance.

After several minutes Lamech was getting winded and Enoch had barely broken a sweat. Totally exasperated Lamech called out, "Judah!"

The master swordsman entered the arena. Lamech ordered, "Teach this insolent slave a lesson or two in humility."

Judah eyed Enoch critically and noticed the wound marks on his legs and body. "Isn't this the prisoner with two broken legs?" questioned Judah.

Lamech sputtered, "Well he's obviously healed now! Take him down!"

Judah spat and threw down his sword. "I will not disgrace myself fighting an injured man. Go ahead and have your sport, but do so without me," he turned and walked away.

Lamech's rage grew and he shouted, "Bring her to me."

Enoch pushed his aching legs for another leap and knocked both of the guards from their hold on Belhah and placed himself between them, Lamech and the frightened girl. Belhah whimpered in fear, still hurting from the previous blows.

Lamech had sworn to not use his Medusa-like glare in this little training exercise. He wanted to save that surprise for a time when life and limb were at risk, but this insolent fool keeping him from his intentions now sorely tempted him. Against his better judgment he allowed the full power of his fiery glare to burn into the eyes and heart of Enoch and Belhah.

Belhah collapsed in an instant, hitting the ground like a sack of fruit, but Enoch stood at the ready, only turning briefly to check on Belhah when he heard the thud behind him.

"What have you done to her?" Enoch demanded.

Lamech was caught off guard but curious at the same time. His secret weapon had no effect on this one; very unsettling indeed. Anxious to regain some kind of advantage he ordered, "It is not for you to know. Take her and leave, be ready for more training tomorrow and remember I hold her life in my hands."

What if there are more like him? Lamech wondered to himself. Such a foe would be difficult indeed to eliminate.

Chapter 38

Apolodon was fairly certain now that Belshazzar and the spawn of Eve had left of their own accord. The gatekeeper himself had not seen them exit the city, but his apprentice remembered a shady caravan of some size leaving early one morning, long before sunrise. The fact that there were no rumors of any kind of their presence in the city or Lucifer's dungeons, was confirmation that he had been betrayed, his pet projects stolen from him.

He could not tell Lucifer anything about his progeny, spawned by a rape of Eve while she slept under Apolodon's protection, or Lucifer would instantly destroy the halflings and him for preserving them.

No, his best bet was to find the triplets and turn them to his will. He had received Lucifer's permission to leave the city under the ruse of finding more beasts to replace the many lost in the recent conflicts, as well as more women for the Dark Lords' pleasure.

Belial seemed to have lost interest in that old pastime of his. He and Lucifer seemed only interested in pleasing each other and raping men now. Apolodon was revolted by such behavior; surely he would not fall that low – there was a limit to his depravity.

"Our formation is readied, my Lord," reported one of Apolodon's messengers. Apolodon surveyed his force. It was still quite a formidable collection of sauropods and great carnivores, giants, mages, trolls, ogres and cyclopes, with his own loyal Dark Lords and sorcerers. He rode upon his own lone red dragon, a mighty beast that inspired great pride in Apolodon and fear to those who opposed him.

"Onward then," motioned Apolodon as he initiated the columns' march out of the gates of the City of Light.

The pale glow of iridescence illuminated the ghastly walls of the fortress and the City of Lucifer in the predawn hours. Apolodon knew he must have powerful allies if he were to ever overthrow this perverted god of forces, which made this trek extremely important if he were to wrest the ruling power from the Father of Lies.

Chapter 39

"You look quite dashing as a Cainite warrior," admired Angela as she observed Trulock in the captured armor of the ill-fated Cainite giants.

"You are right about those stone creatures paying no attention to us as long as we left them to their mining," spoke Trulock as he polished the smudge off of his breastplate of the black, crystalline armor.

Angela and the ten giants who had donned the armor of the slain giants of Cain were now traveling openly. They appeared to be a police unit with a hostage, taking their prize to the city gates. Angela kept her amber armor hidden in her dark robes and remained dormant and dazed looking whenever they encountered questioning eyes.

Mahalial and the remaining giants and great apes followed undercover, arriving at the edges of the woods as Trulock and his masquerading accomplices arrived at dusk with their hostage.

All the tribes of this new earth spoke the same language, but separation had lent itself to different slangs and colloquialisms, making Trulock's background with the Cainites invaluable.

"You arrive late, sir," hinted the gatekeeper, seeking identification from the band of giants.

Trulock spat a huge hock of phlegm at the gatekeeper's feet, "Out of my way, little man. We've traveled long and hard and must get this prize cleaned and scented for Lamech." He thrust Angela's limp body at him, displaying her beautiful face and flowing blonde hair. "I have no time to dawdle with you." He brushed past the protesting gatekeeper, rolling his eyes at the gate guards, his giant counterparts. Trulock leaned towards them and whispered, "Humans!" in a knowing, scoffing way and the Cainite giants laughed at the inside joke.

The gatekeeper's ears turned red and he shot a warning glare at the giant guards, hushing their laughter as Trulock's helmeted force marched by.

Once in the city the little force marched straight to the flowing river in the middle of the town. Once there, Trulock gently set down Angela's now alert form.

"That is where the river flows below the wall," he pointed downstream while the other giants formed a visual screen, ostensibly blocking the view of their fellows relieving themselves in the river. "There is an iron set of bars underwater. You must cut through those to allow the rest of our force to enter the city," Trulock instructed.

Angela nodded and shed her robes, revealing her formfitting amber armor and golden hair before diving into the dark river water. Trulock admired her beauty silently. "If only I were 20 feet shorter," he muttered out loud and shook his head.

Angela used her sonic bubble to form a pocket of air around her, vibrating her armor to propel herself to the iron grid under the wall.

Sure enough, thick iron bars secured the way against any potential intruders. She wrapped her bubble of air around the first set of bars and began to focus a white-hot beam of energy at the base of the bar, melting a hairline crack through it and filling her pocket full of air with acrid smoke.

She sputtered back up to the surface to get a fresh batch of air, coughing and wheezing as she surfaced. Trulock hushed her with his finger to his mouth and motioned her urgently back below the surface. He did not want any hint of amber light showing, anywhere.

Angela gulped fresh air and pushed back down below the water. She realized this was not going to be easy.

Chapter 40

Belhah feigned unconsciousness while Enoch carried her back to his cell. She thought Lamech had been a little too convincing with his blows, but she was not seriously hurt. She had learned from Adah and Zillah to recognize just before Lamech was ready to launch his 'glare of scare' – as they called it – and shut her eyes, pretending to faint, shielding herself from its true effect.

She let her torn tunic slide off her torso, tempting Enoch with her full, naked breasts. Enoch laid her in his bed and cleaned her face and chest of the sand from the arena, then covered her up and left her resting.

She peeked out of hooded eyes and saw Enoch pacing back and forth like a caged lion, obviously consumed in thought.

A bit chagrined that he had not taken advantage of her in her vulnerable, supposed unconscious state – like that pig Lamech would in a heartbeat, she moaned and flopped out from under the covers. He was still preoccupied. She pouted a bit then decided to give a little shriek of fear and pain.

"Enoch, save me!" she cried out in horror, jolting up from her prone position.

Enoch raced to her bedside and she draped her nude body over his, hugging him and kissing him desperately. "Oh Enoch, I was so afraid," she gasped between kisses, hunting for his lips with hers.

Enoch attempted to calm her, drawing her back from his face, "You're okay Belhah, you're going to be okay."

She gazed longingly into his somber eyes with her own tearing orbs. She plumped her lips and took his hand and placed it over her breast. "Feel my heart," she said breathlessly. "It's beating out of my chest."

He lifted his hand and brushed back her hair, "Just breathe, calm yourself, rest."

"What's wrong with this guy?" she thought to herself. "Am I just being too subtle?" She decided to take a more direct approach, throwing off her covers and pressing her soft mounds of flesh into his chest. She kept her eyes on his and reached down between his legs, fondling him.

"Take me, Enoch! Make love to me! Make me your woman!" She squeezed him and parted her lips in anticipation of being smothered with passionate kisses. Instead, Enoch caught her hand and gently moved it away.

"I'm sorry Belhah, my heart still belongs to… " Enoch began.

Suddenly an amber glow surrounded and outlined the prison door and the smell of molten metal filled the air. Enoch shielded Belhah from the heat as the door crashed to the floor.

Through the smoke a glowing female figure appeared, searching through the darkness of the cell. "…Angela!" completed Enoch in shock.

He rejoiced then was filled with dread as he realized he held the naked, trembling Belhah in his arms and the dead love of his life had just freed them.

Angela just stared at the embracing couple, then turned and walked away, saying nothing.

Trulock peeked in as Enoch pulled the clinging Belhah from his chest. Trulock shook his head and tossed in Enoch's old set of amber armor. "I would put this on and get her to put some clothes on now! Mahalial is just around the corner."

Belhah wrapped herself in the linens of the bed as Enoch eyed her coldly, strapping on his armor and sword.

Belhah saw Mahalial burst around the corner and shouted with joy. "My love!" as she rushed lovingly into Mahalial's arms, covering his face with hot, passionate kisses. "I knew you would come for me!" She burst into tears.

Chapter 41

Hera eyed the pile of rotting flesh that the carrion-eating birds and reptiles feasted on. They were the carcasses of giants she was sure. Around the bend she heard the ragged rumbling of stone and ore being broken apart and moved around.

She snuck her sleek lizard mount around for a peek, then watched in open eyed amazement as she watched several forty foot tall stone golems finish loading great carts of precious ore and start pulling them away. The carts moved in a strange direction. Their destination was clearly not towards any city or civilization that she was aware of.

Their progress was cumbersome and left an obvious trail, so they would be easy to follow. She looked again at the pile of devastation close by.

It was too close to be a coincidence. It was caused by the rocky behemoths, so she determined they should stay a safe distance behind the golems to avoid detection.

She returned to her little band and declared, "I found evidence of another kingdom that values metal ore. They must be somewhat advanced." The giants nodded, but they would've agreed to anything Hera said. Hera knew that too but kept talking anyway, "We will follow their trail and see where they take us while we keep enough distance to not be noticed."

Hera had her giants set up an early camp and soon she was luxuriating in the evening sunset while enjoying a light evening meal of fruit and soup.

Any cities past the known territories would be easy prey for her with her superior knowledge and cunning. If she could locate a powerful man or maybe even a ruler, she would quickly win his heart with lust and work her way back into power.

Women in the outer territories would be no competition to her feminine wiles and sexual experience. She examined herself in her silver mirror, admiring her smooth skin and beautiful facial structure, wondering what new world she would conquer.

Suddenly the ground shook and a huge, hulking form strode quickly alongside their camp. Hera's two giants leapt to their feet in defense but Hera commanded them, "Be still! Do not move!" She knew her servants would be no match for this monster.

After a painfully long few minutes the hulk appeared to satisfy itself that they were no threat and strode double-time after the departed caravan.

Hera sighed in relief and motioned her giants to sit back down, "If we don't bother them, they won't bother us," she noted. "We will resume our journey in the morrow."

Chapter 42

"Come on!" urged Trulock, "There is not much time! I ought to leave you behind for the pain you bring to my lady Angela." The giant curled his lips and looked with disgust at Enoch. Trulock knew very little about him, but had become fiercely loyal to Angela.

Enoch's head was swimming as Belhah's deception became more and more apparent. She did not seem to be surprised at all to see both Angela and Mahalial alive and she had proclaimed she "knew Mahalial would come for her."

Enoch held up his hand in an effort to clear the confusion. "Belhah told me Angela and Mahalial were dead, as well as most of the city of Abelton, with the rest enslaved. She has been my nurse since I've been here." He finished buckling his amber armor and hefted his new black crystal blade.

"She was practicing unusual medicine on you," scoffed Trulock as he glanced down the hall and motioned to him to follow.

"It's complicated and it is not what it seems," said Enoch gruffly, dashing into the hall, fighting Trulock for the lead. "I must talk to Angela," he muttered.

"I would concentrate on getting out of here alive first. Besides, I don't feel like she's much into talking just yet," advised Trulock, swatting away a prison guard with his large club.

Enoch disrupted the aim of two archers with an amber blast, knocking them heavily to the ground. "I would never hurt her on purpose Trulock. I believed her dead."

"Why waste time grieving, when you can be polishing the old knob with the first pretty face you see, eh?" Trulock smashed through a makeshift wall of shields more guards had thrown across their path.

"There was no knob polishing. Lamech had just beaten her. I was…" Enoch sighed in frustration. It was just sounding bad no matter how much he explained.

"Well, yes, she looked really seriously incapacitated and could barely move, especially her lips," mocked Trulock as they burst forth into the main courtyard of the prison complex.

It was pure bedlam all around them. A number of giants were clad like Trulock in shiny black armor, but they seemed to be fighting against each other, while other giants clothed in skins joined the battle. Behind them huge gorillas were tossing the prison guards and their lizard-like mounts left and right.

Enoch followed Trulock's pointed finger and saw Mahalial and Belhah mounted on his own saber-toothed tiger. Belhah was blabbering nervously into his ear while a strange look began to appear on Mahalial's face.

Ahead of them walked the glowing female figure, striding forward in anger and cold deliberation, picking off opponents attempting to block the way with her own energy blasts.

Enoch dipped his head and started sprinting towards Angela, dodging a thrown axe as he reached her side.

She glanced at him and he saw cold fury in her eyes.

"How could you!" she shouted, tears streaming down her cheeks. "Do you know all I went through to get to you?" She fought back sobs and put up a blocking shield in front of a squad of dino-riders, throwing them backwards into disarray.

"Angela, it's not as it appears. I need to explain," appealed Enoch, ducking a swing by a black armored guard. He countered, thrusting into his shoulder, causing him to scream in pain and drop his sword. Enoch kicked him aside.

"And Mahalial, how could you do this to him? You know he lives and breathes for that woman and he loves you!" she shouted as she cleared her eyes and glared at him.

Enoch shielded a flight of arrows from Angela's unguarded flank with his amber shield of energy and they fell harmlessly to the ground. "Obviously, this is not the best time to discuss this. You're distracted," said Enoch as he looked for new threats.

Trulock thundered past them, "Run to the river! We will have our best chance of escape there!"

A huge gorilla snatched up Angela and swung her onto his back as he raced after Trulock. Enoch could see his rage filled red eyes peering at him accusingly.

"Another one of her friends," he mourned to himself. His legs ached and he struggled to keep up with the retreating band, now not so eager for him to be joining them.

Suddenly a formidable figure dropped from above, clad in energy diffused obsidian armor, swinging a crystal black blade of his own.

"I see you're feeling better," the familiar figure threatened.

"Judah!" exclaimed Enoch.

Chapter 43

Adam and his royal retinue had just set up camp outside the Cainite city of Enoch. He had sent in his emissary to notify Lamech of his arrival and of his desire for peaceful resolution. That messenger had returned with an offer from Lamech to meet in the morning.

So far, so good. Adam had made good time, bringing only his unicorn riders and camels along for carrying supplies. He had not been able to sleep well so he had left his royal tent to walk in the cool evening air.

He looked up into the star-studded heavens and spoke to the God he had once known face-to-face. "I wanted to thank you for what you did for Eve," he started. "I was a fool, again, trying to solve my own problems by thinking I could do it better than you. Forgive me for my impatience and my pig-headedness."

He stopped for a moment, surveying the brilliant tapestry spread across the midnight sky. "I don't know how many more days I'm going to have with her, but I want them to be good days, days that we honor, respect and love each other. Help me to see what I fail in that so I can correct it quickly."

At that moment, the brilliant streak of a shooting star flashed across the heavens. Was God listening?

"Creator," he wondered out loud, "Angela has told me of how she lived outside of her body when she drowned and saw spirit beings also without bodies. Is that our fate? To be a mist, a shadow, just a hint of our former selves?"

In the old days, when he asked God a question, he could hear the voice of God audibly and see his face. But it was different now. As he sat in the quiet stillness, struggling to hear something, anything, from above, a thought began to form in his mind. It was like a thought of his own, but from a source outside of himself.

"Your end is just the beginning," the thought said.

Adam said quickly, "Is this you, Lord?"

Again the thought came, addressing him as though he was a second party to the conversation. "Your end is just the beginning."

"What does that mean?" Adam questioned. But nothing else came. Adam shook his head and pondered those words. After a while he got up and slowly walked back to his dark tent.

After a few strides towards his sleeping pallet, he sensed a presence – an evil, nonhuman force behind him, in the corner of the tent. Sweet perfume attempted to mask the acrid hint of sulfur in the air, a sure sign that a Fallen One was near.

Adam's bracelets of amber quickly fired up and golden light filled the room as he spun around and confronted Belial.

Now illuminated, Belial stepped forth from his hiding place. "How do you do that?" he questioned in admiration. "I thought my concealment spell would have hidden me longer."

Adam pinched his nostrils together, "You stink, try taking a bath," Adam stated. "Why are you here?"

Belial, affronted a bit by the insult, tried to not let it distract him. "You come for the boy, Enoch?"

"He lives?" Adam's heart jumped within him at the prospect.

"For now," purred Belial. Adam noticed a difference in Belial. He moved and smelled like a woman, but his corporeal body still appeared as a man. Adam noted the strange difference in his mind, but continued.

"What do you want for him?" Adam crossed his arms across his powerful chest and prepared to negotiate.

"I am studying him now," admitted Belial. "You know his power is very unusual. He has caught me off guard several times." He continued to slink around the tent, swaying his hips like a sow in heat.

"What will it take to end your studies?" demanded Adam.

Belial played with a long strand of his snow-white hair, unconsciously twirling it around his little finger. "He may not want to leave the city," Belial plotted his words carefully. "He and that little vixen from your city – Belhah – I think is her name, have become awfully close. They spend a lot of time lying with each other. You know the unbridled passion of these young people," he grinned maliciously, licking his lips.

"Enoch chose Angela. He would never lay with another while she lives, let alone another man's wife!" Adam declared. "I know him well enough to know that."

"You might be surprised at what acts can be wrought through temptation and trickery," mused Belial.

"Then let me speak with him. If he still decides to stay, I will not prevent it," Adam relented. He did not believe Belial's story, but needed to make some progress with the strange negotiations.

Belial held up his hand, in a rather limp wristed way, "Now, now, I'm just saying he might not want to leave. But even if he decides to trade his current bed partner for another, there is still a matter of payment."

Finally, Adam thought. "What is your price?"

"Gold and silver I have aplenty," said Belial coyly. "I would know the secret of Enoch's power and how to protect myself from it. And, I desire a fresh stream of sexual partners from your camp to feed my lust," he demanded.

Adam revolted in shock at his request, "You cannot expect me to surrender my daughters to your depravity. Besides, you have the daughters of Cain, willingly given, to satisfy you."

"Not your daughters," Belial said as he peered at Adam with hooded eyes, smoldering with lust, "your sons. Especially the young, helpless ones."

Adam stood up in revulsion. "Has your evil no restraint?" he admonished Belial. "You mock God by going against the very nature of things!" he shouted.

Belial spun lightly in a circle and raised his voice an octave. "That's my price," he tweeted, grinning wickedly at Adam.

"Rot in Hell!" said Adam coldly as amber energy coursed threateningly up and down his body.

"Tell Angela that she need not worry about Enoch's sexual wants. He will be well taken care of," Belial mocked as he faded into the night.

Adam shook in revulsion as his men, woken by Adam's loud retorts, burst into his tent.

"My Lord," said one, "are you all right? Who are your speaking to?"

"No one of importance," said Adam gruffly.

Another sentry crowded in, "My Lord, Adam," he said excitedly. "There is a disturbance within the city; I think I can see an amber hue."

Chapter 44

Enoch eyed his opponent warily, watching the way he moved his body and sword in preparation for conflict. He quickly noticed this was not some Cainite butcher that relied on muscle and steel, but an opponent with the panther-like style and reflexes of a seasoned Adamic warrior. His armor was well fitted in pure black crystal, shaped to deflect any sonic energy blast Enoch could muster. If he were to defeat him, it would have to be by swordplay.

"I see you are practiced in the Adamic style," observed Enoch as he matched Judah's preparatory dance, willing his legs to ignore their weakness.

Judah acknowledged Enoch's awareness, "These butchers lack classic style, all brawn and no brain," he scoffed as he feigned and thrust a few times, causing Enoch to duck and weave away.

"Why work for them?" Enoch joined in the dance, causing Judah to retreat to avoid a strike.

"They pay very well," stated Judah as he penetrated Enoch's defense posture and nicked his weakened leg, slicing the skin open and causing blood to flow.

Enoch nodded his head and looked down on the minor wound. "Nice move," he complimented. Then launched his own attack, thrusting and winding his body in renewed configurations until he was able to flick his blade across Judah's cheek, opening it up and drawing a trail of crimson.

Judah rubbed the side of his face with the back of his non-sword hand and saw the red tint on his black armor. He was aware now that he faced a skilled warrior. "I might be open for employment." He grinned as he circled Enoch, probing for another opening.

Enoch stated, "I have no quarrel with you. You treated me fairly in the training arena." Enoch dodged another attack, receiving a slight nick across the shoulder.

"You're still a tad slow on your feet," observed Judah. "But you move well considering the recently broken legs."

Enoch launched another assault, twisting and diving past the dodging Judah and managed to nick his other cheek on his way past. "You're too confident that you will be able to pull your head out of danger quickly, thus leaving it exposed unnecessarily," instructed Enoch.

Judah wiped the blood from his other cheek and suggested, "Perhaps we could train each other? Do you pay your warriors well?" He launched another attack that caused Enoch to retreat into a back flip to avoid another wound, making him flinch in pain.

Suddenly, the ground in front of Judah exploded in an amber blast, the force knocking Judah backwards off of his feet. He rolled nimbly to a defensive stance and stared with wide-eyed amazement as a golden, glowing female figure leapt from a huge, ferocious ape, her long blonde hair wafting behind her as she determinedly marched between him and Enoch.

"I do not have time for this!" She fired another blast at the ground beneath his feet, knocking him on his rear. She turned to Enoch and queried him with her flashing eyes. "Are you coming?"

"Judah here was just auditioning for employment," explained Enoch, glad to be speaking to Angela about something other than Belial.

"Men!" she spat and started back to her gorilla mount.

Judah crawled up from the ground, watching her graceful form retreating from them. He looked approvingly at Enoch. "Yours?" he asked.

"My wife," said Enoch, sheathing his razor-sharp blade.

"Quite a fiery one, isn't she?" he laughed.

"You have no idea," Enoch rolled his eyes and started trotting after the great ape. "Sorry about your face."

Judah grinned and ran after him, "I'll get you back."

As they got to the river, they saw the small force had won a little path down to the banks of the water. Trulock was knee-deep motioning everyone towards where the river met the wall. "Dive to the center, there's an opening in the middle."

Enoch joined Angela in firing amber blasts to force their pursuers to keep their heads down and prevented them from launching arrows or spears. They looked at each other as the last of their group disappeared below the deep water.

"After you!" cried Enoch, his voice elevating over the fray of battle.

"We go together," she replied.

Just then, the waters erupted in a cascading fountain and a shrill scream exploded from the mouth of a great ape, trapped in the cruel jaws of a one hundred foot long water serpent.

Angela watched in stunned silence as the ape's chest was crushed in the creature's horrible jaws, nearly splitting it in two. The beast roared in triumph of its conquest. It eyed them menacingly, positioning itself between them and the wall, its long neck hovering above them.

Enoch fired several quick bursts in its face, causing it to recoil from them for a moment. Enoch shoved Angela towards the wall. "Go now!"

He formed a bubble of energy around himself and drifted up to the serpent's ravenous face. "Hey big boy, pick on someone your own size!" he chided, firing blast after blast at the face of the creature.

Angela hesitated as Enoch shouted, "There are more coming!" He saw their armored backs splitting the river behind this one. "Warn the others to flee the river!" Then he was off, leading the enraged creature back to its brothers.

Chapter 45

Adam's men raced to the area of the wall where the amber blasts were most prevalent, where the river flowed under from the walls of the city. As they arrived, sodden apes and giants were dragging themselves out of the black water.

Adam saw the black clad giants and readied for a fight, but Trulock sputtered, "Hold! They are with us!" Adam scanned the fugitives and asked Mahalial, "Is Enoch alive?"

"Yes, Lord Adam," he coughed up water, "he is right behind us."

Adam peered into the dark water hunting for some sign of life. There! A faint amber glow of light came bubbling up from the depths. Soon he made out a glowing form in its center and pulled out Angela who resembled a drowning puppy.

"Girl, you've no idea what an uproar you've caused by your actions!" Adam admonished as he pulled her towards the bank. "Thank God you're all right!"

She sputtered and coughed, "Out of the water! Water serpents are in the river! Out of the water everyone!"

Adam, suddenly on his guard, echoed her warning. "Out of the water, far from the banks, now!" He looked at Angela with dread, "Water serpents?" he knew full well those creatures were without fear, full of pride and armored beyond belief.

"Yes!" She yelled as she struggled with Adam to free herself from the soft mud of the banks. "Enoch is behind, trying to hold them back."

Adam swore an oath, "Fool! These creatures are unstoppable!" he muttered as he helped her from the black mud of the riverbank.

A great mass of scaly flesh pounded the ground just beyond the bog of mush they were mired in, knocking them off their feet. "Join with my shield!" shouted Adam as he threw up a protective bubble around himself and Angela. The great serpent snapped at the bubble but was repelled and screamed out in rage.

Trulock and Mahalial readied themselves to enter the fray as the great beast surrounded and engulfed the tiny shield of amber with its massive body. Belhah was grasping Mahalial's arm urging him to stay away from the monster.

Angela cried out to her faithful band "Stay back! There are more of them on the way! Don't throw away your lives!" she pleaded.

Out of nowhere, a powerful blast of golden energy struck the beast fully in its ferocious face, knocking it backwards from its prey. Drifting down from the misty fog above the black water, was a glowing amber bubble, holding the fully charged figure of Enoch.

"Please exit the river and head to solid ground," advised Enoch as several heads, each as large as two mammoths together, sprouted out of the river. "I'll keep these guys busy a few more minutes." He kept up a constant barrage of sonic blasts at the face of each serpent until they roared in frustration, trapped in their watery boundaries and denied their prey.

Judah ran up to Adam and Angela and assisted them out of the mire. All three yelled at Enoch to join them once clear from striking distance of the giant serpents.

Chapter 46

Lamech quietly bypassed Adah and Zillah's quarters and stealthily headed to their attendants' bedrooms. He was spending more and more time enjoying the variety and pleasures of his newly won population of slaves, but his two jealous wives were getting way too nosey and suspicious of his actions.

Although he made the point that he was the King and had no duty to report to them, they could make his life miserable for weeks whenever they caught him on one of his escapades.

Lamech had noted a particularly voluptuous red-haired servant girl earlier in the day and plotted to find her after hours.

He wore only a light linen tunic, easily dropped from his muscular frame. As he entered the servants' quarters he spotted his target. Her coppery locks spilled over her satin pillow as she slept on her side, snuggled up in the luxurious covers, her back facing him.

He admired her soft, white skin as he softly drew back her blankets and lightly kissed her on her bare shoulder.

"It is your Lord, King Lamech," he whispered in her ear as his hand caressed one of her firm white buttocks.

She woke to his gentle touch and replied, "My Lord honors his humble servant. You have entered my dreams." Jewell had been coached by the other girls and knew that pleasing Lamech sexually was the quickest way to preferential treatment and each one of them vied to attract his wandering eye.

She felt his warm hand squeezing her and nestled closer to his reach. Lamech eagerly accepted the subtle invitation and slid his fingers between her legs.

"My Lord may examine his humble servant," she murmured as she rolled over, stretching and arching her back, moaning. She had this one shot to capture his lust and earn his attentions and she didn't want to miss it.

Lamech squeezed her full, ample breast, "Your skin is as white as pure milk." Lamech was enthralled with her coloring; both Adah and Zillah were swarthy. His own dark hands stood out in stark contrast to her alabaster skin.

"You're like a heavenly angel," Lamech smiled.

Jewell slid her hand between his legs and began to massage him.

"Let your angel cover you with kisses," she pleaded and began kissing him.

Lamech leaned back and closed his eyes in pleasure as her sweet little pink mouth engulfed him.

Suddenly, explosions rocked the city, startling Lamech back to reality. Jewell moaned in disappointment.

"What the – ?" Lamech stood up and searched for his tunic.

He heard his guards running towards the royal chambers, shouting, "Lord Lamech! Lord Lamech!"

Lamech threw on his tunic and called out to his jilted angel, "I'll be back!" Then he bolted out the door of the servant quarters, trying to catch his guards' attention. "Here!" he called, waving at them to come closer. "What's happening?"

"Explosions at the prison my Lord," shouted one guard.

Lamech tried to hush the excited messenger but it was too late. Adah and Zillah's door flew open and the two queens burst out of their quarters, startled by the noisy interruption. Lamech noted their dark brown bodies were glistening with sweat and their faces flushed with that fresh bloom of orgasm. They had obviously been busy.

Adah and Zillah saw him standing in his nightshirt in front of the servant quarters and instantly knew what he had been up to. They shot hostile glares at him and started walking towards him in anger, their naked bodies shimmering in the torch lit hallway.

The guard tore his gaze from the approaching beauties and stammered, "Something is happening at the prison and we found footprints of giants on the riverbanks by the wall." His eyes shifted for half a second back to the exquisite queens.

"Look directly at me, son," Lamech charged. "Release the river serpents, now! And alert the palace cavalry brigade to meet me at the gate. No, tell them to meet me at the river, outside the city walls." Lamech threw his hands up to the furious women. "And you two put on some clothes if you're going to show yourselves to the guards."

"So you think you can just go groping around with our servant girls whenever you want?" accused Adah.

"Which one is it this time?" accused Zillah.

"By God, we will make her pay!" threatened Adah.

Lamech hustled past them, "I don't have time for this." He rushed to his royal chambers to suit up in his armor.

Chapter 47

"It is not wise to push so hard through the night," counseled Enos as their force picked their way along the darkened path.

"The sabertooths have excellent night vision. They lead the way," dismissed Eve. "And besides, my spirit drives me to be at the city of Enoch, now!"

Enos submitted to her authority and replied, "Then I will see if we can pick up the pace." He sprinted his giant red stag back towards the front of the column.

Luna was nearby and spurred her war unicorn up to Eve. "I feel it too. Will we make it in time?"

Eve spurred her brilliant, white unicorn forward into a gallop, illuminating the path ahead with reflected moonlight.

"We don't have a choice," she muttered as she urged the column forward.

"Ride!" she called, "Trust your mounts to find their way!"

The column broke into a faster gait, following their queen.

Chapter 48

Adam, Enoch, Angela and Judah scampered away from the awesome power of the serpents. In Adam's opinion they were most feared creatures on earth.

Enoch searched desperately to find the right words to say to Angela as they struggled to the top of the rise of the riverbank.

"Angela," he stammered. "I…" but as they crested the peak of the hill he was interrupted by the sight below.

A half circle of the Cainite palace guard of snarling, snapping bi-pedal T.rex-like carnivores, mounted by black clad, armored warriors surrounded Trulock, Mahalial, Belhah and the remaining giants and great apes.

Enoch heard the flapping of leathery reptilian wings overhead as Lamech and a squad of Dark Lords landed lightly in front of them.

"Well, well, well," chided Lamech. "What do we have here? Spies?" He walked accusingly in front of the disguised, black crystal armor clad giants, and then he addressed Enoch and Judah. "Escaped convicts and traders? Thieves?" he questioned at Adam. "And Belhah, after all we've shared together, you betray me too?"

Belhah broke away from Mahalial and fell sobbing at Lamech's feet. "Lord Lamech, they forced me to go with them! My body is yours always!" she clung desperately to him.

Lamech kicked her away disgustedly, "You think I want anything to do with you anymore? You sicken me."

Mahalial smarted as if he himself had been insulted and made a half step forward, placing his hand on his sword hilt.

Lamech held his hand up to Mahalial, "No, no, no lad," he admonished. "I'll feed her to my riders if you take another step." Looking down at the sobbing Belhah, "It looks like you still have one fan," he stated, amazed.

"Adam, your emissary told me you agreed to meet with me in the morning to discuss my reward for nursing my prisoner back to health. Now I find you stealing him away in the dead of night." Lamech shook his head dejectedly, "How can I trust you now?"

Angela took a step forward and growled, "You attacked and slaughtered innocents and kidnapped the crown prince of our city. You are the criminal here!"

Lamech approached her. "Well, well my little blonde beauty, I believe you and I have some unfinished business," he said suggestively, licking his lips.

Enoch strode between them, threatening to draw his blade. "Get your filthy, warmongering self away from her," he growled.

Lamech held his hands up in mock surprise, "Whoa, there! You sure spent a lot of time with this tramp while in my care!" he accused, pointing his finger at Belhah who looked desperately at Lamech, Mahalial and Enoch, trying to find a supporter to rally to her side.

"You live in a world of deception and lies," observed Enoch. "You are skilled at drawing others in."

"My kingdom, my rules," laughed Lamech. "I see an entire group of lawbreakers here. I place you all under arrest. Will you come quietly for trial or do I destroy you now?"

Adam surveyed the situation. They were hopelessly outnumbered, with their backs against the roaring, carnivorous serpents, straining to reach them as tasty morsels. Perhaps he and Enoch could escape, but the rest would be slaughtered and he knew Enoch would never leave Angela behind.

"The terms you offered this evening through Belial were unacceptable," Adam retorted. He spat on the ground.

Lamech winced as if struck. "Belial came to you and offered terms?" he asked in real surprise. "He does not represent me," he stated contemptuously.

"You should keep a tighter rein upon your court," advised Adam.

"Don't tell me what to do!" snapped Lamech. "Now surrender to trial or suffer destruction!" The palace guards drew their swords, snarling mounts ready to charge, as more and more troops, giants and beasts were flooding from the gates, reinforcing Lamech's position.

Lamech's supporting Dark Lords crackled with latent black energy, along with his own mages and sorcerers.

Angela whispered in Adam's ear, "He is a man without mercy, surrendering to him is worse than death."

Adam calculated he could extend his sonic shield around the group. With Enoch and Angela's help he might even be able to mount some sort of offensive attack, but that would only delay the inevitable point when they would be overwhelmed.

Enoch glanced up, at Adam, his eyes pleading, "Never give up, never surrender."

Adam said softly, within the hearing of Angela and Enoch, "On my signal have everyone converge on me." He counted down on his fingers, three, two…

Just then a long, lonely blast from a deep bellowing ram's horn pierced the night air.

Lamech knew all too well what that forlorn blast foreshadowed and wildly spun around, searching for the direction of the new threat. "No! No! No!" he shouted, unable to believe additional Adamic forces could have shown up from nowhere.

Enoch seized the opportunity of the distraction to pounce on Lamech, folding Lamech's arm behind his back and sliding his own forearm across his windpipe, applying enough pressure to induce a fit of coughing by Lamech.

Enos, Seth, Eve, Luna and Angel led the horde of Adamic forces, including the woodland animals and their small riders, through the stunned palace guard, parting them with little effort as their attention was drawn to Enoch's rising amber bubble of energy, engulfing Lamech and himself in the air.

Enoch shouted to the Cainite forces, "Men of Cain and all those who follow Lamech, behold your King. Stand back, make way for our passage and he will be returned to you."

Lamech's commanders looked for Lamech's acknowledgment and Lamech waved his hand dismissively, coughing and sputtering, "Let them go!"

Trulock, Mahalial, Adam and Angela and the rest of their party started cautiously moving through the gap caused by their new forces.

Belhah was still on her knees, sobbing and wild eyed, trying to discern where she should ally herself. Mahalial stopped in front of her.

"Oh my husband, my love, take me with you, you are my life!" she pleaded.

Mahalial replied, "I can no longer trust you Belhah, though I still love you, how can I share a life with you?"

Belhah blubbered, "I'll change and I'll be committed to you. Please,

please don't leave me here to be ravaged by these wretched men!"

"You have much to atone for, Belhah," Mahalial hesitated.

Adam noticed a dark haze, almost a shadow, but it was moving separately from where Belhah's shadow should be in the moonlight. It was just there for an instant, then moved back into the heartbroken, sobbing Belhah.

Adam stepped up next to Mahalial and touched his arm, "You still love her?" he asked gently.

"God help me, I do," confessed Mahalial. "But I fear love cannot bloom with such treachery of heart."

Adam held up his finger to Mahalial, indicating that he should wait for a moment.

Adam stood straight with great authority and shined brilliant amber light upon Belhah's tortured, emotionally broken body, exposing the vacillating shadow, now struggling to maintain its habitation in the frantic woman.

"Spirit indwelling Belhah, come forth and address me, give me your name!" commanded Adam.

Belhah screamed and jerked her head around Adam at a grotesque, unnatural angle, her beautiful tear stained face now a snarling mask of rage. She growled and spat at Adam.

"Your name!" ordered Adam.

Belhah threw back her head and tore off her clothes, arching her back in a hopeless attempt to seduce Adam while growling in a deep, baritone voice, "No, she is mine!"

"Give me your name!" commanded Adam, louder and firmer.

Belhah squirmed and shuddered, "Jezebel," she screamed, spitting and drooling.

"By the Holy Creator, Jezebel, release Belhah, come out of her!" Adam shouted, keeping his amber glow on the dual entities.

Belhah's body stood up ramrod straight stretching her arms in the air and standing on the very tips of her toes. "No!" she growled, seeming to almost levitate into the air, her face a grotesquely contorted mask of rage, then she collapsed in a heap on the ground.

Mahalial rushed to her side, covering up her bare body with his cloak of furs.

"She will need to be sanctified," said Adam warily. "If she does not realign her heart, the spirit can come back and bring even more destructive spirits than itself."

Mahalial draped the unconscious body of Belhah on the back of his sabertooth, mounted him, and the entire group of Adamites slowly backed away from the Cainite troops. Roused from their slumber as they were, they were definitely not eager to engage an equal force.

"After we cross past these peaks I will deposit your King safely on that mountaintop. Follow us before then, and he shall suffer for your disobedience," Enoch declared.

After Lamech was brought back down to the city he stormed back into the palace, past his wives' bedchamber and into his own royal bedchamber. What a humiliation to be caught off guard like that before his men.

To his surprise he noticed the beautiful red hair of his earlier attempted conquest. It billowed from her head, and lay on his bed pillows. He pulled back the covers and saw that it was only her head, her face frozen in terror. A card lay beneath her dripping neck from Adah and Zillah.

The card read, "Enjoy your slut." Lamech sighed. It had not been a good start to the day.

Chapter 49

Belshazzar had discovered much about life and death, procreation, spirit and flesh, sound and chemicals, as well as sorcery and dark sayings, but Hades was dwarfing his knowledge. Belshazzar had instructed Hades on how to re-create his old laboratory back in the City of Light and now Hades was expanding on his own old designs and improving on them.

"Zeus's golems are extremely handy aren't they?" Belshazzar noted as he toured the expansive underground labyrinth of caverns and chambers.

"They are handy for the rough excavation work, cutting and carting rocks and debris, but they have their limitations with more delicate work," Hades noted as he took Belshazzar into a majestic cavern. He hummed and crystals of light illuminated, displaying a natural cavern of enormous size that had been expanded. Gigantic stalactites dropped from the roof of the chamber, joining in many places with equally impressive stalagmites on the floor, forming gleaming, seemingly liquid rock columns that appeared to support the arched ceiling.

"This is my training school," Hades beamed proudly. "I am assembling acolytes to assist me in my experiments. I must use mankind for this, but I have to condition their minds to accept what we are doing to their brothers and sisters. I have to desensitize them."

Belshazzar nodded, "I find the dull-witted are the easiest to control. You offer them position, authority and security, then tell them they are better than the rest and they will do anything to keep their power."

"Yes, that is fine for the butchers and the torturers and the enforcers, but I need intelligent thinkers to help me with my research. They can't all be simpletons," complained Hades.

"So what are your thoughts?" queried Belshazzar.

"If I can catch them when they are young," he waved around the cavern, "and educate them with my truth, separate them from their family's influence, then encourage them to submit to the activities that foster spiritual degeneration and moral depravity, they will have no baseline of ethics to compare to. I will be their god, they will strive to please me."

He continued, "The others, outsiders if you will, are the ones to be used and abused, the ones who don't understand and need to be eliminated or changed. That is what I am building this for," bragged Hades.

"What have you discovered about the spiritual realm? Have you found a way to make spiritual weapons?" Belshazzar's interest was palatable.

"Well, as far as I can see to date, the spirit realm is not that different from the physical. It's just at a different vibration level, or sonic dimension. Now as you know, we have gained the ability to manipulate matter, but not create it. If we manipulate matter and energy to a certain vibration level, we can make the spiritual realm accessible to us. The problem is that using our current level of knowledge and technology, it takes time to elevate from one level to the next. Just as when a Fallen One attempts to reincorporate into a physical body, it is a laborious process."

Belshazzar offered, "So weapons tuned to the right vibration or frequency could strike at a spiritual being?"

"Yes, in theory. My experiments here will take a hard look at what happens to the human spirit after I kill its body. See if I can see it, capture it and eventually kill it or evaporate it or render it ineffective. Once we figure that out, the same principle should apply to all other spiritual beings," explained Hades.

Belshazzar nodded and said, "We must make all haste, we don't want to be caught defenseless by either the Dark Lords or mankind. The day will come when they will find us and we must be prepared."

Chapter 50

The banished spirit Jezebel was tumultuously tumbled through the atmospheric heavens like a leaf caught in a tidal wave. It raged and cursed as it helplessly flailed against the unseen power that controlled it, casting it further and further into the wilderness and dry places.

Belhah had been such a perfect host, so pliable, so easily manipulated and so well placed among men for it to exercise its lust and desires. Cursed be those Adamites! How had Adam detected it? Now everything was lost, lost, it had nothing. It was now but a spirit, a vapor, a misty wraith, incapable of touch, feel, taste and pleasure.

Jezebel screamed another silent scream of rage and frustration, the sound not manifesting in the physical world. As a lower-level demon, Jezebel did not have the ability to incorporate into its own spiritual body, but had to depend upon a willing host to meld with. While in the wilderness, humans were few and far between, willing ones even more so.

Jezebel shuddered. Perhaps it could find a simple form of life – a lizard, a snake that had a weakness it could breach and enter into it. But their diet was so horrible and they tended to mate only for procreation and they were so stupid, always getting eaten or attacked by other beasts.

Finally it slowed and was able to come to a stop. It tried to pull itself up from the ground, to levitate, but nothing happened. It tried to step, but each attempt to move met with horrible resistance, requiring so much energy that it was completely depleted after only a short distance. It saw a flickering light not too far away, but in its current condition it might as well been an eternity. Jezebel boiled in anger and pooled into a black, seething haze, resting just above the desert sand in the deep blackness of the wilderness night. It waited. Surely something would pass by, eventually.

The fire had died down to a soft, flickering blaze, already performing its task of heating the surrounding stones. Hera drew another long puff on her ornate pipe, carved from human bone filled with hallucinogenic herbs and weeds.

Cain disliked this habit of hers and she always had to hide it from him or abstain completely until he left on one of his campaigns of conquest. She suspected these excursions were just thinly veiled excuses to bed trashy, outlier young women whose heads were easily turned by nobility. But Cain had always returned with riches and plunder and the reaches of their kingdom grew.

She drifted in her mind as the burning plants took effect, her body relaxed onto her crude backrest consisting of bags and thick furs. Soon she was soaring through lush meadows and over vast seas, flying and playfully hiding from lusty young men eager to pleasure her completely.

She laughed as she frustrated them, tempting them towards her then flying away. "Catch me if you can!" She taunted, easily outdistancing them with her speed and flight.

Then she was in a royal banquet hall, the tables filled with many kinds of succulent foods, rich pastries, brilliant fruits and delightful sauces and wines. She poured a rich red wine freely upon her chest and told the two handsome young men dining to her left and to her right, "Drink, drink my fine wine." Greedily they each took a wine covered breast and began to suckle like newborn babes. "Oh yes," she moaned, "Taste my sweetness!"

She felt the fire building between her legs, when suddenly she sensed a presence. She was not alone in this drug-induced fantasy. She looked upwards and glanced around. She was now sitting on a golden throne, surrounded by huge boulder sized rubies, diamonds, sapphires and jewels of all colors and hues.

In front of her, crouched atop a throbbing, brilliant ruby, sat a fanged viper, looking intently into her eyes, as if it had intelligence.

Suddenly it spoke to her, in a soothing, calming voice, "Don't stop on my account, you are putting on a great show." It smiled knowingly at her.

"How have you entered my dream?" Hera questioned with a mixture of surprise and offence, covering herself with her hands.

"You have opened yourself into the spirit realm with your potions and herbs. You may call it a dream, but we spirits know better," hissed the snake.

"Can you hurt me?" demanded Hera, preparing to smash the offender into a pulp with a rock if need be.

"I can only interact with you on a physical, sensual level with your permission. So, if you wish for pain, I can accommodate you." The snake was flicking its long, forked tongue in and out of its mouth and changing from one brilliant incandescent color to another. It was captivating to watch.

"What if I tell you to be gone, to stop interrupting my dream world?" she commanded.

"I would obey," the snake submitted and bowed low to her. "But first, may I share something with you?"

Hera pondered for a while. The spirit did not seem to be able to hurt her, what harm could it do to listen?

"Are you one of the Fallen Ones?" she accused. "Cain forbade me from ever speaking to any of your kind, but the rumors that work their way back to the city…"

"…spoke of our special… abilities?" finished the serpent.

"Yes, it is said when you meld with a woman, that her sense of pleasure heightens and her rapture knows no bounds," she frowned in disbelief.

"This is all true," confessed the snake.

"Well that is not for me," Hera stated flatly. "I have no problem with pleasure, it is much more important for me to keep my wits about me. I have a life to rebuild, I can't sit around wasting the days on mindless sex. I don't even have a man now in my life."

"Yet you failed to keep Cain true to you, he hungered after other women," the creature reminded her.

"I can keep your man interested in you. With the wonders I can teach you, he will always come back for more." Hera was puzzled. She had always considered Cain's wondering eye his fault, not hers. "Go on," she ordered.

"I can also bring knowledge and secrets from the eons before this earth existed – from Lucifer's original kingdom, that spanned an untold millennium," enticed the reptile.

This would definitely be an advantage, Hera considered. "Was that your world?" she queried.

"Yes. Before we followed Lucifer and his assault against the Creator we had a majestic world. We walked among the stones of fire, enjoyed all sorts of privilege and power. I can bring you secret knowledge from that world to help you control and manipulate your rather simple race," tempted the viper.

"What else?" she demanded.

"I cannot create, but I can manipulate flesh I am permitted into. I cannot prevent death, but I can extend life, make your flesh younger looking, your body more attractive, help you stave off the effects of gravity. You will appear as one with the body of a young woman," promised the spirit.

"I will maintain control, completely?" she demanded. "You may be my guide, my spiritual counselor, but I will make all my own decisions. I will not serve you."

The serpent slyly bowed its head in subservience, "But of course my lady. I live only to serve you and share in your experiences," it hissed.

"What shall I call you, dark spirit?" asked Hera.

"My name is Jezebel," bowed the snake.

"I will give you a trial," she decided. "Finish this dream with me. If I find my pleasure increased enough, I will let you stay."

"As you will," agreed the reptile.

The sleeping giant awoke to a strange set of impassioned cries. He rolled over and looked at the dimly illuminated nude body of Hera, squirming and embracing herself, moaning and whimpering in pleasure as she dreamt.

He shook his head in disapproval. These humans were so focused on needless sexual pleasure. As a serving giant, he had been neutered at birth. But it didn't matter, there were no giant women anyway. Sometimes he wondered if he was missing anything important. At least she might hold down the noise!

He pulled his roughly sewn together pelt over his ears and turned away from Hera's orgasmic fits of passion.

"Humans!" He scoffed and tried to drive Hera's impassioned cries from his ears.

Chapter 51

Angela sat alone on the outskirts of the camp, staring out into the night. She had shed her suit of armor and wore only her white linen tunic, warm, fur-lined boots and wrapped herself in a cloak of woolen skins.

She absentmindedly brushed out her flowing golden locks, tangled from the desperate search for the fallen Enoch.

The picture of Belhah's nude body in Enoch's embrace played over and over in her mind; she couldn't stop it, no matter how she tried.

Her mind told her Enoch had been tricked into thinking her dead, along with most of their people, that Enoch had refused Belhah and her indwelling demon of lust and he was simply offering decent human kindness and comfort to a grieving friend. But her heart was crushed, her trust shattered. How could he have been fooled by Belhah unless he wanted to be?

He should have known she was still alive, searching for him. She had not accepted his death, she had still felt their connection. How could he fall under Belhah's spell so completely? Again, her reason argued Enoch was severely injured and taken hostage by a hostile enemy, nursed back to health by the only friendly face in his captivity. His only connection to the outside world lied to him. How would she have responded?

But her injured feelings snapped her back into indignation. Would she ever be whole again?

She heard a pebble skitter behind her, betraying someone's approach from the main camp. Enoch sat down in silence beside her. She involuntarily turned away from him, unwilling to look him in the eye.

After a long silence Enoch whispered. "I don't blame you for being angry."

She blurted out, angry and hurt, "It was just such a shock! After all I had gone through to find you, to believe you are not dead, then to finally reach you and see her in your arms, in my place." She began sobbing uncontrollably.

Enoch tried to hold her, to comfort her, but she pulled away. He sat beside her helplessly.

"Would you have loved her? Could you have?" she accused.

"I told her I still loved you," Enoch said again, "That it was too soon for my heart to love another."

"But if I was truly dead, could you have loved her?" she demanded.

Enoch hesitated, not knowing how to answer such a hypothetical question.

"I could never love anyone else like I love you, no matter how many centuries passed by. You're my first love and my best love, I want no other," Enoch finally responded.

Neither said anything for a long time.

Eventually, Angela got her sobbing under control. "Enoch, you have to be smarter, you are too naïve. There will always be women after you, trying to steal you away from me, to tempt your eyes. You have to make your mind up to turn them away."

Enoch said simply, "You are everything to me. I only want you, no one else."

Angela finally looked him squarely in the eyes, begging him, pleading to him with her gaze to make her feel loved and safe again with her heart. She saw hurt but also deep and abiding love staring back at her.

"Will you forgive me for hurting you and let me back into your heart?" Enoch looked helpless and so vulnerable before her.

She burst into tears all over again and hugged him, burying her head into his chest. "I want nothing else!" she cried.

Enoch held her and let her sobs slowly subside. "I will always love you," he murmured to her.

After a long time, she finally raised her tear stained face to him and he wiped away the shiny tracks down her cheeks.

She laughed briefly through tears and looked again into his eyes, "Enoch?"

"Yes my love," Enoch smiled.

"I'm pregnant!" she burst out laughing and crying at the same time.

Chapter 52

Apolodon reached down, scooped up a handful of dust, smelled it, felt it and let it run between his fingers. Nothing. The trail of the triplets from the City of Light had vanished into the wilderness. He had to acknowledge supernatural power at work here. Somehow they had scattered and eliminated all evidence of their caravans' passing.

Apolodon straightened up and scanned the horizon ahead, cursing under his breath. If these three developed their full power they would pose a serious threat for overtaking the kingdom of earth and banishing him and his kind to mindless servitude.

He climbed back onto his monstrous red dragon, patting its long closely scaled neck as its massive head bobbed, searching for scents in the air.

He turned to his scouts, mounted on various types of flying reptiles. "Take this point and form a search pattern outward. We will try to cover one hundred leagues before the sun goes down. Meet me back here as soon as the sun sets."

To the commanders of his troops he ordered, "We might as well set up camp here until you have better information on where to go. Form some raiding parties to locate and pillage a few villages to keep the men busy."

The massive giants and lumbering dinosaurs made quick work of building defensive fortifications to protect his force from any sort of fleshly attack, while his conjurers and magi started weaving their dark powers to provide spiritual protection.

Apolodon returned to his thoughts. Yes, he had tried to capture or eliminate the triplets before they grew too powerful. Left on their own, there was no telling what havoc they could create or what powers they could uncover.

He nodded to a couple of red-cloaked mages, "You two come with me. We will see if we can pick up any trace of sorcery, magic or dark energy that might divulge their direction."

The trio's winged mounts leapt into the misty air, their leathery wings pounding torrents of force upon the dry surface, causing clouds of dust to momentarily obscure their rising, before they flew clear of the gloom.

Chapter 53

Lamech fumed as he passed by Adah and Zillah's quarters, furious at the sounds of passion that seemed to endlessly emanate from the royal bedroom. They were so engrossed with each other, they acted as if they didn't even need him or miss him in their games of ecstasy.

He would show them; he would not be the first to buckle. They would come crawling back soon, after they grew tired of only feminine attention.

He burst into his throne room, startling those who waited to attend him.

"What do we have before us today?" asked Lamech as he pushed himself upon his royal throne of gold and onyx. He didn't know how Cain had endured this throne for so many centuries. It was too uncomfortable.

He turned to his court clerk, "Have the royal tailors design some cushions for this accursed throne," he commanded, then he looked around the throne room, wrinkling his nose, "and get me some plans to spruce up the room a bit. This black is far too drab. Who do we see first today?"

"Your son, Tubalcain, comes from the far reaches of the kingdom," announced the butler, signaling the royal trumpeters to sound their welcome. After a few notes Lamech waved them off impatiently. "It's too early for all that," he said, obviously irritated.

Tubalcain entered with a bevy of nude, beautiful women of different shades and colors. Lamech grinned lustfully, waiting for all his new conquests to enter the halls. Unexpectedly, the trail of women stopped, well short of the numbers he expected.

"Are we short of numbers this trip?" questioned a disappointed Lamech.

Tubalcain bowed to his father. "My Lord, many of the villages in our outlying territories are empty – deserted – with no sign of the inhabitants."

Lamech sat up in surprise. "No sign of struggle?" he asked.

"Most appear to have left voluntarily, but we found this on the side of a road near a village not far from the City of Light," stated Tubalcain. He held up a pair of detached, sandaled feet, obviously charred and burnt at the anklebones, despite the obvious decomposition they suffered.

The train of captured women gasped in horror, some crying in shock.

"Get them out of here," dismissed Lamech, quickly scanning the group and picking out an attractive red-haired girl. "Take this one to my special quarters and begin her preparations. Keep her separate and protected from any of Adah and Zillah's servants. If any harm comes to her before I see her, heads will roll. Do I make myself clear?"

The head attendant nodded his head furiously, "Yes my Lord, she will be readied for you."

Lamech turned to Tubalcain, "So you suspect the Dark Lords have broken the treaty and are harvesting our women for themselves?" he asked.

"It appeared that way at first, but we also came upon a large force led by Apolodon, We expected to find them with captives, but they had none. They seemed to be searching for someone or something," observed Tubalcain.

Lamech puzzled, "Perhaps a rogue Dark Lord?" He stood and paced. "How many villages?"

"We ran across almost thirty that had been emptied, but there could be more," Tubalcain reported.

"That's too big of an operation to be done in secret underneath Lucifer's nose in the City of Light," Lamech mused.

"We also discovered one of our mining sites abandoned," continued Tubalcain. "It was greatly enlarged since my last pass through the area, showing decades of work done in less than a year. We followed a trail of heavy carts to the west, but then the trail vanished."

"To the west?" Lamech asked, "Into the wilderness and dry places?" Tubalcain nodded.

"Away from the City of Light," Lamech pondered aloud.

"Take me to Apolodon. I would seek what he knows of this mystery. And bring that new girl along, I want her away from those jealous wives of mine," he ordered.

Chapter 54

"Thank you for coming," Mahalial stood and clasped Adam's hand and bowed lightly to Eve as they entered his simple tent of animal skins.

"Is she any better?" asked a concerned Eve softly, as she brushed past Mahalial and sat down on a pallet of furs next to Belhah, placing her hand on Belhah's fevered brow.

"She's still delirious," answered Mahalial, standing awkwardly and nervously shuffling his feet. "She keeps muttering, 'Forgive me.'"

Eve peered into Belhah's glassy eyes and requested, "Leave us alone for a while, let us women have some time together."

Adam held the door flap open and motioned Mahalial to join him outside. Once outside, Adam said, "Walk with me, my son."

"Have you and Enoch spoken to each other since our rescue?"

Adam asked, gently.

"No, I have been too busy caring for my wife." Adam detected a little bit of extra emphasis on the words, "my wife".

"Will you seek to kill Enoch over this?" Adam asked directly.

Mahalial sighed in frustration, "No, we've shared far too much together and I know now much of this, if not all, was due to the demonic spirit that controlled her." Mahalial exhales slowly then inhaled a deep breath. "It is just hard to separate the emotions from the facts," he admitted.

"Do you doubt Enoch loves you more than a brother?" Adam looked directly into Mahalial's dark brown eyes. He could not have seeds of discord sprouting in his camp, not if he could prevent it.

Mahalial was quiet for a long moment. "I know he does. He has risked his life for me and I risked mine for him many times. I suppose he felt an obligation to care for and protect Belhah in my absence; I know I would do the same for Angela."

"Do you believe him when he says he never laid with her?" probed Adam.

More silence. "He is a stronger man than me," Mahalial managed a small chuckle. "I succumbed to Belhah's charms the moment she gave me the opportunity. I still love her dearly, despite everything that has happened," he confessed.

"Then love her, but hold her to the correct standard of love to be returned. Sometimes love requires you to be strong, even if you risk her anger for the moment. She will respect you more for it," Adam counseled. "She is the weaker vessel. She needs your love, your protection and when necessary, your leadership."

Inside the tent Belhah slowly focused her eyes on Eve's tender gaze as she patted a cool, wet cloth on Belhah's face.

Eve smiled at her and said softly, "Welcome back to the land of the living. You had us worried there for a while."

Belhah grasped Eve's hand. "My lady, it was so horrible, so degrading and humiliating. I knew everything that I was doing was wrong and evil, but I did it anyway. I am not worthy to be accepted back into your kingdom. You should banish me to the wilderness, to my fate among the beasts of the field," she sobbed, heartbroken.

Eve agreed, "Yes, that is what should happen, but what of Mahalial? If he desires his wife, why should he be punished?"

Belhah sighed and sobbed, "I don't deserve him either. I've treated him like dirt. He will never want me again." Her wail was pitiful.

Eve let the pain of Belhah's expectations buffet her for a while, then she asked, "What would happen if you were given a second chance? Would you change any of your ways?"

"I've had many chances, I can't blame everything on that demon," Belhah moaned. "I'm a selfish gold digger and I don't know how to be anything different. I hurt everybody I touch."

Eve hugged her, startling Belhah. "That is the truth my daughter and admitting the truth is the first step in being set free."

Belhah lifted her tear stained face from Eve's breast.

"Free? I couldn't stand for anyone to look at me after what I've done. How can I be free?"

Eve stroked her hair and encouraged her, "I'm looking at you. Mahalial still loves you. He would travel to the ends of the world to earn your love in return."

"I don't know how to love," cried Belhah, whimpering like a scared puppy.

"You can start by accepting someone's love for you. Let him forgive you. Let him love you, then practice loving him back. Do what makes him happy and you will find your own happiness will grow in return."

The tent flaps opened and Mahalial and Adam stepped back inside.

"My love?" Mahalial breathing quickened as he saw Belhah sitting up and awake. "Do you feel better?"

Belhah again broke down in tears and held her arms out desperately, pleading for his embrace. "Can you ever forgive me?" she sobbed, her heart totally exposed.

Mahalial rushed to her arms and covered her salty face with kisses.

Eve arose and touched Adam on his arm. "Let's leave these two to work things out together," she whispered as she led Adam out of the tent.

Chapter 55

Hera was truly amazed at the incredible city that lay before her. Who would've imagined such a structure could have existed this far into the wilderness? Towering, crystal clear buildings soared to the sky, their transparent walls tinted in a rainbow of hues that changed colors depending on the angle of view so that the entire city appeared awash in a rainbow of infinite colors.

People walked on smooth, stone streets that flowed like a continuous river throughout the many dwellings. Mages and aristocrats hovered on shining disks, effortlessly gliding to and fro. There was an abundance of fruits, nuts, produce and prepared soups, sauces, desserts, breads, cheeses and wines in the marketplace.

"Thank you," Hera nodded as a nosey guide escorted her to the expansive guest quarters.

"Are you sure you don't want me to announce the purpose of your visit to Lord Zeus?" the attendant tried one more time to wheedle information out of her.

Hera struck to her plan – a woman of mystery. She believed that it was her best angle. "My business is only for him," she said with royal bearing and authority.

The guide motioned the porter to place her bags inside her room and stated, "Lord Zeus will call you when he has time for you."

"Tell him to give me time to bathe and prepare myself for our visit," she said dismissively as she waved them away. She had to leave her little caravan of beasts and giants outside the city in deference to their city rules and now she could see why. The last thing you want roaming a city of glass would be giants and sauropods.

It took but a moment of conversation to find out Zeus was the prominent leader of the three lords who ruled this wondrous city and she set her sights on him at once.

She shook out several outfits from her traveling bags. The citizens here dressed simply, usually in plain white tunics and flat soled sandals. Few spoke with the distinguished tones of high speech – they seemed on the whole simple country people, almost as astonished as she at their opulent surroundings.

Any one of her queenly gowns would give her an instant advantage over these pretty but unpolished girls. She debated over which pair of heeled shoes to wear, shoes she had devised herself and had specially made for her in the city of Enoch, to allow her to tower above any competition she faced over Cain, as well as giving her a greater air of authority over her staff. She also liked how they shaped her legs and laughed as she remembered the creative ways they had made intimate encounters more enjoyable for her and Cain.

She gazed at her renewed body as she stripped for a bath. The mirrors here were excellent, there was nary a blemish or wrinkle in her reflection. Jezebel was true to her or its word. Hera didn't know what it was, really. But her body had regained every bit of its youthful, flawless beauty. She would definitely be a physical match for any women vying for Zeus's attentions, but she also had centuries of royal experience in posture, intelligence, manipulation, carriage and sex.

She would capture Zeus's attention and soon have him begging for her company. She knew how to tempt and tantalize, pleasure and please, and keep him desperate for more. She grinned as she eased herself down into the warm bath water and exhaled deeply as the dust and weariness of the long travel eased away.

What was the name of the city? Atlantis… Queen of Atlantis. It had a nice ring to it.

It was all Belshazzar could do to maintain his composure at the shock of seeing whom Zeus's special guest was as she was announced.

"Your highness, presenting the former Queen of the city of Enoch, from the lands of Cain, the first son of Adam, Queen Hera!" boomed the deep voice of the royal announcer.

Hera had chosen a deep purple gown, trimmed in fluffy, snow-white furs, six-inch high strapped golden heeled shoes and she carried her golden scepter, encrusted with light purple amethyst jewels. The dress was cut low, giving Zeus a good view of her ample, young bosoms. Her hair was straight and shiny.

She smelled of cinnamon, frankincense and myrrh as she glided towards Zeus's throne. She bowed deeply, her breasts straining to escape their confines and she lightly touched herself at the hollow of her chest to make sure Zeus's eyes were drawn there.

She glanced around at the other women close by the throne. Good, her competitors were already intimidated and she had not even begun to fight.

"I am most honored that you have received me into your marvelous city, Lord Zeus," she said demurely, lingering in her bow until Zeus moved his gaze from her breasts to her face.

Zeus worked hard to maintain his royal composure, even though the new mystery woman captivated him. "You are welcome in my court," he nodded in return, drinking in her presence with his eyes.

Belshazzar saw that he would have to quickly cut in to protect Zeus from her charms. "If I may, Lord Zeus," he nodded to Zeus then turned to Hera. "It is a pleasure to see you again, Queen Hera. What brings you to this wilderness, so far from home?" Belshazzar had to find out if they were discovered.

Hera grinned inside herself, and put on her best "distressed maiden" act. "King Cain, the great ruler of the vast Cainite kingdom and territories, my husband, alas was slain on his quest for immortal life. In his absence I have been banished from the kingdom by his unscrupulous usurpers." Hera let her lip tremble and bowed, again clutching her hand to the hollow between her breasts, drawing a lusty gaze.

Belshazzar interrupted Zeus as he struggled to reply. "Does anyone else from your kingdom know you're here?" he demanded.

Hera looked innocent and hurt at the same time. "I was banished, my Lord Zeus. No one follows me or cares as to my whereabouts unless I return to my kingdom."

Zeus found his voice and made an extravagant gesture. "You will dine with us, Queen Hera. You will enjoy safety here."

"I would be honored to prepare myself for you," Hera bowed slightly again, tantalizing Zeus with her bulging décolletage. "May I beseech you for a few attendants to provide for my needs?" she asked, feigning innocence and helplessness.

Zeus stumbled over his reply, and chided himself. "But of course," he motioned for three or four of his white clad women to get up and attend her, even though they looked incensed to do so.

Hera nodded sweetly, "Perhaps I can teach these concubines of yours some skill in how to bring you pleasure, if they're willing pupils."

Zeus cleared his throat and tried to downplay his excited anticipation. "That would be graciously appreciated," he smiled as his concubines pouted.

Belshazzar touched Zeus's arm lightly and whispered in his ear, "I would be wary of this one, she is up to no good," he looked pointedly into Zeus's lust filled eyes and determined he might as well be talking to a deaf man in a hurricane.

Zeus was well smitten and would not stop till he unwrapped his new prize.

"She'll be fine," he muttered, "What can one woman, all alone, do?" He laughed and patted Belshazzar on his back. "Prepare for lunch."

Chapter 56

"Safe travels," waved Adam as Enos and the warriors who accompanied Eve to the city of Enoch embarked on their journey back to their home city of Carmel.

"I praise the Creator things went well and Enoch has been returned to us," nodded Enos as he saluted Adam in return.

"If you need us for anything, don't hesitate!" encouraged Eve as she hugged Enos goodbye. "And say hello to that pretty wife of yours and all of my grandbabies!" she laughed as he turned to go.

The city of Abelton was abuzz with life as things returned to normal. The great beasts were being unloaded and returned to their dwelling places and merchants were eager to sell their stores of food and fresh wares to the returning riders.

Stories were being shared of what had transpired and families were reunited in joy and thanksgiving.

Adam smiled as he watched Enoch and Angela walking hand-in-hand, Angela aglow with fresh life and chattering like a magpie, while Enoch smiled and nodded, starting to reply, but not finding an opening to speak, so continuing to smile and nod.

Eve touched Adam's upper arm, squeezing it affectionately. "They're going to be okay," she smiled, "aren't they?"

Adam kissed Eve on the top of her head. "They have learned to talk things out between them, which bodes well for their long-term happiness."

Eve turned her face upwards to Adam's and craved a kiss on her lips. Adam obliged her and again noticed how similar Angela and Eve looked to each other. They could be twins except for their slight difference in hair and eye color. He chuckled, "…and of course she takes after her great-grandmother, so she is really hot!" Adam kissed Eve again.

Eve preened a bit before him and said, "So you still like what you see?"

Adam laughed again as he playfully ogled her. Before he could speak Mahalial rode up to him, with the newly restored Belhah mounted behind him. His saber-toothed cat panted furiously, struggling to cool itself and regain its breath.

"Lord Adam!" saluted Mahalial, and before Adam could even acknowledge him he began, "As you know Belhah and I left on the way back from the lands of Cain to start her own life, free and clear from the hurts of the past."

Eve stepped up and gently touched Belhah's calf as she still sat on the back of the laboring beast. "Of course you are welcome here, there was no need to depart so," she assured her. Belhah smiled back, embarrassed yet grateful.

"It's not that we changed our minds..." began Belhah.

"...We came across something very strange," continued Mahalial. "We saw Apolodon's brigade, camped upon the plains, searching. We circled around them, far to their rear and I think I might have found what interested them. I found tracks of huge wheeled carts and footprints larger than any giant's I've ever seen, pressed deep into the ground. The creatures must have carried enormous weight."

"We followed them back to an abandoned mine," added Belhah, "and there was a huge pile of decayed giant bones, still being picked clean by carrion beasts."

"Whatever has been unleashed across the plains is strong enough to slaughter a band of giants. Angela and I saw great stone behemoths on our way to the city of Enoch. I should have said something earlier, it's just was so much happening..." Mahalial hesitated.

"What, my son?" Adam prodded.

"I saw the same kind of tracks again," gulped Mahalial, "and they were headed to Carmel!"

Adam signaled for his war unicorn, "I must get to Enos," he said urgently as he saddled up and turned to shout to Eve. "Call the council together, we must conceive a plan right away!"

Everyone shared Adam's fear. Carmel had been left lightly guarded, with the majority of its troops joining Eve in their mad dash into the heart of Cainite territory.

Such creatures appeared to have no weakness and were definitely belligerent. Carmel possessed a wealth of silver, gold, precious stones and something even more precious – living families.

The hastily convened council was in an impatient uproar. Adam stormed in with Enos in tow and called Angela and Mahalial forward.

"Tell us everything you can about these creatures," he commanded.

"Well, first of all, they are really big! A good ten feet taller than the tallest giant and many times heavier and stronger," Angela reported.

"And they move extremely fast for such large creatures. They had no trouble catching a band of Cainite giants and pulling them into pieces," added Mahalial.

"And you say they were solid stone?" asked Adam incredulously.

"It appeared that way. We saw one's toes smashed and only stone was visible behind the wound, no blood or muscle or bone," said Angela.

"Animated stone, obviously dark power of some kind, the likes of which we have not seen," mused Adam.

Enos interjected, "We must hurry to Carmel, we cannot leave them to battle these things alone."

Enoch suggested, "Let's take a troop of our fastest cavalry, with multiple mounts and try to get some of us to Carmel ahead of these monoliths."

He turned to Seth who agreed, "All of our scouts can join them and we can help with their defenses."

Adam added, "We will follow with our machines of war and catapults. Perhaps we can smash them with direct hits."

"A direct charge of multiple mammoths might knock them to the ground long enough for us to do some rock crushing of our own!" snarled Trulock.

Everyone stood, rushing to his or her assignments. Enoch rose to his feet and spoke loudly, with authority, "We go to face a foe of dark spiritual power. We must seek the God of Light's protection if we seek success," he entreated.

"You are right," agreed Adam. "Bow with me. Great Creator, holy is your name. Forgive us our failings, as we forgive each other. Protect us, give us victory so we may honor you. Amen."

"Amen!" A shout in unison echoed around the room as they rushed out of the council chamber.

Enoch kissed Angela passionately as he readied himself to saddle up on the first of his three war unicorn mounts. He grabbed each side of her shapely rear in his big hands and gave it a loving squeeze. "You can't come with the advance force. We have to ride long and hard to get to Carmel before the stone monsters…it would not be good for the baby," he said patting her still small stomach.

Angela looked into his eyes, pained but resigned. "I know, it still pains me to be apart from you so soon!" she sighed.

"Come with the main force and we will meet at Carmel. After we stop these creatures we can make up for lost time," he grinned and kissed her again, long and hard, leaving her breathless as she watched him mount up and ride into danger.

Chapter 57

"What have you done?" accused Belshazzar as he accosted Hades in his lower chambers. "How far away have you dispatched the golems Zeus gave to you?"

"They are to go till they find what I asked for," said Hades, nonplussed and continuing to work on his experiments. He had manuscripts and charts, bottles and beakers, crystals and charms spread out in a seemingly disorganized manner.

"Have you not thought they may lead others back to us?" demanded Belshazzar.

"I have woven a concealment spell around them. Their tracks will vanish so that no trace will be left," Hades retorted, waving off any concern.

"Well, it's not working that well. Zeus is entertaining a visitor who followed some of your golems back to Atlantis," declared Belshazzar.

"Odd," mused Hades. "Is the visitor a threat?"

"It depends on your definition of a threat, but the fact that anyone found us at all should be disconcerting," emphasized Belshazzar.

"Well, I must have my samples and test subjects. Zeus limits how many citizens I can have now," Hades went back to a manuscript. "Perhaps I should put a shorter fuse on a concealment spell…" He manipulated some figures on the parchment.

"Until you perfect your spiritual weapons we must stay hidden. So, whatever you need to do to fix it, fix it now, " Belshazzar huffed. Hades looked up to him with ice-cold eyes, causing Belshazzar to step back a pace. "For the safety of us all," Belshazzar added hastily, afraid he might have pushed too hard.

Hades blinked and then returned to his work. "I will send a new concealment spell out to the golems post haste."

"Zeus invites you to a luncheon he is preparing for our guest," Belshazzar offered cordially, eager to deflect any possible ire of Hades.

"Tell my brother I must continue my work. I have no time for such pleasantries," Hades retorted and dismissed him with his hand.

Belshazzar left Hades puzzling over his calculations. Perhaps he was off just a little on how quickly his foragers' tracks would vanish, so Hades adjusted his spell and called forth a new servant to his table.

The groaning and twisting of metal assaulted his ears as a shiny brass golem strode into view. "That will never do," he fretted through another book of dark sayings and found a noise-deafening curse. He said the old angelic words and the noise lessened considerably. "There, the concealment spell will do nothing for you with all that racket," he said, pleased with his efforts.

"Here, carry this crystal with you to the troop of stone golems. I have set you on their vibration path. Touch each one for at least thirty seconds with this crystal, then return to me."

The bronze monolith listened impassively; its face not registering any emotion, just a blank, solid unblinking stare. After its instruction, the forty-foot gargantuan rose and started striding purposely to complete its task.

Chapter 58

"So, what is it you are not telling me?" Lamech probed, sensing Apolodon was hiding something from him.

Apolodon turned away and took a few steps to the right. "Whatever are you insinuating?" he grumbled, uncomfortable with the question.

Lamech had located Apolodon and his force looking for something out on the vast open plains. "So you have no idea who looted the mine and destroyed my detail of giants?" he asked.

"I said it was not me and that I am trying to get to the bottom of it," restated Apolodon. He motioned to an incoming scout to come over to the scarlet red command tent where he and Lamech stood under a gilded awning.

"Lord Apolodon," bowed the scout, "nothing from our quadrant."

Apolodon frowned and pursed his lips. "That was the final quadrant," he muttered, puzzled with the results. "It's as if whoever, whatever did this, just vanished into thin air. We must widen the search."

"And that is unheard of to you?" asked Lamech, showing a tad of questioning disbelief. "I believe Belial has encountered a similar phenomenon."

"Yes, but the Adamites would have left some kind of amber energy signature and they have never acted this way before. If anything, this speaks of dark energy, but of a kind unknown to me," pondered Apolodon.

Lamech was flabbergasted. Here was a Dark Lord, a fallen angel – who knew how old he might be – but certainly he existed before the present world. Lamech had expected Apolodon would have seen everything there was to see, and yet, this was unknown to him? It was beyond belief. "How can that be?" he asked incredulously.

"I'm saying, I have not encountered this before," repeated Apolodon. "This world of flesh is new to us – many strange things are occurring in this place."

Lamech's brain was whirling. What was new? Certainly not the creator, not Apolodon's kind. Mankind was new; the half-breeds were new. Something in Lamech's mind clicked. "Your experiments with half breeds – what have you unleashed upon us?" he accused.

"Nothing for your concern," dismissed Apolodon.

"Nothing for my concern?" Lamech mocked. "I've just had a mine pillaged, the workers have disappeared and my police force of giants torn limb from limb. I think I have a right to know what I'm facing," he fumed.

Apolodon motioned for Lamech to come deep into Lamech's royal tent set up on the plains, juxtaposed with the command center set out as his base.

"Are we alone?" asked Apolodon.

Lamech dismissed the thought of the tantalizing young redhead he had prepared for his bed, waiting for him in his royal chambers. He had left his two quarrelsome wives behind with the ruse that this would be a quick trip and not worth all the trouble to pack up and go with him. He had had the young girl hidden away by his most trusted servants, so she could provide him some well-deserved entertainment on his journey.

"We're alone, you may speak freely," Lamech replied as he crossed his arms on his obsidian armored chest.

"I am missing my chief wizard – a runt of a half breed – but very, very intelligent. He was working on some experiments concerning the mixture of angel blood with humankind, trying to improve the consistency of offspring." Apolodon avoided the point of whose offspring. "I'm afraid he discovered something that he either stole or he chose to abscond with it."

"You have no idea where he is?" Lamech probed. "Or what he created?"

"No half breed has ever shown this kind of physical strength," pondered Apolodon. "It must be some sort of dark energy creature, but exactly what, I don't know."

"We need to find this wizard of yours," stated Lamech.

"Don't I know it," muttered Apolodon angrily.

Lamech grunted and spent himself inside of the timid red-haired slave girl. She cooperated to an extent, but he had observed no throes of passion or ecstasy on her face. Her expression was more that of a resignation of her fate. No matter, she had excited him anyway with her fair white skin standing in such direct contrast to his swarthy complexion as he overshadowed her small, delicate frame with his powerful warrior's body.

He had taken his pleasure and now he plopped down beside her on his back, letting his racing heart and sweating body calm itself before he redressed himself in his regal garb and continued the search for the mystery creatures.

Her still, quiet, childlike voice broke his rest and interrupted his thoughts. "You will protect me from them, won't you?" she spoke softly in a begging, pleading tone.

"What?" Lamech grumbled, displeased to be bothered in his repose.

"The stone giants you and that other man were talking about, you will keep them away from me, won't you? If I keep you happy like this? You won't let them find me, will you?" she whimpered like a frightened puppy.

"Stone giants? Tell me what you know of these," demanded Lamech, suddenly paying full attention to the young woman. She was disarmingly beautiful and still fresh and vulnerable, unlike his quarrelsome wives who troubled him so. Her fear brought out something almost noble about him, his desire to comfort and protect. He chuckled to himself that she was in far more danger from Adah and Zillah than any creature of dark energy, but he needed more information about what was robbing his kingdom of resources.

Her delightful green eyes filled with tears as she tried to respond. Lamech patted her head and stroked her full mane of red locks and said, "There, there girl, of course I will protect you. Calm yourself and tell me about the stone creatures."

She gulped down her fear and stated, "I have a name, Lord Lamech."

Lamech looked at her in surprise.

She continued, "If I am to be with you in this way, I thought you might want to know my name," she sniffled as she drew the sheets up around her breasts. "It's Lucinda."

"Of course, Lucinda. Now tell me, what do you know?" Lamech persisted. "From the beginning."

"My father and I were traveling and we saw a caravan from afar, headed towards us. My father had me hide in the woods to the side along with the wares we had purchased from the markets. He was trying to protect me," she began sobbing again.

Lamech sighed in impatience, "Girl, I don't have all day," he snapped.

"Lucinda," she corrected. He noted a little bit of stubbornness in her voice.

Lamech rolled his eyes and calmed down as best he could, "I'm sorry, Lucinda. Settle yourself and try to remember all the details," he urged.

"Well, the caravan was led by a man dressed like a wizard or sorcerer of great importance, along with three very unusual young men," she recalled.

"What made them unusual?" asked Lamech intently.

She brushed back a disheveled strand of her long hair from her face. "Well, first of all was their size. They seemed like just adolescents, but they were already taller than full-grown men. Almost giant size, but not with the rough features of the giant race; they were very handsome.

"One of them was performing feats of great wonder as they walked, forming snakes from sticks, making little statues of stone move like they had life.

"I couldn't hear what my father and they said to each other, but my father got upset with something and spoke sharply to one of them…" She began tearing up again.

"Be strong, Lucinda, you must continue," Lamech held her hand. It was delicate and warm and he liked the feel of it in his.

She wiped the tears from her eyes with her free hand and went on. "And the man-boy's mouth opened up and out shot an all-consuming blue fire that just ate my poor father up, all the way down to his feet." She pulled his hand to her breast and sobbed some more.

Lamech fought arousal as he really didn't have the time for another round of lovemaking, so he refocused and urged her to continue. "That's horrible. Then what happened?"

"Well, I waited for them to pass then went back to my village. It was deserted. I remember the caravan had many people following along, but I was too afraid to look for survivors after my father… I just hid in the bushes, crying my eyes out. "I set up in my village by myself for weeks, living off of the stores we had bought from the market and what I could forage from the land. Then, one day while I was searching for berries, I heard a great rumbling approaching me. I ran and hid in the underbrush and huge monsters of stone walked right by me, thundering when they struck the ground with their massive feet. They looked much like the little moving statues one of the man-boys was making and they came from the same direction that the caravan had been going," she reported, calmer now, but keeping Lamech's hand pressed between her soft breasts. He could feel her heart beat racing with the memory of the horror.

"And that direction was…?" he asked, touching the side of her face, wiping away her tears.

"To the west, the wastelands," she said breathlessly.

Lamech sighed as he was drawn into her vulnerability. Perhaps he had a little time, he thought, as he kissed her lips.

Chapter 59

"This was the place, I am sure of it!" Mahalial stated determinedly, searching the ground for tracks.

The Adamite force had ridden hard to make up ground on the stone creatures' progress to Carmel. Enoch dismounted from his unicorn and felt the earth below him.

Enos and Adam looked intently around them, searching for anything outside of the ordinary. Their entire battalion was comprised of scouts and cavalry mounted on war unicorns, steeds and camels. Because of the need for endurance and speed each man had three mounts and the larger beasts had been left to follow with the main force. Seth was commanding the slower group.

Enoch's hand lit up as amber energy flowed from his fingers into the surrounding dirt. A pale blue light illuminated the earth around him, then began taking the shape of huge footprints.

"A concealment spell," he stated, "from some sort of dark power, but with a different aura than I am used to."

Adam followed the direction of the tracks with his eyes. "They are headed to Carmel, whether they know it or not," affirmed Adam to Mahalial.

"I know of a path through the woods that such large creatures must have avoided. They will have travelled the plains because of their size," declared Enos, eager to get to his home. "Once there, we can use the secret tunnels through the mountain caves to gain entrance into the city. Again, the tunnels are too small for such behemoths."

Adam nodded in agreement. "Let's be off!" he commanded and the riders shot towards the mass of tall trees and tangled undergrowth, trusting and following Enos's lead.

As Enoch mounted a brilliant white war unicorn, trailed by two equally majestic royal beasts attached to his mount with leather traces, he sensed something behind them.

He turned and scanned the horizon. His sharp eyes saw nothing, but he could feel an aura of dark energy. He quickly looked up to survey the skies, but saw nothing, as he squinted in the bright morning sun.

Suddenly a slight movement just at the western horizon caught his attention. There, a small rounded object began to appear. He could feel the vibration of its approach separate from the lighter vibrations of the thundering herd of riders moving off through the woods, like a bass fiddle among a symphony of violins.

He twirled his nervous mount around, steadying it as he kept his face pointed to the distant horizon. The object was huge and headed towards him without hesitation. The head and shoulders arose from the plains and soon an entire shining body of what appeared to be brass armor breached the horizon, striding purposely.

Enos cut the traces on the spare mounts and slapped their rears, sending them off to join the retreating riders. He feared for the carnage this thing could cause on his men in the open field, so he spurred his remaining mount directly towards the marching metal monstrosity.

So far, none of the riders had noticed him staying behind. Good. He would face this creature and see what it could do before he risked any of the Adamites' lives.

As he approached the behemoth he confirmed its massive size, a good forty feet tall. On further inspection, it was not wearing armor, it was armor. The solid mass of animated bronze, its unmoving blank face and sightless eyes like a statue, strode closer .

As he drew even with the approaching monster Enoch circled around it, not seeming to distract or even draw its attention. It was strangely muted, moving very quietly for such a mound of metal. Enoch noticed that even though it imprinted the earth deeply with each heavy step, the footprint left behind filled with a pale blue light and was brought back level to the ground, erasing any trace of its passage.

Around its solid neck it had a necklace of some type of crystal, glowing amulet, and kept its face pointed solidly in the direction of Carmel. Once behind it, Enoch dismounted and touched the vanished footprint with his amber glow. The same blue aura as before arose from the ground. This creature and the stone giants had the same origin, he determined.

As soon as his amber glow issued forth from his gauntlets the brass statue stopped in its tracks and turned towards him with surprising speed. It apparently could sense his energy and saw him as a threat. In a heartbeat, it slammed its massive fist down towards Enoch.

Enoch shouted a golden bubble of protection around himself and the fist slid off, striking the ground with such force it threw him up into the air in one direction, and his mount upwards in the opposite direction. The stunned beast landed with a thud and didn't move.

Enoch struggled to his feet and fired a few blasts of amber energy bolts at the towering figure. At each point of impact the blast ignited a corresponding blue light that seemed to dissipate and absorb his attack.

Enoch barely had time to frown in dismay before the creature launched another round of blows, attempting to squash him like a bug. For now, his energy shield was deflecting the blows from direct hits, but the pure force of the shockwaves of the bronze behemoth fist hitting the earth tossed him like a ragdoll.

Each time he landed, he bounced to his feet and prepared for the next assault. He could not see the exertion affecting the monster at all, its face was an impassive mask of calm, its flat eyes unblinking. He wasn't going to be able to wear it out.

Enoch focused his attack on the earth beneath the giant's right foot, suddenly creating a gaping hole beneath its extremity. The creature toppled to the right and fell heavily to the ground in a resounding crash. Enoch rushed upon it, dodged between its flailing arms and tried stabbing the monster in its eyes, but his crystal sword just clinked as if striking solid metal. The creature started swatting at him and struggled to rise.

Enoch readied himself to leap back off when he saw that the crystal was attached with a braided rope of some kind. He sliced the cord with his sword and successfully detached the crystal, which was throbbing a blue color and about half the size of a loaf of bread.

Bronze hands felt frantically for the crystal around its neck, then its head located Enoch with its sightless eyes and it gathered itself to charge him.

Enoch dashed to his recovering unicorn and prayed it had only been stunned. "We have to fly, mighty one. Can you run?" he asked out loud as he leapt onto its back and kicked its sides with urgency.

The startled steed needed no encouragement and snorted in fright as it bolted away from the fast approaching brass giant. As the gargantuan's metal fist slammed behind them the unicorn used the shockwave to launch itself into the air then landed solidly at a full gallop, fleeing the creature's wrath. Enoch turned his face back, trying to gauge the top speed of the pursuing creature, and with some dismay saw the creature was gaining on them.

He secured the crystal by plopping it into his water bag and began firing amber blasts at the ground just ahead of where the creature planned to place each foot, causing it to stumble and slow its gait to try to avoid falling to the ground. This opened up a little distance between them and he scanned the horizon for the plume of sulfurous smoke from the liquid mountain.

From what he knew of metal, it was impervious to blunt force but was weak to intense heat, which could cause it to lose its shape and power. The hottest fire he knew was a vast boiling pit of molten rock deep in the bowels of the liquid mountain. He would have to gain a larger distance from the chasing giant as his tiring steed would not be able to negotiate the top of the peak and he would have to climb the last distance to the top by hand.

They raced across the plains to the tell tale column of haze and fumes spewing forth from the belly of the mountain. Hours passed and Enoch was able to keep the giant stumbling to regain its footing. He could tell by its heavy breathing and slathered sides that his war unicorn was beginning to tire. He tried again to throw a barrier of sonic energy in front of the gargantuan, but it easily crossed through it with sparks of blue light energy.

Enoch resumed his attacks on its footing. He turned ahead and saw the liquid mountain closer on the horizon.

"A little bit further, old boy!" he urged his lathered mount. "Don't quit on me now!" He patted the hot, sweaty neck of the majestic unicorn, encouraging it to the goal.

As they neared the mountain, the terrain became rockier and the creature raised a new threat. It would pause to scoop up a boulder and launch it at the fleeing rider and his steed. The first few missiles fell too far away to concern Enoch, but with practice the creature was getting closer to hitting them.

Enoch gauged the next one would strike them head-on and urged his mount to the left while blasting the massive rock with sonic energy, deflecting it to the opposite side. In this manner they picked their way higher and higher up the mountainside, dodging and weaving until Enoch had to snatch up the water bag from his mount and send the exhausted steed off on its own path away from him, back down the mountain.

Enoch noticed the metal giant finally slowing just a bit as it struggled to pull its massive bulk up the sheep climb to the top of the liquid mountain, but Enoch himself was tiring as he had to take four steps for every one of the towering hulk's.

As Enoch reached the lip of the huge bowl that encircled the steaming vat of fiery ore, he felt the creature hot on his heels. After one glance at the boiling inferno he rolled over on his back, struggling to pull the crystal out from his water bag.

The metal monster gathered itself to pounce on him and rip him to shreds as Enoch managed to gain control of the blue glowing pendant and toss it high over his head into the frothing liquid rock.

The creature adjusted its leap from him to intercept the crystal, showing remarkable agility by snagging an outcrop of rock with its other vice-like hand. Enoch scrambled to peer down into the pit and saw the creature beginning to pull itself back up onto the outcrop.

"You have got to be kidding me!" exclaimed Enoch.

Enoch shouted out a narrow, laser like beam of rock slicing energy, a skill he had learned first from Adam as he crafted huge blocks out of the mountain to build the majestic city of Abelton.

In moments, the outcrop crumbled and gave way to the massive weight of the beast, which fell into the boiling pool of molten ore.

Enoch struggled to catch his breath as he watched the creature sink into the bubbling muck, diffusing into a melted pool of brass for a few moments until the red-hot rock wiped out every trace of its metallic existence.

Enoch paused and gave exhausted thanks to the Creator. "I bet Adam never used the rock cutting beam like that before!" he gasped to himself, scarcely noting a tiny shadow streaking by him, cast from far above.

Chapter 60

Her bright green eyes were thrown open wide with pure horror and her light brown body glistened with the sweat of terror, thrashing against its bonds. She was stretched out on her back, her arms and legs bound at the wrists and ankles. "Please, please," she whimpered, "please let me go."

At seventeen years of age she had fallen into the throng of people who followed after the new gods. They were so exciting and could perform miracle after miracle. The city of Atlantis was a miracle in itself, so clean and majestic. But she had drawn the attention of one of the new bureaucrats who had been installed as the ruling class in the city. He had demanded her to "service" his need for sexual relief and she had refused him. He was an arrogant pig. Hours later she was arrested and handed over to the dungeons of Hades.

She now was laid spread wide on a cold marble slab, bound and helpless. Hades frightened her, he seemed inhuman, so she turned to the two assistants who appeared to be human like her. "Please don't hurt me!" she begged.

"Remove that and prepare her body," commanded Hades as he

pointed to her simple white tunic.

The male assistant ran a razor-sharp blade down the cloth from her breasts to her groin, slitting it open and pulled it from under her.

"No, no, no!" she screamed as she squirmed and twisted.

"Should I gag her, Lord Hades?" asked the other, female, assistant as she began to smear thick gelatinous substance over her torso, covering her body completely.

"No, I rather enjoy their last words," reveled Hades, as he adjusted some controls and crystals around the table.

"I'll sleep with the officer, I promise! I will be good to him, just let me go!" she cried as they finished rubbing in the viscous oil and started attaching needles and tubes to her skin.

"You should've done that earlier. It's too late now," said the male assistant, who appeared to enjoy rubbing a lot of oil on her breasts, squeezing them as they heaved in fear.

She squirmed and entreated, "You, you can have me! Let me make you happy! Just let me go, please!" The female assistant replied with disgust, "We can have any of you whenever we want you. Down here you can win no favors with your body. We own you."

Hades finished adjusting the crystals and lifted a long black blade. It seemed to glow with a pale blue light.

"Run this last tube down her throat to catch her last breath."

"No! No! Urghh," she gargled as she felt the glass tube slide down her throat.

"Now lift her left breast just a bit so I can have an unobstructed thrust at her heart," Hades instructed as he placed the razor-sharp, spirit infused blade tip under her left breast, its point drawing blood just by touching her skin.

His groping assistant pulled up on her breast and Hades prepared to thrust his knife deep into her chest. Suddenly, the blue aura around the knife flickered and extinguished. Hades pulled the knife back and looked at it curiously. "Well, that won't do."

He put the knife down on the table and walked over to a crystal the size of half a loaf of bread. Its bright blue glow had faded to half its intensity. "This won't do it all," he muttered.

Hades looked over at the male assistant, still groping the girl on the table. "Stop playing with the subjects, Carl. Clean her and take her back to the holding cells. Keep her pure…a virgin. Do you understand, Carl? We will need her to be unblemished for our next try. Keep her healthy," Hades ordered.

Something had happened to the other half of his power crystal, something very bad, and he had to fix it.

Chapter 61

Lamech tried to listen as Apolodon droned on and on covering the pointless results of search quadrant after search quadrant. His mind kept going back to Lucinda's luscious body. She was so young and fresh, so willing to give herself to him without reservation. He was obviously her first and she was so eager to learn how to pleasure him.

"So that leaves the flyer from the smoking mountain still to report," finished Apolodon. Lamech shook his head and refocused, brushing back his tangled hair. "When do you expect to hear from him?" he queried.

The telling screeches of the leathery winged scouting reptiles sounded in the moist air.

"That will be him now," stated the ruby armored Dark Lord, pulling on his golden viper helmet over his long snow-white hair, his red eyes flashing in anticipation of news.

Lamech and Apolodon stepped out of Apolodon's command tent and waited for the security guards to clear the scout. In a moment the scout hurried over and bowed low.

"My Lords," he snapped urgently. "I come from the smoking

mountain, known as the liquid mountain to the Adamites," he reported.

"Yes, yes, I know, I sent you there," said Apolodon impatiently. "Go on."

"I saw a battle between a lone Adamite and a huge brass giant, a good forty feet in height," he claimed.

"Brass? As in 'armored with brass'?" asked Lamech.

"No, solid brass. Brass that moves by itself," the scout stated.

"Not stone?" queried Lamech.

"No, brass," repeated the scout.

"Well, it sounds like our Adamite friends have also discovered these monsters are not just made of stone," Apolodon noted. "What happened?"

"The Adamite led him over the edge of the pit and it fell into the smoking depths. It looked like he melted in the pool of rock," stated the scout.

"Those Adamites are resourceful ones," marveled Apolodon.

"Let's not get all starry eyed here," scoffed Lamech.

"Well, we have a direction, and we know the creatures can be defeated. I say we go," declared Apolodon.

"Let's mount up! To the smoking mountain!" cried Lamech, excited with the promise of adventure and more time away from his contentious wives to explore his new toy.

Chapter 62

Belhah sat all alone by the campfire. She was withdrawn, staring out into the blackness, seemingly at nothing. She was wrapped in one of Mahalial's fur cloaks left behind for her.

Eve nodded to Angela, "Go ahead, you need to talk to her."

Angela hesitated, "I don't know what to say. Part of me hates her for what she did to try to win Enoch's heart, while the other part of me feels sorry for all she's gone through."

"She is cleansed of the demon for now, but her heart needs to be healed if she is to stay free. She needs forgiveness and she needs friends. All will shun her if you shun her. Everyone respects you," Eve admonished.

"How can I look her in the eye and forgive her? How can I ever trust her the same as before all this happened? It seems impossible," argued Angela, turning away from the lonely figure in the flickering glow of the waning blaze.

Eve shrugged her elegant shoulders and wrapped herself tighter against the chill evening air. "Forgiveness is just as much for the forgiver as it is for the forgiven. You harbor bitterness, she harbors guilt; neither are whole, neither can heal."

Angela started to defend herself, then admitted, "I am very bitter and it kills me whenever I see her. It even casts doubts into my relationship with Enoch," she bemoaned.

"I wasted centuries harboring bitterness," sighed Eve, "and it ended up costing me Cain and Abel. I fear this world of conflict and violence owes much of its origins in my bitterness," she exhaled a long breath and brushed her honey blonde hair back from her face. "I would give anything to have those centuries back, to have the relationship with Adam then that I have now. But you my Angela," she patted her hands, "You are young, you don't have to repeat my mistakes, you can learn from them if you choose to."

Angela bit her lower lip. "Aren't I running the risk that everyone may think I was wrong or that I'm weak?"

"Of course you are. You can no more force her to give up her guilt than she can force you to give up your bitterness. Each of you must concentrate on what you can do for the other," Eve counseled.

Belhah started to stand up and head to her small, nondescript little tent. Eve prodded Angela with her elbow, "Go!" she urged sweetly.

"Belhah," Angela called as she walked towards the crackling logs.

"Do you have a moment?"

Belhah stiffened, then nervously brushed her cheeks with her hands, steeling herself for a conflict. "What do you want?" she responded curtly.

"Belhah, Mahalial and Enoch were and are best friends. I suppose if they can forgive each other, you and I should give it a try," she offered.

Belhah shook her head, "I don't deserve forgiveness. If you knew half of the evil I've done since that day I left the city, you would turn around and never speak to me again."

Angela softly touched her arm as Belhah tried to walk away. "Can we at least talk?" she pleaded earnestly.

Belhah snapped, "Talk about what? How I threw away the love of a good man? How I spread my legs to Lamech and his wives? How I tried to steal your husband? How I betrayed the city to Lamech? How I led hostages to their death? What would you like to talk about?" she fumed in a boiling rage.

Angela gulped in shock, unsure how to respond.

"Oh, cat's got your tongue now?" mocked Belhah. "It is a wonder Mahalial still wants me, but for some reason he still desires me and I will cherish his love from this point on. Any sight I have of the rest of you just reminds me of my other feelings of failure as a person," tears began to well up in her eyes and she furiously wiped them away.

"Belhah, what has happened has happened. We can either let it keep on destroying and eating away at the lives we have left or we can try to learn from it and become better, stronger people because of it. You are a powerful woman with a strong, survivor personality. How many women could have gone into the belly of the beast and lived to tell of it? I would count myself blessed to have you as an ally and a friend, rather than as an adversary." Angela was somewhat amazed that these words were coming out of her own mouth. She agreed with them, but she never thought she could a voice them without her anger and bitterness shutting her down.

Belhah looked back at Angela's steady gaze and could see truth in her words. For the first time she could sense there might be a way out of her horrible guilt and her feelings of utter failure.

For just a split second, a moment frozen in time, Belhah saw a path towards redemption, a chance for a life free from the horrible weight of guilt, disappointment and devastation. She was a survivor – she reached for it.

"Angela, from the first time I saw you, I hated you for your beauty. I envied how Lucifer chose you instead of me, how you got the crown prince and I got a common man, how you rose to lead the city against Lamech while others followed me to their doom. I wanted to destroy you and take your place. Can you honestly look me in the eye and say you forgive me? Could you ever trust me again?" She looked in Angela's face, her eyes filled with desperation and vulnerability.

Angela paused, a flood of doubt, bitterness and anger overwhelming her. A voice foreign to her echoed deep inside to not let this evil woman off the hook; to hate her, despise her; that she was deserving of Angela's scorn and disgust. Belhah had admitted her hatred; now was not the time to be weak, but to hold onto the anger, the hate, and to be strong!

As this voice raged and roiled her senses, a gentle, more calming voice overwhelmed it and simply told her that freedom comes from forgiveness and trust, but to hold others accountable. The calm voice had broken through. Angela knew what she had to do.

"I forgive you, will you forgive me and my anger and bitterness towards you?" Angela grasped both Belhah's hands in hers and returned her gaze.

Belhah burst into tears and she hugged Angela as relief surged through her soul like a tidal wave. She choked back her sobs long enough to utter, "Forgive you? My lady, you have earned a servant for life. I will lay this life down for you," and she knelt on one knee and bowed.

Angela quickly lifted her up, "I don't want a servant but I will accept a friend."

Eve watched the two girls sobbing and hugging each other and she smiled.

Chapter 63

Twelve stone golems, each one forty feet tall, stood motionless and equidistant from each other in front of the walls of Carmel. Their blank faces displayed no emotion and they turned neither to the left or the right.

The amber walls of Carmel reflected the setting sun, giving a golden glow to the valley.

"How long have they been there?" Adam asked Irad. Irad was clad in the familiar amber armor of the Adamites. His red hair and green eyes were uncovered as he held his silver helmet in his hands.

"They arrived yesterday at sunset," Irad answered. "They are beyond catapult range, and have made no threatening gestures yet, other than surrounding the city."

"So they've not moved at all?" asked Adam, stroking his chin in thought.

"We have eyed them all night and all day. They've not moved an inch since they arrived," said Irad, brushing back his long hair from his face.

Enos turned to Adam in the cooling evening air. "Should we go out and investigate them?" he asked.

Adam cautioned, "Mahalial and Angela say they moved incredibly fast when provoked, so for now, let's try not to do that. We need to get all our defenses prepared, load the catapults and be ready to launch. Have your mammoths armored and ready to charge."

Enos nodded and added, "We can have the women and children drawn back into the caves, safe and out of the way of combat. Do you think they will have a chance of breaching the walls?" he asked.

"From a purely physical standpoint, I would guess a creature of that size and weight would severely test the walls of Carmel, but your amber shielding should swing the balance in your favor," mused Adam as he smiled with raising confidence towards Enos.

Irad interjected, "When the sun completely sets, you can just make out a pale, blue aura around them, an energy source I've not seen before."

Adam turned behind him, "Where's Enoch? Have him come up here and see if this is the same energy pattern as what disguised their footprints."

Adam's messenger dispatched himself to find Enoch.

Enos turned as well, "It's unusual for Enoch to not be up here with us, in the thick of things."

The group of Adamite leaders stood atop the massive amber covered walls surrounding the city of Carmel. They had reached the secret mountain tunnels and made it to the city safely, but not in time to beat the stone goliaths. Fortunately no attempt to attack the city had been made. It was as if they were just watching, perhaps content with intimidating, or maybe they were… learning? Collecting information? Adam pondered as he waited for the messenger to return with Enoch. The cool mountain breezes lifted Adam's long chestnut hair and billowed his flowing golden robe in the air. There was not even a hint of sulfur in the air, so often detectable whenever the Dark Lords plied their trade.

After some time, the messenger returned empty-handed. "No one has seen Enoch for a while," reported the messenger. "The last place anyone remembers seeing him was just outside the path through the woods."

Another messenger leapt up the flight of stairs to the top of the wall. "My Lord, we found Enoch's two spare mounts; their traces were cut. They apparently came into the city with the rest of us, but there's no sign of Enoch."

"Show me the mounts," Adam ordered and took off quickly, following the hasty gait of the retreating messenger.

Once there, Adam gave the heavily breathing unicorns a quick going over. "They're not injured in any way and this trace has been cut with the blade. Enoch sent them along to us. He must have found something interesting to follow," deduced Adam.

Chapter 64

Zeus thrashed and squirmed; finally calling out from his newly constructed royal palatial bedchambers, "Enough, enough Hera I am spent!" He laughed as he pushed her head away.

His chambers rose high above the city, with walls of pure transparent glass. Viewed from the outside, the glass was opaque, changing colors and hues from different vantage points. From the inside, the chamber itself provided a majestic view of the city of glass against the turquoise sea and far off cliffs that sprang from the edge of the city.

Hera giggled like a schoolgirl and kissed her way up his groin, stomach, chest and neck, then kissed his panting mouth. "Have any of your slave girls provided you such ecstasy?" she pried, confident of his answer.

Zeus gasped between passionate kisses, "I have never encountered one such as you, you're definitely the expert."

Hera nestled on top of Zeus's chest and looked alluringly into his bright blue eyes. "This is just a taste of what I can provide you. Make me your Queen, Lord Zeus, and your pleasure will know no bounds."

Zeus chuckled as he looked at her gorgeous face, still flushed with exertion and into her deep brown, almond shaped eyes. "If giving pleasure was the only criteria, you would win your throne hands down. But there is more to being a Queen, you know."

Hera rose quickly and covered her body as she began to gather her clothes and re-assemble herself. "I have been a Queen for five centuries, there is no one in your kingdom more experienced than I, including you." She turned her back on him and stepped into her dress, pulling it up over her torso. "You are toying with me. If I do not please you and you do not see my value as a partner then I shall leave you to your little girls. Good luck in your endeavors."

She adjusted her deep purple, silken dress and smoothed it over her shapely hips, tantalizing Zeus with his last glimpse of her.

"Hera, wait!" Zeus dragged himself up from the rumpled bed, disheveled from the hours of passion he had never experienced before. He certainly did not want to lose this regal woman who carried herself with such poise and authority but could also cause such pleasure and pain in so many imaginative ways.

Hera continued to arrange herself and headed for the door. "You will not be opposed if I court other suitors, your brothers perhaps?" She tossed her shiny dark hair with a flip of her head.

Zeus was overcome with a jealous rage. He stormed towards the door, trailing a bed sheet from the large rumpled nest of lovemaking. "Hera I said wait!" He roared as he grabbed her arm roughly.

Hera burned a hole in his eyes with the heat of her glare. "Are you going to hurt me?" she demanded.

Zeus dropped his head in surrender. "Hera, I don't want to lose you. I don't know much about love, it is an emotion I have little experience in."

Hera laughed roughly, "Love? You do not need to love to choose your Queen." She grabbed him below, firmly. "Do you love what I can do with this?"

He moaned in agreement.

"Do you doubt my intelligence, my will? Am I resolved to make your kingdom mighty and powerful, to overcome all impediments in your path?" she persisted.

Zeus nodded in agreement. "You are indeed an exceptional woman," he groaned as he again began rising to her gentle touch.

"Then name me your Queen, before someone else takes your place," she tossed his flesh aside and turned to walk out the door.

She strode quickly down the halls of Zeus's magnificent abode. He certainly was a master architect. She would miss him, but there were Hades and Poseidon to try next. She was confident whoever chose her, she would make him the dominant brother.

As she reached the exit doorway, the head servant bowed low to her and spoke, "Queen Hera, your King, Lord Zeus, wishes to discuss which chambers would be most befitting of his new Queen."

She smiled and cocked her head, cutting her eyes back behind her. "Tell my King I will return, I have wedding plans to attend to."

Chapter 65

Enoch raced his exhausted, lathered white war unicorn towards the walls of Carmel. As he approached the plains before the city he was dismayed to find the giant stone creatures already arrayed like great monuments. He slowed his struggling mount as he drew near to the middle pair of monsters, positioned in front of the massive amber gates.

The cautious steed picked its way carefully up to and beyond the goliaths. Enoch held his breath in silent expectation praying he would not have to press his stallion any harder.

He could see heads and shoulders of figures scurrying around on top of the walls and he waved to the gatekeeper, high above the gate, holding his forefinger in front of his mouth in the universal hush sign. As he approached the gate a small door opened, just large enough for a dismounted man and his mount to walk through. Enoch kept an eye on the stone giants as he hopped off the worn-out unicorn and handed its reins forward.

"Take care of him, he has been ridden long and hard," he whispered, while backing towards the opening following his mount. As he turned away he saw Adam and Enos, their arms folded upon their amber armored covered chests, looking at him for an explanation.

"Well?" stated Adam simply.

"I sensed another kind of these at the point Mahalial brought us to," began Enoch. "I thought I would explore it a little to see what I could find out."

"Please continue," Adam urged, now interested to learn more rather than reprimand.

"It was a creature made of brass, of the same energy as those stone ones. It was drawn to me when I used my own amber pulse. It was very fast and absorbed my attack blasts with no effect." He rushed his report. "I was finally able to lead it into the pit of the liquid mountain where it met its doom. The brass one had a blue crystal of energy around its neck, these seem to have no such adornment."

Adam and Enos looked at Enoch in open-mouthed surprise. "You felled a bronze monstrosity like one of these since we've seen you last?" Adam asked in wonder. He was having a hard time believing these things could even move, as he had not yet seen it himself.

"You can keep them off balance by blasting holes in the ground below their feet; their balance is limited," added Enoch as he finished his report. "Oh, and I wouldn't activate the shields of the city. It will make them charge."

"If they are drawn to a discharge of our energy…" began Enos.

"Then maybe we could lead them away from the city," finished Adam.

"Like flies to honey," agreed Enoch. "But they're very fast and surprisingly agile. I don't know if I could lead these all the way back to the liquid mountain, my animal would surely tire."

Enos thought for a moment. "There is a vast canyon to the west of here, a drop of well over two thousand feet. Would that cause them to shatter?"

"It's worth a try. Can you guide me?" asked Enoch.

Adam gathered himself to lead but Enoch touched his shoulder. "Father Adam, you're needed here in case Enos and I fail. This ride calls for speed and knowledge of the land, not numbers. Let us do this and under the grace of God, we shall succeed," he pleaded earnestly.

Adam debated within himself, then finally commanded, "Find six of our fastest steeds, the most rested. Take three apiece – that should get you to the canyon?" He looked at Enos for confirmation,

And Enos nodded.

"Get as big of a head start as you can," Adam added.

Chapter 66

"I spotted the lone rider heading to Carmel," recounted the flying scout as he stood before Lamech. "So I flew ahead and found twelve of the stone behemoths, poised outside the city walls."

Lamech snacked on a cluster of grapes while Apolodon stood with silent reserve, contemplating their next action.

"They were not attacking, just standing there?" Lamech confirmed.

"No my lords, they were just planted there like statues," assented the scout.

"We do not have a large enough force to engage an Adamite fortress," stated Apolodon, clicking his ruby red armor with a long, black, claw like nail.

"But I am curious to see these things. Especially if they attack the city walls," confessed Lamech. "Could you assemble a fast platoon of riders strong enough to protect us while we spy on them? We could circle to the west of the city and observe."

"It could be done," stated Apolodon flatly.

"Give me a few minutes and then we ride," Lamech rose and headed to his tent. He was developing strong feelings towards Lucinda, his little slave girl. He walked into his royal tent and spied her sitting on the bed, brushing her long locks of reddish hair.

"Lucinda," he announced as he entered the room, scanning it for anything he needed for the trip. "I'll be gone for a while, I have business to attend to. Stay in the tent, do not go outside in my absence. Do you understand?"

Lucinda nodded as she asked, "I can't go with you?" She stopped brushing her hair and looked plaintively at him with her large green eyes.

"No, it is a trip that will be fast, hard and dangerous for one as delicate as you. Stay here, stay safe. And if for any reason you are told Adah and Zillah are coming, run. Run for your life and I will find you," Lamech warned. "You should be far enough away but one never knows with those two."

Lamech grabbed his helmet and dashed out, stopping to speak to the guards at his tent. "Keep her safe," he ordered. "At any hint of Adah and Zillah, secret her way to the City of Light. I will find you there."

The guard saluted.

"I don't want to find this one's head detached, I want to keep her intact, understand?" added Lamech, flashing a brief glare at the guards.

"Her life is protected by ours, my Lord," they submitted.

Lamech strapped on his dragon helmet and mounted his reptilian steed. "Let's go!"

Chapter 67

Zeus hurried to his throne room, eager to receive the guest whom he was sure would be a grateful and exuberant Hera, ready to share more of her wares. When he arrived he was somewhat crestfallen to see his brother, Hades.

Hades observed his dejected air and replied, "Sorry to disappoint you, brother, but I have somewhat of an urgent issue."

"What do you request?" Zeus tried to recover some regal air of authority.

"I've lost the brass golem," stated Hades.

"Lost? It should respond to your signal and return to you wherever it is," Zeus chided.

"I know that, but for some reason it is not responding. I sent it on a mission to upgrade my concealment spell on the stone gatherers and it vanished." Hades flopped his hood back over his disheveled crop of jet-black hair and let out an exasperated sigh. "And that's not the worst of it."

Zeus grew more intent, "What could be worse?" he asked gravely.

"The bronze golem carried part of our power crystal to reprogram the stone golems. The crystal is gone as well.

"Without that crystal, I know my control over the stone golems is hampered. I need to find them, reestablish control and update their instructions," Hades concluded.

"You don't know where they are? What if they wandered into the lands of our enemies, unconcealed and uncontrolled? They could lead our foes back to Atlantis before we are prepared!" fumed Zeus.

"That's why I need to track them, find them and fix the problem," Hades paced the floor and made an exaggerated chop of one hand into the other palm. "You claim to be able to make these golems out of almost any material, is that right?"

"Just about. I have not yet mastered crystal or living matter like wood or flesh," Zeus stated.

"I need one of air or cloud, one that can ride the winds for greater speed. I will travel with it in spirit and find these hampered ones and bring them back. I will also search for the crystal that is missing," explained Hades.

"We can do that?" questioned Zeus.

"It's a simple spell. I will just be asleep in my flesh and it will interrupt my work," complained Hades.

"Well then, let's get started. I will send you the air golem when I construct it," exclaimed Zeus.

"Brother," bowed Hades as he left the royal chamber, passing a rather stunning beauty with jet-black, long, shiny hair. She seemed taller than most and when their eyes met for an instant he felt a kindred spirit, of immense age, not fitting at all in such a young and supple body. She was waiting to be received and nodded to him as his gaze lingered.

He gave a half smile to her and hurried on his way. She would be an interesting one to have on his table, he thought in passing.

Chapter 68

"Are you ready?" Enoch sat astride the first of his three royal matched unicorns. They snorted and pawed at the soft earth, eager in anticipation for the breakneck ride that lay ahead. Their brilliant white coats reflected the early morning sunlight.

Enoch had shed his cloak of sewn furs and was adorned in his complete suit of amber armor. He wanted as much coverage as possible to draw the greatest amount of attention to himself that he could.

Enos's role was to guide Enoch through the unfamiliar terrain, so he wore simple linen clothing to not weigh down his midnight black stallions. He checked the traces that attached his two additional mounts to ensure they were tight. "As ready as I'll ever be," he nodded.

They slowly walked past the stone monoliths that had stationed themselves around the semicircle walled city of Carmel. Once they were well past the giant figures, they mounted up and prepared for their headlong flight to the massive canyon that formed the western border to the Carmelite lands.

"Let's get started then," declared Enoch as he took in a deep breath and fastened his amber and silver helmet.

"The Lord is our shield!" shouted Enoch, igniting the amber glow of his golden hued armor.

He eyed the gray speckled stone creatures but saw no movement. "I thought you said they were drawn to your energy?" said Enos.

"Hmmm. The other one was..." puzzled Enoch as he thought. "Perhaps we should move a bit closer." They gently urged their nervous plains riders closer.

Suddenly, Enoch noticed an eerie blue glow emanating from a swift moving, dark thundercloud passing overhead.

"Where did that come from?" Enos queried as he noticed the passing shadow from above.

"This is unnatural, it shares the same signature of these creatures," warned Enoch.

Without warning, blue shots of light crackled like pale bolts of lightning from the center of the cloud into the chests of the stone golems. The creatures began to animate as one took initial steps towards the city walls.

Enoch yelled, "Don't activate the shields," not thinking anyone could hear him over the thunderous footsteps of the stone gargantuan. He shot repeated blasts from his hands, aiming one at the backs of each of the creatures. Sure enough, as the amber balls of energy struck, a pale blue light flared up and dispersed the attack. It had the desired effect as they instantly turned and started running towards Enoch and Enos.

Enos's eyes widened as he turned Enoch and said, "Let's ride!" kicking the flanks of their skittish mounts who were poised to flee. No extra incentive was needed as the animals bolted away from the approaching behemoths. The race was on.

Chapter 69

"I see an amber glow. Look, just at the horizon, see it?" gasped Angela as she, Seth, Eve, Luna and Angel rode at the head of the Adamite force assembled to protect the city of Carmel from the stone giants Mahalial and Belhah had discovered while heading that way.

Seth peered from the back of his giraffe like mount. "You have sharp eyes Angela. I see the glow and there appear to be riders going full speed at its center," he observed as he watched the figures move across the plains to the west.

Eve stood up in her stirrups and squinted to see behind the riders. Of the five, she alone wore the brilliant white dress and billowing robes of royalty, bedazzled with a rainbow of gems and precious stones. The others were outfitted for war and Angela wore her newly crafted suit of amber armor while her golden cape fluttered in the gentle breeze.

"What is that? I see shapes of some kind, chasing them?" asked Eve, pointing her elegant finger at the horizon.

Angela sat astride Maverick, the huge saber-toothed tiger that had accompanied Enoch in so many of his journeys and battles, but had to be left with her as his massive power and bulk were ill fitted for the mad dash across the land by Enoch and the other riders. She shifted her gaze to where Eve was pointing.

"It's them – the creatures! That must be Enoch!" she cried as she kicked Maverick's flanks, bolting away from the main force. Maverick flared his nostrils and caught Enoch's scent, giving him another burst of catlike speed.

"He's in trouble!" she yelled as she clung to the streaking feline.

"Angela!" yelled Eve helplessly. "Wait!" But it was too late.

Angel and Luna dug their heels into their mounts and took off after her.

"We'll keep an eye on her, follow as you can!" shouted Luna, looking back to Eve and Seth.

Angela heard voices shouting behind her but they grew distant and too faint to understand as the wind from her swift advance cut around her ears. She made an impressive sight, a beautifully formed female figure covered in perfectly fitted amber armor with her long golden tresses of hair and golden robes billowing out behind her while she leaned forward on the tawny, powerful cat, urging it faster and faster, putting the startled Adamites further and further in her wake.

Maverick was eating up the distance between them quickly, and Angela marveled at how such a powerful beast could achieve such speeds. "Don't wear yourself out," she said, patting his neck, "Save some energy for when we get there."

Maverick, veteran of many battles, was already settling down into the ground-covering pace he could maintain for hours. He growled an earth-shattering roar in anticipation.

Enoch heard the distinctive roar of an enraged saber-toothed cat above the consistent thunder of their own mounts' hooves and the earth-shaking creatures behind him.

He turned to his right and his sharp eyes caught the advancing figure of a golden amber figure on a massive feline – Angela!

Desperation flooded him as he now saw the mass of Adamites also advancing, still far behind her.

"Whatever you do, don't activate your amber energy!" he screamed futilely in his head, as he knew that's exactly what she would do. Sure enough, she and the cat lit up in an amber hue.

He looked behind him and saw a group of six of the straining creatures break free from the back to address the new threat, thundering towards Angela.

Enoch yelled at Enos, "Ride to Angela, tell her to turn off all amber energy. They are drawn to it! Hopefully those six will turn back after me!"

Angela was already firing blasts of golden hued energy at the charging stone goliaths, frowning in puzzlement that her blasts seemed to have no effect on them.

Enos peeled off from Enoch and streaked on his midnight black steeds towards Angela, yelling and waving his arms to get her attention. "Stop! Stop!" he screamed. She stopped firing her bolts of sonic energy but kept up her defensive shield. The behemoths kept coming towards her. Enos finally got close enough for her to understand him. "They are drawn to your sonic energy, they will destroy you!" he gasped.

"What is Enoch doing?" she demanded.

"He is leading them to the great canyon that borders the lands of Carmel. We hope to lead them to their doom," Enos warily eyed the stone giants approaching.

"I know the place," said Angela as she brushed a stray strand of golden hair from her face and deactivated her shield.

The giant creatures slowed for an instant. Far behind Angela, Enos's force of casters activated their sonic amber shields by shouting out words of faith and the creatures redirected and started charging the main force.

"Enos, they will tear them apart! You must run to them and tell them to drop their shields. I will follow and try to draw them back to Enoch," she commanded.

"My lady, I cannot allow you…" he began.

"Enos, only I can draw them. You have no shield. Now go, race like the wind and save your people, go!" she ordered.

Enos acknowledged her reasoning and bolted towards the main force.

Angela urged Maverick out of the way of the earth shattering creatures. "Rest while you can, boy. We will need all of your power in a moment."

Seth ordered his catapults to unlimber. "We will need your best aim!" he urged as the crews struggled to assemble the great machines before the stone destroyers were upon them.

Eve shouted, "A rider is coming from Angela, while she stays. The creatures have passed her, thank God, but they are now heading towards us."

Enos met Luna and Angel, quickly informed them and all three of them charged ahead of the rock titans, splitting up to get the word out quicker.

Angela watched in heightened desperation as the stone death mongers got closer and closer to the main force of Adamites. Finally, the amber bubbles of energy began shutting down one by one. She waited until the last shield dropped then charged at the stone figures, firing blast after blast and screaming at the top of her lungs. "Hey, hey! This way, follow me!"

The lumbering creatures turned to meet the new threat behind them and Maverick threw on the brakes and quickly changed his direction nearly unseating Angela in the process. She repositioned herself astride him and patted his neck, "I'm okay boy, go! Go to Enoch!"

She twisted her neck backwards to ensure all six of the golems were following her, then she gave Maverick his slack and let him run.

Enoch rolled his eyes as he watched the events transpire to his right. As hard as he had tried to keep his pregnant wife out of harm's way, here she came with six fearsome, gigantic stone demons hot on her trail. He admired her determined, shapely form as she sprinted towards him, her long blonde hair and golden cloak flowing behind her.

As she pulled up beside him she nodded a polite greeting, "Enoch, good to see you in one piece."

Enoch grinned and shook his head. "I guess it's too late to request that you stay home out of trouble?" he asked.

"Well, I just thought I would go for a ride, get some fresh air," she said casually.

"Mmhmm," nodded Enoch. "I see. Well, I have no idea where I'm going. You just sent my guide off in the opposite direction."

"Just follow me, sir. This way to the great canyon," Angela smiled as she nudged Maverick into the lead, ahead of the wild-eyed war unicorns.

Chapter 70

Lamech and Apolodon received a frantic scout, soaring in on his pterodactyl beast. He jumped off the landing creature and threw back his dark hood.

"Sirs! They are headed straight for us!" he warned hastily.

"Slow down. Now, who is headed right towards us?" urged Lamech, disturbed that his silent observation mission was turning into something more troubling.

"A small group of riders," he stated, then hurried to complete his report in response to Lamech's "So what?" look. "They are followed by a dozen huge moving stone statues."

"They are leading them?" Apolodon asked.

"It looks more like they are being chased by them, Lord," corrected the scout, fidgeting before the two authoritative leaders.

"Set up a defensive perimeter," motioned Apolodon. "We will

prepare a welcoming committee to greet these interlopers."

Enoch spied the dark forces spreading out before them. "We don't have enough time to stop and talk," he called Angela, pointing ahead.

"Power up your shield to its maximum level, join with mine, and we will blast our way through the middle of their lines," he instructed.

"Fire up your dark shields!" ordered Apolodon. A dark bubble of black power formed around the Dark Lords' and Lamech's forces, blocking Enoch and Angela's path leaving them trapped between the powers of darkness and the stone destroyers.

"Now, focus everything at the dead middle of the force field, give it all that you have!" Enoch bellowed. Angela screamed, Maverick roared and Enoch shaped their combined energy in faith to form a sharp wedge of power, splitting through the Dark Lord's defensive shield and forming a pathway through Apolodon's shocked defenders.

Apolodon cursed and yelled, "Stop them!" as he fired black blast of power from his mouth. Lamech tapped the angry Dark Lord on the shoulder and stated. "Uh, Apolodon, I think we have bigger problems right now!"

Apolodon turned and watched the living stone statues tear into his screening forces, scattering them like rag dolls. Lamech stood open mouthed as he saw men crushed and pulled asunder. They were like pesky bugs being swatted away.

Any dark energy caster was routed out immediately and crushed by the stone giants. Apolodon saw that any dark blasts reaching the rock warriors just defused into a pale blue light.

Before his entire force was completely decimated, he blasted an order above the fray.

"Stop your dark energy! Shut down your shields, stop your blasts!" Apolodon screamed.

The giant granite blocks of power paused for a moment, then re-focused on the two fleeing amber riders and resumed their headlong pursuit.

Enoch looked over at Angela as they rode furtively ahead, attracted to her womanly shape, her face flushed with excitement and her flashing brown eyes. "Have I ever told you I think you are quite attractive?" he smiled.

Angela stole a quick glance at him and grinned, "Now you tell me, really?" She waved her arm over her well- sculpted armor, highlighting every curve on her body. "I just threw this old thing on, and my hair is a mess."

Enoch sighed, "Well, after we take care of this catastrophe, how about a picnic?"

"Are you going to cook?" she challenged.

"I'll cook," he agreed, "if you don't mind eating simple fare."

"You know I'm pregnant," she reminded, "I could eat a horse."

"You certainly don't act pregnant," declared Enoch, laughing. "How about we just ride the horses and don't eat them?"

She pursed her lips and looked back, checking the distance from their pursuers. "I'm just saying you'll have to be gentle with me," she smiled demurely.

"Yes, my lady, your wish is my command," Enoch doffed his helmet towards her and they shared a mutual laugh before turning more serious.

"We have maybe another twenty miles or so. How long can Maverick last at this pace?" Angela asked, a bit concerned.

"He is well rested, he will be fine. I do think it is time for me to cut this one…" he eyed the lathered steed beneath him, "…loose and hop on number two."

Enoch drew near to his next unicorn and pounced on it, reaching down with his crystal dagger and cutting the traces to his first mount, slapping its rump.

"Go back home, boy!" he urged as the exhausted steed peeled off to the left, leaving the chase. The stone creatures paid it no attention.

Hades flew along, his consciousness embedded in the cloudy air golem, watching the life and death chase below. He wished now that he had been more creative with the scripted instructions he had installed into Zeus's stone creatures. He had not known what situation he was going to find them in and had gone for a quick fix in lieu of taking the time to get more elaborate.

Things seemed to be going well. These two riders could not escape his killers. Their mounts would tire and that would be their end. The trail of the stone goliaths was effectively erasing itself quickly now. The forces far behind would not be able to follow.

He was intrigued, though, by how these two faced their certain death. They did not seem frightened or resigned to their fate, although they must know as well as he that their plight was hopeless. He thought he would stay for a while and watch them die.

His assistants would keep his body safe and cared for back in Atlantis, so just a little while longer should be fine.

The time flew by and Angela finally spied her landmark. "Here! We turn to the southwest now and we will soon be at the edge of the lands of Carmel."

Enoch spied the creatures making the adjustment with them and replied, "They are still close behind."

"Good, "declared Angela. "What are we going to do?" she asked.

"We are going to jump," Enoch stated matter-of-factly.

"Jump? Where?" demanded Angela.

"Into the canyon," smiled Enoch.

Chapter 71

Seth quickly had the catapult crews reload their weapons onto their wagons and they started off after Enoch and Angela.

Luna and Angela rode up to meet him. "It's so odd, the great stone creatures' footprints are just vanishing but fortunately we can still see Enoch and Angela's tracks."

Enos pulled alongside, "I know where they are heading. Follow me."

The Adamites took off at full speed towards the great canyon, the faster units separating from the heavier ones, but all moving at top speed.

From the left, atop his galloping high perch, Seth noticed three riders coming from Carmel. He pointed towards them, declaring, "Queen Eve, riders approaching!"

Eve raised her hand to shield her eyes from the sun and strained to make out the trio of approaching men. Soon she recognized Adam on his white war unicorn, Mahalial on his saber-toothed tiger, and that swordsman, Judah on a stallion of pale gray. Adam had on his full amber armor with his silver helmet and flowing golden robes. Mahalial wore leather scouts' armor with a cape of animal skins. Judah wore a dark brown hooded cape over his black obsidian armor.

They drew up alongside the head of the pursuing force. Adam leaned over to Eve, shouting to make himself heard over the thundering hooves, "What news? Have you seen – " then he eyed Enos, also at the head of the column. "Enos! What happened?"

Eve waved her hand to refocus Adam back on her. She shook her full head of honey blonde hair and drew back a stray wisp with her hand. "Enoch and Angela are drawing the creatures towards the gorge; Enoch is leading us there as well."

"Angela! Enoch, why did you let her…?" Adam pointed a finger at Enoch.

"No one 'let' her. You know how impetuous she is," chided Eve.

Adam nodded then wisely changed the subject. "Trulock and his band are not far behind us," he said as he thrust his hand behind his back.

"Good," said Eve, her determined face causing Adam to give thanks to the Creator for giving him such a strong, beautiful woman as his partner. "We will need all the help we can get," she stated.

Soon, the leading edge of their force came across the remnants of slaughter that had until recently been Apolodon and Lamech's screening force.

Adam held up his hand and slowed them to a walk as he surveyed the torn and crushed bodies of men, giants and beasts, cast about in a bloody hodge-podge of guts, legs, arms and torsos. The smell of offal and the rusty, iron like smell of blood filled the air.

"By the Creator!" gasped Eve. "What could possibly give these creatures such power?"

"It is not of this world," stated Mahalial. "No flesh could do this."

Adam heard the rustling of a bush and instantly twisted in his saddle and fired up his armor for a devastating blast. "Come out from behind that brush or suffer your doom!" he shouted.

Lamech held up his hands and waved Adam down from red alert. He walked out with a considerable limp. "Half-breeds," he winced as he walked up to them.

Adam quickly searched around their party for any kind of accompanying force or ambush. "What happened to you?" he asked, satisfied that Lamech was alone.

"I was thrown from my mount when those creatures attacked us. Damned Dark Lords left me behind," coughed Lamech.

Eve pulled up alongside Adam and inserted herself into the interrogation. "Half breeds?" she asked, "You said 'half breeds'?"

Lamech fought what Eve's beauty was doing to him; she took his breath away and turned his knees to jelly with those intense blue eyes. He tore his gaze away from her face and looked back at Adam. "Yeah, half breeds. Some experiment of Apolodon gone wild," he grumbled.

Adam puzzled, "We have seen half breeds, giants, trolls, ogres, sorcerers, even some twisted beasts, but nothing capable of this." He shook his head. "Those stone creatures look like no half breed I have ever seen."

Lamech stole a glance at Eve's perfect form. Oh how he wished he could be Adam for a night! She made Adah and Zillah seem like homely has-beens. "The stone creatures aren't the half breeds. They were made and empowered by some new kind of magic or power."

Lamech paused and looked back at Adam. "Are you going to give me a ride?"

Adam frowned at Lamech's lingering glances at Eve and waved to Enos. "Find him a mount, we must keep going. "

Lamech climbed upon a borrowed sorrel steed. "Mind if I tag along?" he insisted as he pulled up alongside Eve. "I'd like to see how you fare against these things."

"Come up here with me, Lamech. The great mother doesn't need your company," ordered Adam, pointing beside himself.

Lamech stole one last glance at Eve then bowed and saluted to no one in particular, "By your leave, Great Father."

The force kicked the flanks of the their various types of mounts, war unicorns, horses, giraffe creatures, sabertooths, camels, mammoths and rhinos, and took off, following Enoch's trail to the great canyon.

Hades looked over the fleeing pair, then suddenly it dawned on him what they were up to. He saw them heading directly towards the great canyon that separated the western wilderness from the lands of Adam and Cain and the Dark Lords.

There were going to sacrifice themselves by throwing their little amber charged bodies over the cliff, hoping to draw his golems along with them. "How noble," he thought, but he could not let that happen.

He had not thought of this contingency when he had formulated his new instructions and there was no time for him to get back to his laboratory then return here to alter his golems' behavior. He would have to use this air/cloud golem he was tied to. He conjured strong winds and rain and focused them against the racing couple. He cursed as he saw them form an amber shield and cut effortlessly through his attempted interference.

Angela looked wide-eyed around herself and Enoch, "Where did this come from?" she asked incredulously. "It is only around us!"

Enoch shouted, "There is a presence above us. I feel it working for our demise," as he modulated their combined shielding to offset the attack of the weather.

Suddenly, a massive bolt of blue lightning struck between them, supercharging the air with static electricity and an explosive sound. The blast threw the mounts and their riders high into the air and Enoch struggled to maintain his consciousness in the sudden flash of blinding light and thunderous resonance.

He caught Angela's body along with his own in a cushioning field of amber to break their fall somewhat, but she and the beasts were stunned into a stupor. The golems were almost upon them and Enoch could sense murderous intent on their blank, impassive faces of stone.

"Angela, wake up! Wake up!" he urged. He hoisted her limp body up over his shoulder and started running towards the gorge, just beyond a jagged row of cliff tops. A great hand came crashing down in front of him and he was barely able to stop in time to keep from becoming a human pancake.

He desperately searched the surrounding terrain for a way of escape. Angela gurgled and pointed groggily, "That way, there is a small cave that leads to the edge."

Enoch leapt ahead and fired a blast at the base of a huge column of stone, collapsing it on top of the closest creature, momentarily immobilizing the golem under tons of fallen rock. It gave him the moment he needed to gain entrance to the mouth of the cave, giving them a few second's respite.

He sat Angela back on her feet and she was able to stand.

"Are you alright?" he asked as he looked her over, searching for any serious injuries.

"I'm fine, I'm fine. Let's go!" she expressed dismissively and hurried him away just as huge hands smashed into the opening, grasping blindly for their soft bodies.

They fired up an amber energy glow and hurried along through the now illuminated darkness, hearing the massive golems ripping away at the mountain behind them.

The interior of the cave through the mountain ran at a steep incline, causing them to climb in a struggle to make decent progress. They were deafened by the horrendous rending and crushing of rock all around them as the golems tore through the rocks below.

Long moments passed as Angela picked her way through the tunnel. "This was much more fun when I was a kid," she panted as she scaled another wall.

Enoch listened to the heavy thumping above them. "Some are climbing over. They attempting to beat us to the other side!"

Suddenly, huge hands burst through the ceiling of the cave, blindly clutching for them. They dodged the groping fingers and kept up their furious pace to the tunnel's end.

After anxious minutes, Angela finally saw sunlight flooding in from the canyon's side opening.

"It's up ahead!" she shouted as she scrambled to the promise of freedom.

Enoch saw a massive shadow darken the exit and pulled her back just before a giant hand exploded inward, knocking them both backward with a misplaced knuckle.

Enoch glanced behind them, saw the clouds of rock dust and felt the thunderous tumult of sound approaching from behind.

"We're trapped!" cried Angela.

"Over here!" he urged. "Focus your energy blast as narrowly as possible against this wall. The goal is to cut a plug from the inside to the outside. They won't expect us to come out there."

They both shouted the words of faith that pierced the darkness and burned through the resisting rock wall.

As their beams met Enoch yelled, "Now, let's push out with a broad blast," as they dodged a clutching stone fist.

Far above Hades was pleased with his golems' performance. Their prey were moments away from destruction. It was getting late, he needed to get back to his experiments. He was so close to developing the right mixture of matter, energy and frequency to capture a human spirit. He had to slaughter so many of them to get this far.

Disposal of the bodies had become a problem as Zeus didn't want the truth of his wanton bloodletting to become public knowledge, but Poseidon had come to the rescue, calling huge carnivorous sea creatures that feasted on the remains of test subjects. They congregated so thickly at his feeding point that no one dared to enter the waters around his side of the city of Atlantis, even though his feeding station was well hidden and distanced from prying eyes. He was just about to wrap his endeavors up and head the air golem back home when a piece of the mountainside began glowing with an amber hue.

"What t – ?" proclaimed Hades.

If the doomed couple were trying to escape this way, there was no ledge, only a steep fall to certain death. The glow burst into an explosion as a great cylinder of rock shot out from the mountainside. The golems quickly adjusted to seeking the new source of amber energy.

"Now! Let's go!" shouted Enoch as he grabbed Angela's hand and led her, racing to the new opening.

"Really?" gasped Angela as they shot out of the cave and into the canyon.

"No, no, no!" bemoaned Hades as he saw the two figures dive out of the circular opening, barely evading two sets of stone fingers trying to snatch them from the air.

Angela screamed as she hurtled through the air, thousands of feet above the hard rock floor below.

Enoch shouted up his bubble of energy and pulled her close to him, narrowly avoiding a falling mountain of writhing stone.

Enoch pulled further away from the side of the mountain and the huge rock golems, faithfully following their programming, futilely leapt after them and plummeted to their demise far below.

Angela clutched Enoch breathlessly as she watched the last of the gargantuans crash into a pile of rocks and dust on the distant floor of the canyon.

She looked up into Enoch's face, also flushed with adrenaline and excitement. "You're going to have to teach me this one," she gasped and then smothered his face with a long, desperate kiss.

Enoch floated the bubble back to their newly formed exit and softly set them down, holding her gently to him. "How about that picnic?" he smiled, stroking her soft face with his hand.

Hades glared furiously at the embracing couple. He had been

caught off guard and had to watch powerlessly as his golems faithfully followed his instructional program to their own doom. Who were these creatures? Why didn't he know about them? His anger grew. He still had control of this air golem and could cause wind, rain and lightning.

He roared as he shot a bolt of white-hot electricity at the unsuspecting pair.

Enoch sensed the presence again as he kissed Angela. He raised his eyes to the sky and saw a cloud forming into a face and a torso, lifting its arm to form a flashing sliver of light. Enoch grabbed Angela and threw them both roughly, deeper into the tunnel, narrowly escaping the blast of lightning.

"It looks like we're not through running just yet," he shouted as they tumbled and stumbled away from the bolts of lightning flickering after them. The cloud creature was following them into the cave, shooting crackling strings of energy ahead, attempting to burn them to a crisp.

"We have got to get out of this cave!" said Enoch as they raced through the tunnel, now greatly enlarged by the work of the mining golems' efforts.

Chapter 73

Adam held up his hand as he viewed, in awe, the entire side of a mountain ripped away.

"This must be the work of those monsters," exclaimed Luna.

"I think I see a cave through there," exclaimed Mahalial, peering into the dusty haze surrounding the mountain.

"The canyon lies just beyond this," affirmed Enos.

"Form a defensive perimeter facing this opening, pull up the catapults, then be ready to send this whole mountaintop over the edge if need be," shouted Adam to his commanders.

Lamech shuffled off to the side, trying to stay out of the way. He was amazed at how orderly the Adamites made preparations, each man expertly going about his task as if his job was the most important one. There was no visible fear, just desperate, grim determination. No wonder his troops were so out fought whenever they clashed with these men. Perhaps there was more to being a king than ordering people around using fear and intimidation.

"There!" shouted Eve. "In the cave, there is flashing light and movement!"

"Prepare yourselves!" yelled Adam as he fired up his amber shielding. The smell of ozone from crackling electricity filled the air.

Enoch and Angela burst through the now huge opening at the cavern. Angela saw the Adamites circled in a defensive formation around the base of the mountain.

"Run! Get back!" she shouted and waved, motioning them away desperately.

Hades poured out over them in a cloudy, billowing mass, raising himself hundreds of feet into the air. Enoch watched in horror as the dark, brooding vaporous mass reformed and shaped itself back into that same vacant, expressionless face and torso of a stone golem. Its mouth opened and a white-hot spout of flames struck the mountainside. Instantly the solid rock was transformed to liquid, and tons of red-hot lava and flames were sent directly on top of the two crouching figures.

"Lord help us!" Enoch shouted in a desperate attempt to form a protective shield.

Eve screamed as she saw the entire side of the mountain melt away and collapse in flames on top of Enoch and Angela.

"God help them!" she cried.

"Hit that cloud!" shouted Adam. All of his energy casters fired amber energy into the blank looking golem in the air, but it seemed to pass right through the vaporous form.

The creature reformed itself and began to open its mouth again.

"Activate your shields with everything you have!" warned Adam.

Suddenly, the air creature turned and peered back into the inferno at the base of the mountain. It released another superheated flood of fire on top of the already burning rocks, bursting boulders and melting more stone around them.

"Look!" shouted Eve, pointing into the midst of the fire. "Wasn't it just Enoch and Angela there before? Now there are three, walking in the midst of the blaze and the third is like the Son of God!"

All the Adamites peered, squinting into the white-hot furnace of flames, glimpsing the figures walking forward unharmed.

The creature above loosed a third torrent of superheated fire upon the trio. As it rushed downward, the figure that appeared to be Enoch lifted his head, opening his mouth, and an amber flood of heavenly fire rushed upwards, meeting and struggling with the creature's own issue of flame.

Then, slowly, inexorably, the amber flames began to force the bluish white fire of the creature upwards. The air golem thundered in protest as the blast from Enoch forced its way higher and higher until it filled its mouth and exploded, instantly vaporizing the dark cloud into nothingness.

Hades awoke in a sweat, his confidence shattered. "Beelzebub's balls!" he gasped, cursing and shaking. "I never would have believed the power!"

Chapter 74

Enoch and Angela walked out of the inferno of flames and magma, their forms glowing with confidence and power. The third figure was suddenly gone as if his work was finished for now. As the victorious couple strode towards Adam and Eve the entire Adamic force, in awe of what they had seen, dropped to one knee to worship who they saw as new gods.

"No! No!" shouted Enoch desperately. "There is only one worthy of your worship and that is the Lord God Almighty! He is your deliverer this day. Rise to your feet and give God the glory!" He raised both hands in the air, urging them up to their feet to praise God for their victory. The Adamites shouted with one voice, a shout of praise and exultation.

Enoch looked at Adam, urging him with his eyes to take over, to be their leader, their example, the earthly father they all so desperately needed. Adam, shaken yet nodding in acknowledgement, accepted Enoch's unspoken prompt and turned to the crowd.

"Glory to God in the highest heavens!" he shouted. "And on Earth, peace and good will towards men."

Eve rushed into his arms, Enoch and Angela hugged each other and the raucous praise and celebration continued.

Lamech was in awe of such magic. If he could control such power, his subjects would truly worship him as a god! For years he had discounted the powers of the spirit world and valued only cold hard steel and overwhelming force.

Although he accepted some of the more useful half-breeds such as giants and trolls, he never realized how powerful the spiritual side of these special creatures could be. He had to master this power if he was going to be the ultimate sovereign of this world. He allowed himself to fall behind in the spiritual weapons race and gain comfort in the brute force and size of his army, but they would be helpless against powers such as these.

Lamech looked over Enoch critically. This man had been his prisoner, powerless before him. Enoch was just a man: he bled, he had broken bones, he was just as frail in body as himself. Where did such power come from? He was not of angel blood. It had to be that armor. The girl wore it as well! It must be blessed, or tied in somehow to the spirit world. Lamech decided he would need armor like that. The old set they had pulled off of Enoch must have been damaged. Belial could not make it do anything.

And who was that figure in the fire? Eve had called Him the Son of God. He knew the sons of God were angel-like beings. The only angels who he had ever seen were the Dark Lords – and this one did not look anything like them – they were fallen, outcasts from the highest heavenlies, so that was not surprising.

Lamech's mind raced. What was the difference between sons of God and the Son of God. That title hinted at only one, special son. Was it that being who gave Enoch such power?

Lamech trembled at the thought of confronting that being, the third figure in the fire, the Son of God. No, he would have to work around him, not set him off and risk unleashing that power until he knew how to counter it, to defeat it. Until then he must avoid any such contact.

The Adamites seemed totally distracted in their celebrations. This would be a good time to leave quietly. In might be hours before they even noticed he was gone. He didn't relish the thought of being reunited with Enoch, especially after their last encounter.

Lamech quietly led his mount away from the mountain and began the long ride home.

Chapter 75

Lucifer had felt His presence, like a shattering burst of light and pain in his spirit. It was not right! It was too soon! It was only for a few moments and then the Word was gone, back to the heavenlies, but there was no denying He was on the earth, in Satan's domain.

Lucifer was not ready to take Him on. He was supposed to be coming from the seed of Eve. If He came in the flesh, Satan felt sure he could use that weakness to defeat Him, to kill Him. But he had not sensed His spirit in any man so far. He didn't know if the prophetic King of Kings would be a random genetic event or specific, directed choice, but now he knew for sure he would know when He was on the earth.

Lucifer struggled with how he could overcome the prophecy against him. If the seed of Eve would be his undoing, he could try to wipe out that seed. Even if he could accomplish that he would then have no subjects to rule over and besides that, God kept a barrier – a "suk" – a hedge of protection around many of these beings, preventing him from taking their lives. If he could not kill them all, Lucifer's next choice was to corrupt them enough that he could control them and perhaps even make God so grieved at their behavior that, if he did not destroy them, he would at least remove his protection from around them.

He had made great progress with the Cainites. He even speculated that he could have succeeded in making Cain immortal and could have ruled through him forever. Adam and his blessed descendants had thwarted that plan. Many of those in the Adamic camp had God's protection around them. That's why Satan desired Adamic women and now defenseless boys for sexual conquests. If he could so pervert them with pleasure to lose that protection, they would fall under his control and he could do what he liked with them. But getting them away from Adam's protection was so difficult.

Such protected prey rarely appeared among the Cainites, that is what made him so interested in the blonde girl Belial had lost to the Adamites. He guessed the seed would come from one of these protected ones, so he would have to defile and debase as many of them as he could in hopes to pervert the line the seed was supposed to come from.

Dragging the blessed ones down into despair was not as easy as he had once thought. He had not counted on forgiveness and redemption occurring within these human creatures. Despite some of his best work, repentance, forgiveness and redemption ruined his ploys and made him start all over again.

"Belial!" Lucifer yelled, "Come to me!"

"Do you desire me, my Lord?" flirted Belial.

"I need you to search out what happened that drew in the Son of God. I felt His presence on this earth and I need to know why!" commanded Satan.

"Yes my Lord," bowed Belial, disappointed that Lucifer was not requesting him for pleasure.

"And fetch me that blond girl you lost to those Adamites. She was interesting to me," added Lucifer.

"But what about – " stammered the Belial.

"I am Lucifer, King of this earth, I can do whatever I want and I don't need to explain it to anyone, least of all to you!" Lucifer dismissed him with building irritation.

"My Lord," acquiesced Belial.

"How is that assignment plan going…you know – a spirit for every man?" queried Satan.

"Our spirits are not always the most cooperative," began Belial, hesitantly.

"I grow tired of these excuses. Send me Apolodon, I will have him take over this task. Now go, accomplish what I have demanded," ordered Lucifer.

Even though Belial was beginning to tire him, Lucifer had to admit Belial's efforts to spread homosexuality were going well. Nothing swung men to a reprobate mindset quicker and more thoroughly. Once they crossed that natural barrier of behavior, they were his to control. That, and the shedding of innocent blood virtually assured his takeover of a soul. But to many, those acts were too much against their spirit to manifest right away. Others needed smaller steps to perdition. Lying, fornication, gossiping, covetousness, theft and anger could all lead man down his path.

Again, the only thing that could turn a soul back once started was repentance, forgiveness and redemption. He hated this "spark" of God in humans. It was proving to be a growing problem. If not for that, they would be such easy prey to deceive and enslave with threats and promises.

His minions announced that Apolodon had arrived in response to his summons.

"See him in," ordered Satan. Here was a Dark Lord he could rely on – strong, of few words, and ready to accomplish what he was assigned.

"My Lord," bowed Apolodon as he came before Satan.

"I need far better information and influence over these humans. They are growing in ways we did not expect. The same for our halflings. Too much is going on without my knowledge," explained Lucifer. "I want you to start assigning every human and halfling a demonic spirit to watch them, to influence them into debauchery and violence, and to report their progress and any movement towards God up the ladder of command. Assign higher lords to seats of power and positions of authority. If we can control rulers and decision-makers, it makes the earth that much more vulnerable to our authority," decreed the Prince of Lies.

"I will appear before the Lord and point to each one's sins and accuse them night and day, forcing the Creator to turn them over to my kingdom because of their failures in faith," Lucifer gloated. "Not one will be worthy to be in the Kingdom of Heaven. He will have cities with no souls to inhabit them. I will rule the kingdom of the damned."

Chapter 76

Enoch clasped Mahalial's shoulder, "Are you sure this is what you both want to do?" he asked, looking him in the eyes.

"I think this is best for Belhah and I," he smiled. "We will be king and queen of our new household, whatever we build will be ours to rule."

"There are many dangers in the wilderness my friend. There will be times you may need some help; don't hesitate to call upon me," offered Enoch.

Angela hugged Belhah, both crying. Belhah smiled through her tears. "I want to see that baby," she said, patting Angela's barely showing bump.

"I'm sure I'll want an excuse to get back out again, after the birth,"

Angela laughed.

Mahalial promised, "I'll have a nice guest quarters built by then and you will all be welcome to come see our progress."

Belhah sidled up next to Mahalial and hugged his waist. "God willing, we will have a little bundle on the way ourselves, right my love?"

"Well, it sure won't be from lack of trying!" exclaimed Mahalial enthusiastically. Belhah slapped him playfully on his rear. "Behave yourself in front of the crown prince, dear," she scolded.

They all laughed, then Enoch took both of their hands in his and Angela put hers on top. "Seriously, we are closer than brothers and sisters. Anytime, anyplace you need us, just send word. Will you?" said Enoch solemnly.

"You have my word," Mahalial looked at Belhah's beaming face. She had become a completely different person. Her bitterness and anger were gone. She seemed to be at peace and eager to explore what adventures lay ahead.

"I'll be interested to see how you top the whole walking in fire bit," grinned Mahalial, raising one eyebrow.

Enoch handed him a small, yellow tinted crystal. He had the other in his hand. "These are a matched pair," he explained. "In time of need, just sing 'The Lord is my Shield.'" Both rocks lit up and glowed a soft amber light. "I will know you need me, or I need you."

"Thank you," nodded Mahalial, "I will guard its use for only exceptional need."

After a last round of hugs, Belhah and Mahalial climbed upon their ox drawn cart, his huge saber-toothed cat trailing behind them.

"Goodbye and Godspeed," waved Enoch as the newly reunited couple headed south to the unknown.

Enoch hugged Angela from behind, gently squeezing her belly. "I guess I need to get started on our new room, don't I?"

"That's right, the time is set. No more traipsing around the country for you," she scolded him playfully.

Enoch and Angela turned and walked back into the amber city of Abelton. His mind was churning with the significance of the events of the last few days. He feared for Mahalial and Belhah's safety as he did for all who chose now to live beyond the great walls of the cities. What manner of power was now loose on this world? Where did they come from? This energy signature of blue was unlike anything he had seen before.

And then there was that brief encounter with the Son of God in the fire. Though he communed with God's Spirit every day, he was in awe yet felt such peace in the actual presence of the Son. Enoch had no idea that he had the ability to erupt such power from his mouth, but the urge to do so had been innate, reflexive. And then He was gone. To where? Enoch was sure the Son was tangible, physical, and that he could reach out and touch Him. He was not a spirit.

Enoch thought of how Angela described what happened to her when she drowned and her ability to be out of her body and see the spirit world. That presence in the cloud, was it a spirit? It was certainly not God. He got the feeling that he had not seen the last of it, nor the last of those massive moving statues of stone and brass.

He felt Angela squeeze his hand and forced his concerns to flee for the moment.

"I'm still waiting for that picnic. When do you think you can deliver on that offer?" she looked mischievously at him with that sparkle in her eye. "Do you think you can get off from your promise by saving the world?"

Enoch laughed and gave her a deep, long, passionate kiss, leaving her cheeks flushed and her breath rushed.

"We're off!" he shouted as he scooped her up in his arms and let the troubles of the world melt away in her embrace.

Chapter 77

Eve snuggled her radiant face against Adam's naked chest. "I feel you might have planted your seed this time," she purred, squeezing him tight.

Adam raised her face to his and questioned "You can tell this soon?" his expression startled.

"Sometimes I can, it's like a feeling of life, of new potential, it's hard to explain," she said then kissed his lips. "But after last night in your embrace, I feel it more strongly than ever."

Adam smiled and hugged her tightly, "Well good, we could use the sound of little footsteps running around the palace. Will it be a boy or girl?"

Eve laughed and replied, "I can't be that precise. Does it matter to you?" she asked insistently.

"I will be blessed by whatever God gives us," declared Adam.

They held each other in silence for a while, both grateful that the years of coldness in their marriage had thawed.

Adam seemed deep in thought.

Eve tickled him and broke his silence, "What are you thinking about?" she queried.

"I was just processing some things Lamech said while he was with us," replied Adam.

At the mention of Lamech's name, Adam noticed Eve's body stiffened almost imperceptibly. "I don't like that man, the harm he has done to our family, our city, the way he leers at me like I'm some piece of meat. What could he say that has value?" she scoffed.

"He spoke of how those creatures were the result of Apolodon's experiments with halflings, how Apolodon was breeding smarter and smarter halflings, far exceeding the capabilities he expected," Adam recalled.

"We have to find a way to end the parade of women into the Dark

Lords' camp," he groused.

Eve's heart raced in panic as she recalled what she had tried so hard to forget, the icy penetration of Lucifer, disguised as Adam in her dreams, the intense feelings of pain and pleasure she had never encountered before, the feeling of life as his foul seed exploded into her. She shuddered in the guilt and horror of the memory. Adam could never find out, he would never look at her the same way again if he knew.

"That would be a monumental task," she responded softly. "Many of these women go of their own free will with their families' blessings. They offer such power and riches to entice the girls."

Adam blew out a breath in exasperation. "But even Lamech has seen the horrendous evil that has been created already. We can't have this demon seed spreading across the earth," he looked into her eyes, and for an instant was puzzled at a faraway look she had. He so desperately wanted to ask her about her time as a hostage in Apolodon's spire in the City of Light.

He could clearly imagine why she was taken, and the conversation with Lamech only confirmed it. If Apolodon was experimenting with breeding halflings, what better, more pure womb could he desire but the Queen Mother of all mankind, the one woman created straight from the hand of God. Mix her seed with a high Dark Lord, or even the ruling Cherub himself, Lucifer, and there was no telling what offspring could be produced.

Luckily, he had rescued her quickly and the years following had proved no such union, had it happened, ever bore fruit, but he shuddered at the disastrous potential.

The few times he had tried to probe at what happened she had shut off and collapsed emotionally so he promised her he would never broach the subject again. He suspected she had been raped, maybe repeatedly, but he wanted her to know he was so sorry he had let her fall into their hands. He wanted her forgiveness for being lax in protecting her. He wanted her to know that as long as he had breath, she would be safe and protected against the vile plans of the Fallen Ones.

But for now, so much had to remain unspoken. He did not want her to ever experience that emotional collapse into depression again. He abruptly changed the direction of his musings.

"I'd like a little girl," he smiled, "One as beautiful and loving as her mother." He kissed Eve gently on her lips.

Eve relaxed in her spirit as the dark memories faded for the moment. "Then I will do my best to ensure you get your desire," she said as she sat up and straddled him. "Perhaps we should try again, just to make sure?"

Chapter 78

The royal wedding was as grand an event as Hera could achieve with only simple country people to work with. She had supervised every aspect down to the minutest detail. She had the city covered with flowers and it took four score ladies in waiting to carry the train of her brilliant white wedding dress.

They had written their vows to each other and each presided over the other as there was no greater power or ruler than they themselves to declare their oaths to. She certainly didn't want to enforce any foolish country beliefs of a Creator and definitely wanted to give no credence to the Dark Lords. No, she and Zeus would be their own gods and his brothers would have their places as well. Gods needed no priest or intermediary to proclaim to them.

The fact that she was almost five centuries in age and he not even two decades had not been difficult to overcome. The melding with the dark spirit of lust, Jezebel, had given Hera's body new youth and sexuality. She had looked good before, but now she was absolutely irresistible. Zeus followed her around like a puppy, desperately craving their next moments of lust and expectations of pleasure. He would agree to almost anything to get her back into his bed, pleasuring him in ever-expanding and newly exciting ways.

She primly opened the door to Zeus's royal chambers and gracefully glided to the throne next to Zeus. She wore a silken dress, black with golden flowers woven into its bodice, the long flowing skirt hiding her height boosting heels. Its hem was also laced with gold and she wore a dangling golden obsidian necklace that draped over her ample bosoms.

Hades, Poseidon and Belshazzar all stood – Belshazzar and Hades rather impatiently – before the thrones. Hera ignored their irritated looks and took her time, bowing low to Zeus, making sure to show even more of her décolletage to his lusty eyes, then took her time settling in her throne, adjusting the folds of her gown just so.

"What do we have before us today, my husband?" she asked, feigning submissiveness as she smoothed her dress.

Zeus nodded to Hades, "My brother has something to share with us."

"Yes and it is very important," he snapped, obviously disgruntled.

Hera looked coolly at Hades, he was obviously immune to her charms, an entity to be wary of in the Atlantean court. Hera felt like a frog on a dissection table when under the gaze of Hades. She would have to work on belittling his power in her kingdom.

"Are we to hear of another one of your failures today, little brother?" she asked with a disinterested tone.

Hades ignored her and took a step towards Zeus. "Our kingdom is under grave danger," he warned.

"What has he done this time Belshazzar?" Hera interrupted and redirected the conversation. If she could implicate him as well, she could kill two birds with one stone. She rolled her eyes as if she were dealing with an unruly child, then smiled at Poseidon. She liked Poseidon and he obviously enjoyed looking at her. Had Zeus not succumbed to her charms, he would have been her next conquest.

Belshazzar spoke briefly, "I think you need to hear Hades out," he encouraged.

"There is a power like none I have ever encountered, nor even knew existed. It resides in the land of Carmel, in the mountains east of the Great Canyon," Hades announced.

"What kind of power do you speak of?" asked a curious Zeus, leaning forward on his throne.

Hera sensed his keen interest and didn't want to lose her position of influence in this discussion, so she swiftly rose and walked to the side of Zeus's throne, resting her delicate hand on his forearm. "Yes tell us everything," she said as she lovingly stroked his skin.

Zeus placed his hand over hers and probed Hades further, "Was it a Fallen One, a spirit, a beast, our father Lucifer?"

Hades hesitated, "It goes against everything I have studied and have been taught." He cast a sideways glance at Belshazzar. "But it was as if the power that created our universe was suddenly, if only for an instant, paying attention to us. For a moment, it was aware of us, like a whale passing by an amoeba and seeing it, focusing on it before it was lost in its wake."

"Preposterous!" announced Hera. "I know of this legend," she scoffed. "He has long ago lost interest in this world and moved on to other things. We run and rule this world. He has been absent for hundreds of years, what could possibly interest him here?"

"Not only did he find something of interest, but he lent his power to oppose me. There can be no other explanation," surmised Hades.

"Are there no other sorcerers more learned than yourself?" Hera countered. "You are awfully young to be taking on experienced casters and spirits out in the world. Could you simply have been outclassed and are now afraid to admit it?" she accused, moving her hand to Zeus's shoulder, squeezing it tightly.

Hades dipped his head and glowered while he spoke to Zeus, "Why is she here? Must I be subjected to her foolish banter?"

Zeus stood quickly, placing himself in front of Hera protectively. "She is your Queen, Hades, you will respect her. What she says makes sense. This is your first real sortie beyond our walls and you have made horrible mistakes with the golems I allowed you to use."

Hades shook, trying to control his rage. "I know what I did wrong with the golems, I can fix that. This power that I confronted is different and it is immeasurable!"

"Well then," surmised Zeus. "Until you find out a way to counter it, I suggest we stay away from the location where it manifested itself. We will call him the 'God of the Mountain' and give him a wide berth."

Hades held his response, his brother was too enraptured with his new bride for now. He would be patient, and his time would come.

Chapter 79

She didn't know if escaping Hades' infernal machine and knife was a blessing or a curse. She shivered, naked in a cold rock cell, dug out of the inside of a mountain. She could smell the sea through a small hole in the corner of her cell, the only place she could relieve herself and not soil the rough floor of her tiny abode.

Her long, chestnut hair was matted and soiled, her body still covered in the thick, oily ooze that they slathered on her for the horrific experiment planned to take her life and maybe her soul.

This paradise of Atlantis was nothing that it appeared to be. Any citizen at any time could be accused and just vanish into the corrupt criminal justice system. On the outside people were grateful the High Lords were keeping criminals off the streets. She knew now it was a sham, a system designed to ensnare, enslave, and cause fear in everyone's heart, while giving those in power a "legal" excuse to take what they wanted and eliminate whomever they wanted.

She should have just slept with the man. But would it have ended any differently? Would he have imprisoned her in here anyway, after using her? Probably so. At least she had denied him his pig-like satisfaction; she at least had that small victory.

Far below, between the moans and wails of the other prisoners, she thought she could hear waves crashing into the mountain. It was maddening. Freedom, the surf, the sea was tantalizingly close. She could hear it, smell it.

She was from a small country village, swept away by the miraculous coming of the triune gods, but she remembered something from her childhood – stories from her great-grandmother – something about a Creator God, the author of all that there is.

"Patty," her grandmother would say, "Always know that you are special, God created you for a purpose. You seek that out and He will bless you."

Patty hadn't done very well. She thought she knew so much more than that foolish old woman, but Patty's way had led to this and this was not working out at all.

She looked up to the short rock ceiling above her head and cried, "God of Grammy Sarah, I was wrong not to put my faith and my trust in you. I thought I knew better, but I was so wrong. Forgive me, please, and help me at least save my soul from this horrible place."

The dim glow of a light in the hall, creeping through the joints of the door, just barely lit her solitary cell. Over some time her eyes adjusted to the dark and she could begin to see the details of her prison. She needed to use the hole in the cell, so she squatted ingloriously over it and tried her best to hit the opening. As she stared at the ground, concentrating, she thought she saw a faint crack, running in a semicircle, in the floor next to her latrine opening.

"Maybe the crack goes deep," she thought.

Grimacing in disgust, she reached into the filthy, smelly crack and leveraged her fingers against the edge and pulled upwards. She thought she noticed the slightest hint of give. She positioned herself, sitting on the floor, her feet braced against the wall and pulled again. Harder and harder she pulled and then it began to move, creating a loose edge. She pulled and kept slipping her fingers further down the edge of the cap stone until she was finally able to lift the chunk of loose rock.

The hole was filed with the smell of urine and feces, but at least it was hers. She smiled grimly as she reached down a small opening. It was tight, but she was slender. She might be able to squeeze down the opening. She knew it led to the sea, she could hear it.

"God, if this is your rescue plan you sure have a poor sense of humor," she said out loud.

She slid her legs down the narrow hole, dragging the loosened rock with her, working her way down, further and deeper into the tiny opening. She got far enough that she was able to drag the stone to its hole and then plopped it back into place.

She tried to push it back up but it was now wedged firmly back into the opening. She had a brief surge of panic, but there was no turning back now.

She snaked herself backwards, seeking the opening beneath her feet. She pushed herself with her hands, inching herself backwards towards the sounds of the crashing surf. She was grateful now that she was nude and covered in oily slime, as it helped her slide through the constricting tunnel far easier.

At one point it seemed that her shoulders and head were not going to fit, but she pushed up a bit and lifted both arms high above her head and twisted until her ear popped past the constriction and the rest of her head and arms followed.

The surf noise was getting much louder now and she was getting whiffs of fresh air through the stench.

Suddenly, her feet found no more rock and she started sliding downward towards – nothing! She desperately tried to grasp the sides of the tunnel but the ooze that had helped her move now prevented her from stopping herself.

In horror, she found herself falling out of a small hole in the ceiling of a wave carved cavern, far above the crashing surf. She fell into a rising wave as it surged towards the cavern wall.

The door to Patty's cell was thrown open and Hades' two assistants stood speechless. Hades peered inside between them.

"Where is she?" he asked the two stunned apprentices.

The female caught her voice first. "It's him! He raped her and was afraid you would find out she was no longer a virgin!" she accused, shaking her finger at the male apprentice.

"You man hater! I saw how you looked at her, you took her yourself!" he railed.

Hades shook his head and turned to his guards. "Take them both, it looks like we will have two tonight for my quest for answers. Prepare them!" he ordered.

"Wait, master! No! No!" they wailed as the guards stripped them and dragged them into the laboratory.

Hades shook his head, immune to their cries for mercy.

"Good assistants are so hard to find," he mused as he prepared his instruments.

Chapter 80

The little boy played in the sand by the seashore with his younger sister. The small village by the salty water was remote, settled by Adamic descendants only a decade ago.

"Look, Kiki!" he cried. "This time my wall will stop the mighty waves," he bragged.

Kiki laughed as she saw the tiny wall struggle then collapse into a pile of sand against the onrushing water.

"Oh no, you suck as a builder!" she teased.

Her brother feigned anger and started chasing her into the crystal clear surf. She laughed and ran from him until inexplicably he stopped, his eyes flung open wide and his mouth dropped to his chest.

She whirled around to see a huge figure rise like a mountain in the ocean behind her. They watched it grow and grow until it blocked out the sun, then with a thunderous belch it vomited out a glob of mucus onto the beach. Then it turned and majestically returned to the deep.

The children looked at each other and then ran as one to the fallen heap left behind and looked with great curiosity to see what could have so disagreed the mighty beast.

"Look Kiki, something's moving!" he shouted.

"It's a white mermaid!" she squealed in a delight. "Go tell Mama, quick, she needs help!"

Patty looked at the small, silver mirror in the crudely fashioned beach hut. Though the children's parents had let her scrub and scrub to get the filth and vomit smell finally banned from her hair and skin, three days in the belly of the beast had bleached her hair and skin snow-white. Only her bright green eyes showed their original color.

She turned to the family, "Thank you so much for your help, the bath, the clothes…" she gushed.

"Oh, believe me, the bath was our privilege," said the husband.

They all laughed, "Your story is incredible, surely God is smiling upon you," marveled his wife.

Only the children seemed disappointed she wasn't a mermaid.

"I have a message I must take to the great father Adam," Patty said slowly. "A great evil brews to the west and I have truly been in the belly of the beast."

Chapter 81

Apolodon thundered and dark lightning flashed around his massive ruby armored figure. Lights sparkled like brilliant scarlet diamonds all around him. His eyes glowed with ancient hate and cold malevolence. "I have been told that some of you don't like the orders you have been given," he bellowed.

He looked across the vast boiling pit of fiery lava in the midst of the smoky mountain. Millions of Belial's servant wraiths hovered over the inferno, quivering with fear at the change of authority.

Apolodon and his Dark Lords stood at the brink of the inferno, forcing the demonic spirits to suffer from the heat and smoke. It was a physical reminder of what he was threatening in the spiritual realm.

"I know that many of you slavishly scurry around, seeking a dead body to pathetically stumble around in just to have touch, feel, taste. Others of you settle for soulless animals that eat filth and are eaten by greater animals, all in the hopes of once again experiencing some glimpse of life. How far you have fallen, you selfish, self-serving fools!"

Apolodon strutted back and forth as thunder crashed and black lightning continued flickering around him.

"Well that stops today," he ordered. "Today, we have a plan that will be executed, followed and obeyed. No exceptions. You see below you a bubbling Inferno of molten rock. No fleshly body could withstand it. Many of you have been in flesh when it burned and you suffered the pain with your host. I tell you today that there is also such a place like this for the spirit."

A gasp of horror rose from the demonic assembly. "Lucifer has discovered it and knows the way to entrap any spirit there," Apolodon threatened. "And I can't wait for one of you maggot dwelling scum to try me one time so I can make an example of you. Who rebels against Lord Satan's plan, so I can deal with you now?" he bellowed.

A deathly silence covered the already hushed satanic congregation.

"No one? This is your chance. Oppose me now, if you will. No more backbiting, disobedience or grumbling. Follow today or from this day forward be banished forever to the lake of eternal fire."

Apolodon stopped and gave a deathly gaze across the slinking multitude of fiends.

"So I can assume by your silence that you agree to pledge your all of yourselves to King Lucifer, but know you must give your voice and your action to that pledge. Around this cauldron are twelve Dark Lords, ruling angels who have sworn their allegiance to the ruling Cherub that covered the throne of the Creator. Divide yourselves into twelve equal groups, report to your ruling Dark Lord and give him your oath to Satan. Now!" commanded Apolodon.

The wraiths scurried to obey while Apolodon nodded in satisfaction. After this, he would have each Dark Lord perform a census of his assigned territories, sending out the wraiths to account for every living soul.

With that information, he would assign one or more demonic spirits to begin their work to capture every human spirit into the kingdom of Satan – his helpless, willful subjects. Finally, he would have an information network he could somewhat dependent on. He would still filter what information reached Lucifer's ears, but this would help him find his lost progeny, the offspring of Satan.

This was the kind of command structure he would have implemented himself once he took over things, so it did not hurt his plans for eventual dominance.

He hoped the threat of eternal fire would force these subservient demons to take their oaths more seriously than he had taken his. His oath to Satan was just to buy time to accomplish his revolution.

There was also the rumor of some great power being unleashed at the western mountains. It seemed to shake Lucifer, hence his fortuitous takeover of this massive force of spies and influencers. The story was that it was an appearance by the Son of God.

Apolodon scoffed at such a thought. There was no way the Creator would have any interest in this pool of broken beings. He was all about perfection and righteousness. This world had long ago fallen into such evil, the Son of God would not risk getting his hands dirty here.

The preposterous thought amused him. Oh, the Adamites might have discovered some of the Creator's magic, as he himself had, but they would never warrant a connection of His interest. He was perfection and any contact with imperfection would instantly destroy it.

No, this was the Devil's playground, and he was determined to become the chief devil, the ruler of this little blemish on the ass of the universe.

Chapter 82

She made a rather striking, unique image, standing before the ruling council of the Adamites in the majestic city of Abelton. Her hair was snow-white, her skin a bleached, powdery hue. If not for her green eyes, one would have thought her a female Dark Lord, but none had ever existed to the knowledge of man.

Adam satin his full royal splendor, accompanied by Eve, both in their white cloaks encrusted with rainbows of precious gems. Adam wore his amber armor beneath while Eve was dressed in an elegant white gown. Enoch, Angela, Jared, Seth, Angel, Luna and the high governess flanked them.

Adam began, "Welcome to Abelton. I understand you bring news and that you arrived on the outskirts of our lands in quite a miraculous way. Please introduce yourself."

"My name is Patty, from the village of the matron Sarah. I am honored to meet you all," she bowed.

Adam introduced the council, then requested, "Tell us your news."

"You no doubt have noticed my appearance. I looked this way after spending some time, I'm not sure how long, in the belly of a huge beast from the sea. I was miraculously brought to your shores to warn you of what I have escaped from, obviously with the grace and help of the Creator, our Lord God.

"Not many months ago a caravan of three unusual halflings and their followers came to our village. They were still youthful in appearance, but well over thirteen feet tall. They were able to do spells and wonders and spoke of a new world they were going to build, where everyone would have no want or need and we would all love each other freely.

"Most all of the young people left and I fear now what happened to those who stayed behind. We headed into the setting sun. We picked up many more young people along the way and we were continually amazed by their magic, enthralled with their promises and speech. Eventually, we stopped at a beautiful coastline, where the mountains met the sea and Zeus, the leader of the three halflings, created great creatures of stone to build a shining, gleaming city of crystal and glass.

Adam held up his hand, "Describe these creatures," he requested.

"They were like huge stone statues brought to life. Zeus made little ones, at first, like toys. But these others were as tall as four men and extremely strong and powerful."

The Adamites all looked at each other with knowing nods.

"We have seen these creatures, they have already trespassed on our lands," acknowledged Adam.

"The city was built almost overnight and we were all assigned our duties with leaders to rule over each of us. The leaders soon proved to be selfish and cruel, ordering supplies and food, demanding service and submission to their rules. The three halflings forced everyone to worship them as the only true gods and all who refused were sent to the underground, to Hades' subterranean lair under Atlantis, and they were never seen again."

The emotions of her distress began catching up to her narrative and she fought back tears. Eve graciously arose and moved to stand by Patty, hugging her and helping to support her.

"It's okay dear, you are safe now," she soothed.

Patty dissolved in her arms and broke down, sobbing. "My Queen, I was so scared," she cried.

Eve held her until she regained her composure a bit and then moved to the side, her arm staying around Patty's shoulders.

"Finish your story," urged Eve.

"Well," she said. "One of the city leaders, a man given position, tried to make me have sex with him and I refused. He had me arrested and I was sent to Hades' prison. It turns out that Hades is experimenting on us, torturing and killing us to find out how he can catch, hold and destroy our spiritual essence once we die. He is trying to create a spiritual weapon, to be able to move and control the spirit realm.

"I was stretched out nude on his laboratory table, hooked up to his infernal contraption, with a glowing blade poised to plunge into my breast. Suddenly, the knife stopped glowing and he could not complete his test so I was stored away for a later attempt." She fought back her sobs and then told of her escape.

There was silence in the hall for a few moments.

Enoch then asked, "Did the glow have a color?"

"Blue," she answered quickly, "I'll never forget it. Pale, light blue."

Enoch thought for a while. "The timing of her story coincides closely with the appearance of the bronze golem with the blue crystal," he pondered. "It could be that when the crystal perished in the liquid mountain it disrupted the power supply. "

Adam stated, "Whatever it did, it wasn't permanent. The creatures were able to reanimate. And that air creature still had incredible power."

Angela added, "Enoch, you said you felt a different presence in the air that was not in any of the other monsters?"

"It was not like a Dark Lord," acknowledged Enoch.

Angela continued, "I know the spirit may separate from the body, it happened to me when I drowned. If this Hades is experimenting in the spirit realm, he might have discovered how to do this himself. It might have been his spirit in that cloud being, much like a lesser Fallen One can inhabit a body of flesh."

"If it was Hade's spirit, then destroying the creature probably only rid him of his host. We have probably not seen the last of him," continued Enoch.

Suddenly Patty's pale white body stiffened into a ramrod straight pole.

Eve fell backwards in shock as a burst of deadly cold emanated from Patty's frame. The stiffened girl's once green eyes were overwhelmed with a pale blue hue.

Enoch ran to pull Eve away from the albino-like figure now glowing, in a pale blue aura.

Patty's face became an impassive mask, reminding Enoch of the unblinking visages of the animated figures of stone, brass and air.

A deep, reverberating voice rumbled out of Patty's chest.

"Well, well, well," it growled, using Patty's eyes to look herself over. "So here is where you have gone to. Quite impressive, how you escaped my lair. But you are mine now," the voice triumphed.

Adam motioned for his guards to block all the exits and windows and then addressed the personage in the rigid girl, "Who is the spirit that is controlling Patty?"

Patty's cold, expressionless face turned its attention to Adam. "So, this is Adam? You don't look so impressive. I expected you to be taller," it scoffed.

It lifted a limp finger towards Adam and shot a bolt of blue white lightening directly at his chest. Adam's amber shielding instinctively activated, deflecting Hades' attempt.

Enoch jumped protectively between Adam and the glowing blue form.

"Hades!" he shouted, guessing who had taken control of Patty. "Look at me."

Her cold stare fixed on Enoch and he thought he saw a spark of recognition in her expressionless, glowing blue eyes.

"That's right, you recognize me, don't you?" Enoch stated.

Patty slowly pointed her arm towards him, crackling with latent blue energy. Enoch stepped forward and grabbed Patty's wrist.

"You have no power here," he said as he activated his amber energy shield and began to use its power to encompass the helpless girl. The two lights crackled, starting where Enoch touched her, then the amber began overwhelming the blue, slowly moving up her arm.

"That's right, we both know how this ends, don't we. We've danced this dance before," challenged Enoch.

"But the Son is not here, how can you – " the girl stammered, the voice showing some distress.

Enoch continued, "And you have no claim to this girl. She fled you and your evil desires. She is a child of the Lord of Hosts. Now, be gone!"

Patty's face contorted and shrieked with a hideous, defeated scream, then she collapsed. Exhausted, battered, but free.

Chapter 83

Again, there was a day when the sons of God came in to present themselves before the Lord, and Satan came also among them to present himself before the Lord.

And the Lord said unto Satan. "Where have you been?"

And Satan answered the Lord, saying, "From going to and fro in the earth, and from walking up and down in it. What is this new power you have unleashed upon the earth?"

"I have unleashed?" said the Lord.

"Well, I certainly have nothing to do with it," declared the Father of Lies.

"I suggest you take greater stock of your kingdom before you accuse," thundered the Lord of Hosts.

Satan took the rebuke, bowed low and left the assembly full of questions. How had he unleashed the new power upon the earth? It was certainly a threat to his own control, but what was it? Was that the reason the Son had visited the earth? He needed answers, and he needed them now!

The End

Acknowledgements

So much has happened since the publishing of "The First Immortal: Dark Angel," the initial book in the series, that it is mind-boggling to try to acknowledge all, but here goes.

Of course I have to thank my lovely wife, Angela, who served as the inspiration for the character of the same name in the series. You are my inspiration and my muse; thank you for your support and standing by me "all the way."

I also want to express my appreciation for all of you who have taken the time to review this tale on Amazon or on my website at *www.stonepalatin.com*. Your effort to tell others what you liked about the book has done wonders in getting the word out into the community at large. Keep up the good work and thank you. I find it amazing that all of you are anxiously awaiting this second installment of "The First Immortal" series, "Angel Blood." I pray it does not disappoint.

To all my family and friends who encouraged and congratulated me on this, thank you. Many of you contributed to having a very successful Barnes and Noble book signing for a first-time, non-celebrity author. We look forward to doing it again."

"The First Immortal: Dark Angel" has made it into the hands of a playwright as well as a movie production company and is in the queue for their review. I look forward to seeing what the professionals think about such unusual materiel.

A great big thank you to Mick and Diane Prodger of Elm Grove Publishing who have helped so much in getting this project off the ground and into your hands to enjoy as well as to Elena Kalashnik who has graced the covers or our books with her majestic vision of the various angels in the stories.

Lastly, I would like to thank the real Yeshua, the Holy One of Israel for His inspiration and the creativity He placed in me to tell these stories in an entertaining way. I pray this tale awakens your *inner warrior* and leads you to fight for truth and justice – no matter what the odds.

–S.P.

Continue reading for a preview of

Book Three of the fantasy trilogy

THE FIRST IMMORTAL

Chapter 1

The gargantuan statues of stone, crystal and bronze were systematically destroying Apolodon's expeditionary force of dino-riders and Dark Lords. The teeth and claws of his large T.rex-like attack force seemed powerless against these expressionless creatures with their blank emotionless visages.

"Use your black energy bolts!" bellowed Apolodon to his fellow Dark Lords, clad like him in ruby red crystalline armor, their black, hooded robes cinched at he waist.

He directed their attack against the forty-foot tall creatures that were decimating his army of giants, trolls, halflings and dino-riders, who were being pulled apart like roasted chickens on a feasting table of famished warriors. The smell of blood, sulfur, guts and offal filled the air, while his men's screams of terror and death stood in stark contrast to the behemoths' silent carnage.

Just as the combined force of his platoon of fellow Dark Lords shot their hot, dark lightening towards the enemy, three smaller, twenty foot tall golems of pale blue crystal strode forward into the fray. They were composed of a translucent material, like rough-cut diamonds. They shared the same unblinking visage of their brother creatures, and glowed with a pale blue light. The bolts of black lightening were drawn to the three crystalline beings, swirling and crackling around them as the stench of sulphur fouled the air.

Then, as one, they seemed to lift the black mass of energy seething around them and hurl it back at the small band of Dark Lords taking up defensive positions around Apolodon. The massive bolt struck in their midst and hurled them into the air, scattering them in all directions.

Apolodon righted himself while hurtling through space and landed lightly on his feet. Apolodon was one of the highest levels of fallen angels, just below Lucifer, the ruling Cherubim that covered the throne of YAWEH, the Creator. Only Seraphim like him and of course the Cherubim Satan – or Lucifer as he was named in the world before – could will themselves from spirit into physical beings.

In this incarnate form they could enjoy the pleasures of this physical world with taste, smell, touch and ecstasy, but they became vulnerable to an extent because of their fleshly, incorporated bodies. If destroyed in the physical it was a long, painful process to re-animate into the fleshly form again. This was an experience none of the Dark Lords relished and avoided at all costs.

He unsheathed his black metal sword and clothed it with demon fire, bellowing to his startled compatriots. "Draw your swords; our dark energy alone is to no effect. We must use steel and magic!"

A great stone hand reached down to snatch him up and he swung his powerful frame, his muscles bulging with the effort. The effect was encouraging, as he sliced off several joints at the end of its fingers. The heavy digits thudded upon the hard wilderness ground, sparsely covered with dry brown straw-like stubble.

"To my command tent! We'll form a defensive perimeter around it!" he shouted, leading the Dark Lords backwards. He cursed that he had brought his favorite three concubines with him this time. He had allowed Lamech, the King of the Children of Cain, to influence him. In the past he had always ventured forth in quests for battle devoid of all the comforts of his home in the Fallen One's capital, the City of Light. But this time he allowed Sulak, Zupah and Axnec along so he could indulge himself in his lustful desires while he was searching for Belshazzar and his wayward student halflings.

He had put the women in danger, and Axnec, he had just found out, was bearing his child.

His troop kept hacking and chopping away against the monoliths of stone, having some limited success. But soon they more and more surrounded Apolodon as they finished the slaughter of his fleshly forces.

One of the brass giants who towered over the fifteen foot tall Apolodon reached down and snatched up the command tent by its top and threw it behind him. The three golden-skinned, bald, naked concubines were suddenly exposed to the impassive monstrosities. Apolodon fought with renewed vigor, leaping on top of a giant stone golem, slashing and hacking at its neck until the great stone head severed and fell like a boulder from the creature's shoulders.

The clang of metal rang solidly in Apolodon's ears from behind and he saw a brass monster swatting away several of his Dark Lords, unaffected by the demon swords. The giant extended its hand towards the horrified women. In a flash, before his eyes, Apolodon saw again visions of his men being torn in two. Unable to cope with his concubines suffering that same fate, he sprang into fevered action.

"No you foul beasts, NO!" he cursed and fired a white-hot blast of black energy-fueled Armageddon fire, concentrated on the extended giant hand of brass. The black blast struck its target squarely, melting brass fingers and palms. The creature unblinkingly raised up its melted, dripping stub on its now mutilated arm.

"Melt the brass ones, chop the stone ones down!" shouted Apolodon, ducking a smashing fist of stone. For a moment or two it looked like they were beginning to turn the tide as the metal and stone behemoths began to fall.

But then ropes of brilliant blue energy streamed forth from the mouths of the 3 diamond shaped figures.

"Enough!" the middle one shouted as the ropes of light encircled each of the struggling Dark Lords, binding them in glowing cocoons of pale blue light.

The middle crystalline creature grasped Apolodon's squirming, encapsulated form in both hands and held him up like a child to his eye level. The impassive diamond face suddenly materialized into the face of a man, clean-shaven with piercing blue eyes and glossy silver hair. "So this is a Dark Lord," spoke the human face projected on the crystalline creature. "Do you have a name?" he asked.

"I am Apolodon," he roared, struggling mightily to free himself from his blue capsule prison.

"By the way," the face uttered, noticing his struggle. "You won't escape that. It feeds off your spiritual energy, draining you to sustain itself. You will be trapped in your physical form, unable to draw on any of your powers of spirit or magic."

The diamond image smiled approvingly at his work then proclaimed. "My name is Zeus, uncle, I have grown up."

"What, how...?" Apolodon stammered.

The other two diamond giants approached, faces also materializing over each creature's impassive visage. "You've been searching for us – you have found us." They spoke as one.

"Hades, Poseidon! What is the meaning of this?" Apolodon shouted, demanding an answer.

Zeus continued, "We know you were trying to find us. You wanted to control us or destroy us before we became too powerful. Well, as you can see, you are too late."

Apolodon cursed and writhed in his bonds. "What do you think you are going to accomplish? If you destroy this incorporated fleshly body my spirit will escape and I will be back to destroy you." He laughed at their helpless plight.

Hades looked at the group of captured Dark Lords. "Yes, we thought of that, that's why you are not going to be destroyed. You are going to come to Atlantis and help us strengthen our kingdom."

"You're crazy, why would we ever agree to do that?" sputtered Apolodon.

"You won't have a choice, I'm afraid," sighed Hades. "Those cells are quite impenetrable you see. I know you are aware that we, as halflings – half man, half angel – have the potential of the best of both species. But my brothers and I are the only three in our kingdom. We need more."

"And as you know, we halflings are sterile, we cannot reproduce, not for the lack of trying!" laughed Zeus lustfully, grasping at an imaginary male organ non-existent on the shining crystal figure.

"So," finished Hades, "we need a constant source of demon seed as we breed a race of demigods to rule this earth." He pointed to the struggling, captive Dark Lords. "That will be your function for the foreseeable future; it should be quite enjoyable for you, really if only you'd be awake to enjoy it."

The energy fields kept sapping the Dark Lord's powers cruelly and Apolodon felt himself slipping away into unconsciousness.

"You see," finished Poseidon, "we couldn't allow you free to cause harm to our city or our breeding stock, so you will be in a coma, a brainless vegetable, while we harvest your seed from time to time to grow our army of rulers and gods."

Satan took the rebuke, bowed low and left the assembly full of questions. How had he unleashed the new power upon the earth? It was certainly a threat to his own control, but what was it? Was that the reason the Son had visited the earth? He needed answers, and he needed them now!

"My concubines...?" Apolodon gasped, struggling to stay alert.

"Oh, they'll be fine, we need as many breeders as we can find. Now bye, bye! When you next see us it will be because we've decided we don't need you anymore and have figured out how to destroy you," said Zeus to a rapidly weakening Apolodon, and then everything went blank.

Watching from the cover of darkness, a fair skinned, red headed maiden hid in the rushes by the creek where she had been sent to for water for Apolodon's concubines. She watched the creatures stride off to the west. Lamech, her lover, had left her behind by when he went off with Apolodon in search of the massive elemental monsters, and he had never returned for her.

Now she was cold, alone and free, but she longed for Lamech's embrace. She must find him. She set her face towards the lands of Cain and started walking.

About the Author

Stone Palatin attended Spring Woods High School in Houston, at the time the largest high school in Texas. After securing his Bachelor's degree at Hardin Simmons University in Abilene, he attended Southwestern Baptist Theological Seminary in Fort Worth.

During his twenty years service in ministry, Stone encountered many spiritual battles in his own and in his parishioners' lives. Discovering that "flesh out of control is spirit" allowed him to help many people to achieve victory in their struggles over spiritual bondage.

Stone Palatin is married with four children and three grandchildren and currently lives in San Antonio, Texas.

THE FIRST IMMORTAL

Coming Soon!

visit www.elmgrovepublishing.com for details

9 781943 492183